Mixed Signals

Adele was high enough on the stink of working men and the titillating mystery of Paul and his boyfriend to want to goad Jude further. It was absolutely the wrong time and place and that just made the thought of mischief seem more seductive. Jude smelled of sawdust, and his sweat had washed his skin clean in tempting streaks of pink and white where it had run in rivulets. He looked like a melting ice-cream, she thought, smiling at him. His eyelids, previously dipped in an expression of contrived cool, lifted and showed more of the blue iris, so that he looked even younger, and eager.

She smiled again and crooked her knee further so that her skirt rode higher. She realised that there was an advantage to this ridiculous outfit. No matter how she loathed the discomfort of wearing it, he liked it and was paying close attention to the lace top of her stocking. She doubted he'd look twice at her if he passed her in the street while she was wearing a T-shirt and jeans, but she wouldn't turn down an opportunity purely out of feminist pique. He was too pretty to pass up. She nearly laughed. Seemed that both sexes had an equal capacity to be shallow.

Mixed Signals
Anna Clare

BLACK LACE

Black Lace books contain sexual fantasies.
In real life, always practise safe sex.

First published in 2004 by
Black Lace
Thames Wharf Studios
Rainville Road
London W6 9HA

Design by Smith & Gilmour, London
Printed and bound by Mackays of Chatham PLC

ISBN 0 352 33889 x

1

Adele Western was nearly seventeen on the day she found yet another ritual taunt pinned to the door of her school locker. It was a crude drawing of the Eiffel Tower with a giant lipstick drawn beside it. In case she didn't get the joke, the legend 'Goldie's lippy' was scrawled beneath it. Hysterical. She sucked her thick, pale lips into her mouth and scowled. There were faint titters from behind the girls' toilet door opposite and, beside her, Kim turned on his heel and yelled, 'Oh – you think you're that fucking good, don't you?'

'Uh, yeah. I do actually.'

Adele didn't turn around but she heard Sharon Bircher's voice. Quite the little artist Sharon was shaping up to be, but just looking at the drawing made Adele feel tired and bored. Surely they were all too old for this crap?

'Why don't you just fuck off and get your toxic twat fingered by that knuckle-dragging boyfriend of yours, bitch?' Kim spat.

There was a startled hiss from Sharon. 'I'll tell him you said that, gayboy.'

'Go ahead.'

'Kim . . . leave it,' said Adele, fearing trouble. Sharon's boyfriend Neville was a six-foot throwback to the Ice Age who would have had no trouble beating seven shades of shit out of Kim. But Kim seemed to have no worries. He was not one to avoid a potentially dangerous situation if a juicy insult were to be enjoyed.

'How does he do it, I wonder?' he went on. 'Fuck you

from behind and wear a blindfold so the sight of your spotty arse doesn't make him spew?'

'Leave it,' Adele said firmly. 'She's not worth it.'

'You are *dead*,' Sharon threatened, from the toilet doorway. Her group of gaggling bitch buddies were struggling with various facial expressions as they tried to avoid laughing and show appropriate fury at the things Kim had said.

'Better dead than a spotty-arsed skank.'

'Kim!' Adele screwed up the drawing and tossed it in Sharon's face. 'Grow up,' she told her resignedly. She dragged Kim off down the hall with her, followed by yells and insults.

'Get a life, goldfish lips!'

'I will!' she called over her shoulder. 'Want me to get one for you while I'm at it?'

'Fish-mouth freak!'

She bit her lips again, a habit she'd fallen into over years of cruelty. Her lips struck her as unavoidably blubbery – thick, fat and full. With too many childhood taunts ringing in her ears she hadn't yet realised that they were sexy and that many women paid good money to be injected with collagen so they could fake such a pout.

'You should have ignored her,' Adele said, as they walked out of the main entrance into the ugly concrete quad that fronted the school gates. She half believed the lie – it was the right thing to do. Ignore them and they'll go away. One day it had to work, even if it never had in the past.

'That doesn't work,' Kim said, glancing over his shoulder to check Sharon hadn't followed. 'Ignore them and they'll just keep jabbering away.'

'You shouldn't provoke them. They're not worth it. They're just immature.'

'Immature?' Kim sniffed. 'Yeah right. Look, Sharon

Bircher will be like a side of old mutton by the time she hits twenty – rough old slag.'

Adele laughed. 'But you won't live to see your twenties the way you're going.'

'Live fast, die young and pretty, babycakes,' Kim said, slipping his arm into hers and turning off the pavement onto a small woodsy footpath. The scraggy nettles and coarse grass were strewn with cigarette butts and crushed Marlboro packets, evidence of half a school's covert nicotine habit.

Kim unzipped the top pocket of his bag and pulled out a contraband packet of cigarettes and a pink plastic lighter. He passed one to Adele and lit up with the air of a lifelong addict.

'God, I have *got* to quit. This is the fifth one today.'

She lit up her own cigarette. 'It's my second. Dad's given up again and Chris tells me to buy my own – mean bastard.'

'That's nice, considering he's got a job and we're stuck here in this hellhole learning to be skint students.'

'And skint actors.'

Kim stuck out his lower lip. 'I'm never going to be a skint actor. I'm gonna be a *star*, sweetie. A fucking *star*.'

She believed he would. He could act the backsides off most of the dopeheads and slackers in his drama class and had a high tenor singing voice, regularly showcased in school productions. Kim liked to sing passionate torch songs; his delicately pretty face porcelain fine even under the unflattering lights of the school hall. His parents were less enthusiastic and were trying to make a chef of him in order to continue the family business. 'Yeah, a fucking kitchen skivvy,' Kim complained, often and loudly. It didn't help that he could burn water and so he was almost always relegated to kitchen portering, unless he started a fight. Then Adele would be left to hang around awkwardly in the hall while Kim thrashed it out with his father.

'I reckon you'll do it,' she said.

Kim blew out smoke. 'Of course I will. I'll shag the right people. Casting couch, hon. That's the way it goes.'

'You're terrible, Kim.'

'No I'm not. I'm fabulous, darling.'

He headed off down the path towards town. Adele followed, smoking. 'Did you see Sharon's face?'

'I know. Fucking classic. Fat old troll.'

'Don't you think she's pretty?' Adele asked hesitantly. She hoped for an honest opinion. She had known Sharon Bircher since primary school when she was an angelic curly-haired blonde moppet; she had steadily grown into a beautiful girl whose reputation as 'the pretty one' preceded her.

Kim snorted. 'No. She used to be pretty in year nine. But most of that was because she had big tits when she was twelve and let everyone feel them. Now she's got really bad skin.'

Adele nodded. 'Puts her make-up on with a trowel.'

'Wrong shade too. On a bad day she's orange.'

They both laughed.

'Orange and pitted, like the surface of Mars,' Kim bitched; he found a mental association he liked and began to sing. '*It's a godawful small affair, to the girl with the mousy hair...*'

She laughed at his David Bowie impression and they carried on down the path, into the underpass towards town.

It was already warm and dusty for the late spring and the grass was beginning to show a parched look, dusty on roadside verges where the traffic fumes touched it. It was cool and smelled of booze in the underpass, the walls daubed with unimaginative graffiti – circled As and declarations of love and hate, announcements that so and so was a slag. Adele hated the town. It was too small to qualify for city status, too large for people to know each other in anything but a bitchy, sidelong, circumspect way.

While she and Kim nurtured grandiose fantasies of taking London by storm, Adele cherished childhood memories of the coast. It wasn't a big enough dream for a sixteen-year-old so she kept it to herself, but in the down-at-heel normalcy of home, with its blocky 1950s houses and bland concrete thoroughfares, she found herself yearning for her childhood home by the sea. Buildings there were concoctions of Victorian whimsy, rich with shabby genteel resonance. The air had smelled of the sea, and the horizon blurred on hot days so that you couldn't tell where the Channel ended and the sky began – a reflection of distance and endless possibilities.

That was home, not this armpit of the Home Counties that fate had dumped her in. Everything was squat, ugly and boring in town: the grey grubby bus station, the mangy pigeons that congregated outside McDonald's, the flat ordinary shop fronts. The most fun you could have was floating condoms off the top of the multistorey car park.

They smoked two more cigarettes on the steps of the War Memorial and watched people walk by – a cluster of tenth-years that hurled chips at each other; morsels that the pigeons fell on like vultures. There was a couple of old ladies walking arm in arm, each walking as if the other was made of the finest bone china.

'This place is the pits,' Kim pronounced.

'Yup.' Adele stubbed out her cigarette on the step.

'If we don't get out of here we'll die,' he declared dramatically.

'Just another year or two,' she said. Time would slip away fast enough. Weeks slid by much the same as one another. Pottery class, tutor group meetings, cigarettes and drunken weekends.

'Not soon enough,' Kim complained. 'There's absolutely fuck all to do.'

She sighed. 'We could always buy condoms and drop waterbombs off the car park.'

Kim rolled his eyes. 'Oh, be still my beating heart.'

'OK. We won't.'

'I didn't say that.'

'Well, what then?'

Kim stared at his shoes. 'Buggered if I know.' He yawned and stuffed his cigarettes back into his backpack. 'You know what would be cool?' he said eventually.

'What?'

'If you could fill condoms with half-melted ice poles. That would freak people out.'

She grinned, imagining the reactions when an ice-cold waterbomb splattered on a person or the pavement in an explosion of red synthetic strawberry or blue raspberry. The idea seemed inspired. 'The blue ones.'

'I thought the green ones.'

'How about the brown cola ones?'

Kim bounced to his feet. 'Yes! They'll look like refrigerated turds. Excellent!'

Galvanised by the prospect of a little childish mayhem, they skipped across the square to Boots. It was clean, pale and scented inside the chemist's, making the mess they meant to make seem all the more appealing. The perfume counters were filled with squares and circles and fan shapes of eyeshadow – colours that looked almost edible, candy pinks and chocolate browns, bright fake raspberry blue.

She side-stepped the lipsticks, pink as poked-out

tongues, red and deep cherry dark, sticking up like cartoon penises in their little white plastic holders. They were too much of a reminder of the cruel school legend that she needed a lipstick the size of the Eiffel Tower to cover her enormous lips. Even if she consciously knew it was childish and stupid, it still made her cheeks burn and the nape of her neck prickle. She knew she couldn't spend her life with her lips bitten and her head bowed, but it felt like such a struggle to tilt her chin up.

Make-up had never been her thing, anyway. She had seen enough of the popular girls' make-up mistakes. Although nobody commented that Tara Raymond's over-plucked eyebrows and lacquered fringe made her look wildly startled or that Sharon Bircher's face occasionally looked like a cross between the Tangoman and a kabuki mask, people had to have *thought* it often enough.

Nobody ever said anything to their faces because they were the alpha bitches of the school. If Adele walked through the gates in the morning wearing make-up that made her look like a burns victim, she knew she would never hear the end of it. That was the realpolitik of school life, and in order to survive it you sometimes had to accept it.

It wasn't fair. Kim told her often enough that she was gorgeous, and her father told her that she was pretty. She paused and peered in a mirror at a cosmetic display, with the pretence of looking at pressed powders.

'Come on,' Kim said, tugging at her sleeve.

'Wait,' she told him.

At times like these she sensed the difference between them. Kim liked nothing more than to break a rule as soon as he encountered it. The teachers named Adele as a good influence on him. She knew she was slower, steadier. Kim was the type to excel or crash and burn, with no in-betweens. He'd either be the star or the *enfant terrible*, a capricious whirlwind of demands and dirty deeds. Adele had learned not to draw attention to herself early in her social interactions. The victim of bullying could not be obtrusive or obvious. The greyer and less significant you were, the better – in order to escape further torment. She'd survived thus far and felt as though that time was gone. She was too old for realpolitik. She wanted to be looked at as a girl rather than a curiosity. She wanted to turn a few heads.

'Wait?'

'Yeah. Wait.'

Kim shrugged and went along the line of nail varnish testers, pronouncing judgement on each shade. 'Boring, boring, boring, boring, cat vomit, car accident ... why don't they have any green?'

'Dunno,' she muttered, her attention elsewhere.

The various compacts, pencils, brushes and cases were alluring, packaged in pale grey and gold; pretty feminine things she'd sneered at before as the only girl in an all-male family. It was hard to explain how she felt, even ten years later when she was twenty-seven and in bed with her lover, Paul, on a Sunday afternoon. It was as if she was walking a wire. That was the only way she could explain it.

Realising you were no longer a child and had, in some way, become a woman was like stepping onto a high wire stretched across a canyon. On the other side of the canyon lay the plain of smooth certainty of knowing who you were, but you first had to tread the precipitous walk of the teenage years, wobbling over a chasm of alligators and jagged rocks. Paul said that only she could think of alligators at a cosmetic counter and asked her if she thought the wirewalk had been worth it. Meaning, of course, 'Do you love me?'

She told him yes, but admitted that she might not be

off the wire yet. 'It might be that we're always walking it. We just get so good at it we don't know we're doing it. Like Blondin at Niagara.'

It was more or less inevitable that it was going to be complicated, but she didn't see it, having something of a Damascene experience at that cosmetic counter, that day. The clarity of it was as delicious as the eyeshadow compacts and pointed lipsticks with their seductive shapes and dazzling candy colours. After so many years of the complex minuet of hiding in plain sight and trying not to draw attention to herself, to accept that that was no longer the way of things was exciting and frightening. A fragile epiphany.

Kim wanted to buy condoms and yanked her sleeve again, impatient. She shook him away and told him to wait again.

'What are you looking at?' he asked.

'Just looking at these,' she said dreamily. She nodded to the cosmetic display.

'Hmm.' He sounded sceptical.

'Don't sound like *that*.'

'Like what?' He looked infuriatingly innocent. 'Anyway, it's about time you started wearing make-up.'

'I *do* wear make-up!'

'No you don't.'

'OK, so I don't put it on with a trowel, but I do wear it.'

He looked at the compacts. 'With your skin I'd say you should go for pinks and browns. Blue if you're feeling really slutty.'

'I don't want to look like a slut.'

'Why the fuck not?' asked Kim.

She liked his attitude. That seemed to be his mantra – 'Why the fuck not?' Red had to be the way to go if one wanted to look sexual. The vamps and bitches in films always wore red; always a discreet mocha or coral shade for the sweet heroine. You could tell the bad girl by her red lips the same way you could identify the villain in silent films by his kohl-lined rolling eyes and twirling moustache.

The lipsticks reminded her of the sweet variety, the hard candy ones she'd licked and reddened her mouth with as a small child. She had only vague recollections of playing with her dead mother's lipstick – bright poppy red.

'All right,' she said, and reached for the scarlet tester, painting a streak across the back of her hand in the accepted fashion.

Kim's eyes were wide. 'Whoa. Bright.'

'Too bright?'

'No way!' he shouted. 'It's a lucky colour, red. Wards off evil.'

'Oh really?' she snorted, already imagining the hell Sharon Bircher would give her if she walked into school with her lips painted peony red.

'Lucky,' Kim confirmed. 'And it's like a labial mimic.'

'A what?' she asked, laughing.

'Labial mimic. I read it in this book: red lips are sexy because they remind men of a woman's bits when she's aroused.'

'Oh, shut up!' Adele interrupted, shaking her head.

'No, it's true!' Kim insisted. 'There was this thing about this dancer in Paris – cancan girl, I think. The traditional cancan was done without knickers, so they'd flash their fannies with every high kick. I read this thing about a dancer who used to paint her lips – and not the ones on her face . . .'

Adele stared incredulously at him. 'You read some weird books. Do you know that?'

'It was a different book.' Kim shrugged. 'And it's not

weird. Makes perfect sense when you think about it. She used to paint the rouge on her twat in front of all the guys in her dressing room and turned them on like crazy.'

'I'm sticking to what I said about the weird books, Kim,' she said, nerves slightly jangled by the eroticism of the image. She looked at the smudge of red lipstick on the back of her hand and shivered. 'You really think red?'

'Definitely. You'd look like Joan Crawford.'

'Who?'

'Never you mind, ignorant peasant,' Kim sniffed. 'Now . . . you need a couple of pencils and a brush . . .'

'What about condoms?'

He shook his head. 'Naa. Fuck it. This is more fun. How much money have you got?'

They had enough between them to buy a lipstick, two coloured pencils – one red, one black – and a mascara. They headed back to Kim's to try out their purchases and mess around with the stuff in his make-up box.

Kim lived in a house behind his parents' restaurant. It always smelled good, of incense and spices. Kim grumbled about the constant stink and entered the house furtively, lest he get caught and dragged through the adjoining door into the kitchen. No such luck. Kim's mother poked her head out and summoned him in sharp Cantonese, ignoring Adele. He argued back in his parents' language and Adele followed him into the kitchen while he argued about something with his father, who was doing something to a duck.

Kim's mother caught hold of Adele's hair and bundled it up under a plastic cap. 'Hygiene,' she said brusquely.

'Sorry,' Adele said.

Kim's mother nodded and tucked stray curls under the cap. 'Pretty hair, but not in kitchen.'

'No. No. Of course not.'

She looked over at the delicate curls of spring onions that Mrs Qing had been preparing.

'You help me?' asked Mrs Qing, surprising her. Usually she struck Adele as surly, obviously thinking Kim and Adele's relationship was sexual.

'Could I?' she said. 'Thanks.'

Mrs Qing smiled a brief, tight smile. 'Wash hands,' she said, pointing to a small basin labelled for the purpose.

Adele scrubbed her hands with bright green soap from a wall dispenser, looking forward to helping out. Kim was still talking furiously to his father and she was excluded from overhearing by the language barrier, making her all the more grateful for Kim's mother doing something to include her.

Mrs Qing put her to work chopping onions, showing her to how to cut them in half, cut slits in them almost to the root and then slice in the opposite direction, so that they fell apart in neat little diced segments. She cut them up uncertainly, wishing she had the skill to show a touch of flair at it. It was a job she would have liked to have, learning to cook fabulous dishes and earning a bit of money.

Maybe Kim's parents had somehow considered she might be the best they could do for him, since he repeatedly said he didn't want to marry some nice Chinese girl. The thought of Kim marrying anyone was farcical. He was still a virgin and unhappy about the situation, saying he wanted some man with big hands and a kissable mouth to fuck his brains out.

No sooner had she settled into a rhythm of cutting up the onions than Kim stormed across the kitchen, yanked the hat and what felt like most of her hair from her head and angrily announced that they were getting out of there. His parents yelled. Her school shoes clattered on the pavement and Kim's fingers remained locked around her wrist.

'Ow ... let *go*!'

He stopped next to the petrol station. 'Fucking hell.'

'What?'

'Arsehole. He wants me to go to fucking chef school.' Kim raked a hand through his hair and let out a primal-sounding scream, probably learned in drama class. 'Dammit. Where are my cigarettes?'

He rummaged in his bag that he had snatched from the hallway on the way out.

'One problem,' Adele said. 'You can't actually cook.'

'No. *I* know that. You think *he'd* have figured that out by now.' Kim lit up with shaking fingers. 'He wants to make a silk purse and doesn't recognise a sow's fucking ear when it's staring him in the face.'

She pulled a face and sighed, not knowing what to say. It certainly wouldn't be a good moment to say that she personally would have leaped at the chance of going to catering college. 'Come on,' she said. 'We'll go to my place.'

It was a walk right across town, but Kim sulkily agreed. Compared to his home, Adele's was Liberty Hall.

It was a small house, built of that yellowish brick common to sprawling estates, and had a look of neglect about it. There were no flowers in the garden and, when you opened the squeaky gate, the dog barked to be walked. He was an overfed Border Collie cross named Tips, and licked too much for Kim's liking.

Adele leaned down and stroked his ears, offered her face for a licking. 'Tipsy tips,' she crooned. 'Show me love, baby.'

'I don't know how you can stand it,' Kim said.

'Aww. He's a good dog.' She rubbed his ears and peered into his sad dog eyes. He had the needly nose of a collie and the soulful eyes of a black Labrador. 'No, I'm not feeding you. Lie down. Lie down!'

She yelled a hello to whoever was in and stomped up the stairs with Kim in tow. 'He'll blag a meal from everyone who comes in the door. I feed him, Dad feeds him, Chris feeds him, Tony feeds him and he eats four meals a day. No wonder he's so lardy.'

She was glad to be home, in her small bedroom with all its familiar things – the Indian bedspread, the poster of a kohl-eyed and clinically depressed Kurt Cobain on the wall. It smelled of dog and her attempts to mask the stench with joss sticks had made her father throw fits. He complained that they smelled disgusting and, whatsmore, they were dangerous. His job made him obsessive and Adele and her brothers were continually being told to check the cooker was off and cigarettes were completely crushed out. She hid ashtrays under her bed and set off smoke alarms, not showing the proper respect a firefighter's daughter should, despite being told from infancy never to play with fire.

Kim said it was her element, because she was a Leo, and that she was a fire dragon in Chinese astrology. He was a Pisces, a water sign, and Chinese year of the snake. He still held onto his superstitions, believing that it was fitting for an actor to be superstitious. He squeezed a blob of make-up onto his index finger and dotted patches on her cheeks, nose, chin and forehead. She stared self-consciously at the ceiling as his small, round-tipped fingers worked over her face, patting the stuff in place with a delicate fingertip under her eye, smoothing it firmly across the wider planes of her cheeks and forehead. She had never had anyone put make-up on for her before, and it felt strange and awkward. She hadn't had much practice herself. Her brothers liked make-up and short skirts on their girlfriends and her brothers were pricks and their girlfriends simpering airheads, so she had wanted to try and be as different from them as possible. She hated the thought of having sisters-in-law. She didn't like women at all – in her experience they were sly, nasty, catty, petty creatures.

Kim brandished an eyepencil. 'God, you're going to have to do something about your eyebrows, Del.'

'What's wrong with my eyebrows?' she said, trying not to move her lips too much lest she disturb the film of foundation sitting on her skin. She began to realise why they called it pancake. It looked like a thick gluey batter on Kim's fingers, and sat on her face like a stodgy Shrove Tuesday pancake with holes cut for the eyes and mouth. Squeeze of lemon and a spoonful of sugar and she'd be all set.

'Too thick,' Kim said. 'You got any tweezers?'

'You're not plucking my eyebrows.'

'Go on. It'll make such a difference to your face.'

'No. It'll hurt.'

'*Il faut souffrir pour etre belle.*' Kim reeled off one of the few French phrases he knew well. In class he would sarcastically drawl through the verbs, *je vais, tu vas, il va, elle va.* He didn't see why he had to do French. He was already bilingual and fond of telling teachers that Cantonese was spoken by more people than French, statistically speaking.

'I don't want to suffer.'

'Life is suffering, sweetie,' Kim said dramatically. 'Get over it.'

'I haven't got any tweezers anyway.'

'I've got some at home.'

'You would have.'

Kim laughed unexpectedly. 'We're all wrong. I'd rather

be a girl and you'd rather be a boy. If we could switch bodies we should. Right . . . nearly done.'

When she looked at her face in the mirror, her initial desire was to scrub it all off, because she knew how her dad and her brothers would tease.

'What do you reckon?' Kim asked.

'Um . . . yeah,' she said, looking at her face, rendered mask-like by the make-up, smooth and matte like the girls on magazine covers. She was afraid to admit that she quite liked it.

She waited until late at night when she was alone in her room to try it again. Her mind was still focused on Kim's story about the French dancer, putting on her make-up in the dressing room in front of all her would-be lovers. She knew how her face looked with her lips painted in a blatant invitation to kiss, and thought maybe she did get what putting on make-up was about after all – highlighting every aspect of one's body to extend an erotic invitation.

Hot and restless, she switched on the bedside lamp and sat down at the cluttered dressing table, sucking her lips reflexively at the sight of her reflection. Her hair covered her breasts, thick hair that Mrs Qing had said was pretty. She supposed it was – thick, curly and dark. She dragged a brush through it and looked thoughtfully at herself, her lips sucked into her mouth in a self-conscious ugly line. Irritated, she forced herself to relax, pouting back at herself. It looked better and felt sensuous, holding her lips soft and pliant as if she were about to kiss a cherished lover.

She tried out a thicker, softer pout and was startled to discover that it looked sexy. Her lips looked soft and delicious and her skin was pale and pure in the lamplight. Daring a little more, she put down the hairbrush and pushed back her cloud of dark hair, exposing her breasts to the mirror. Her nipples were paler than her lips. She bit her lips, chewing on them in her old, bad habit, then released them so they sprang back ripe and pinker than before – the only method of lip rouge that had been acceptable to Victorian ladies, who had advised young girls to bite their lips and pinch their cheeks before they entered a room. Adele supposed rouge was the slapper's solution – the loose women who didn't have the 'moral fibre' to bite and pinch themselves in that strange world where if it hurt it was good for you.

Sod that, she thought, rejecting it out of hand. Life was hard enough without having to cause yourself more pain. She'd prefer to use a touch of paint and powder, save herself the pain and make her lips redder than was respectable. She imagined herself as the French dancer, making up in her dressing room, revealing all to a pack of horny men, all unable to take their eyes off her and saluting her with their cocks. It was an exciting thought and prompted her to take the red lipstick out of the drawer and paint her lips with it, her hand trembling slightly because she was thinking about how it would look if she painted herself the way the dancer had. With her lips painted, her eyes looked darker and brighter and her skin pale and flat like pale clay, a blankness that was both exotic and erotic. She was like a canvas on which she could paint her own fantasies.

She slipped off her sensible black cotton pants – the only thing she was wearing – and caught a glimpse of her dark pubic bush as she sat back down at the dressing table. Her legs seemed to refuse to stay together, so she let her thighs sprawl open against the low stool. Putting on lipstick was alien enough to her, but doing it naked was even more so, and even more exciting. Probably the way that provocative cancan girl would have done it – making up her face in the nude, maybe wearing a pair of frilly garters to offset white thighs that she flashed as brazenly as her tits.

Emboldened, Adele applied the lipstick to her nipples, painting them so that they stood out like targets for a man's hungry mouth. Her breasts looked like they were designed to be stared at.

She bit her lip again and the greasy flavour of the lipstick reminded her that she shouldn't do that any more. That was her old self, not this fabulously sexy creature that she could be, naked and painted. Her thighs felt loose and restless and she was surprised and pleased by the pleasant swollen sensation between them. Perhaps, for the first time, she was aware of her own femininity as a gift rather than a hindrance, and understood, certainly for the first time, why Kim coveted it.

2

It was psychological warfare. You had to go in there with your head up high because those angry, lonely sods in polyester would make you feel as small as they possibly could in order to make themselves feel better about being hated. Adele faked nonchalance as she skimmed over the boards – lousy jobs that wouldn't even begin to cover the rent on the kind of property she could live in. Even the better paid nine-to-five positions in offices would see her living in a coffin-sized bedsit like Larkin's Mr Bleaney. Miserable bastard, that Larkin. She'd read his poems at school and disliked his cynicism because she didn't care to believe that was the truth of the world.

All the catering positions were asking for meaningless vocational qualifications she didn't have, because her father had insisted she worked on far more useless achievements, certificates to prove she knew how to read and write, and stuff about xylem and phloem and the causes of the Second World War. It was all so mind-numbingly dull she felt like slapping herself. Assistant chef. GNVQ. What the hell was a GNVQ? If she remembered correctly it was something they made the dense kids do when they repeatedly failed to show up for regular GCSE classes. All you needed to cook was a basic food hygiene certificate.

Showtime. She joined the queue behind a skinny middle-aged man with a heroically advanced case of fag-finger and greasy, thinning hair scraped back in a ponytail. His fingers, drumming impatiently on the edge of a board, were the colour of mahogany and she thought he could save himself cash on cigarettes by sticking his finger in his mouth and sucking. You had to keep your eyes peeled and notice details about people in here in order to stop your brain turning to cheese. That was the way they wanted you – numb, mindless sheep to be herded into a pen.

And what type of work are you looking for?

Like you'd know. In a world where you were defined by what you did, why pin yourself down to a category? Chef, office wonk, tomato picker, hairdresser. These people viewed life like a game of Happy Families. Mr Bun the Baker, Mr Stamp the Postman. Round here it was more like Mr Pancreatic Shutdown the Alcoholic, Mr Spliff the Stoner, Mr Mitty the Barefaced Bar-room Bullshitter and Mr Don't Fancy Yours Much, the Last Twat In The Nightclub.

Monsieur Continental Cancer the Powerful French Fag Smoker in front was signing his name before heading off to the pub, assured of another cheque in the post. Adele sat down. It was a boy this time, not the patronising woman with the red frightwig and no eyebrows that she usually encountered. His nametag said Steven and he had a soft young face covered in little pimple scabs, and one of those downy moustaches that adolescent boys cultivated.

'Good morning,' he said, briskly tapping on a computer keyboard.

'Hello,' she said, already realising she sounded snotty and bored. There was something about a nineteen-year-old in a suit and a boring job that depressed her. Lost cause already. Poor little sod.

He was clicking his mouse and peering at the screen.

'How are you?' she asked, deciding to see how he

responded when treated like a person instead of a Job-centre clerk.

'Um ... fine,' said Steven, looking disconcerted. 'Right ... uh ... your job review, Ms Western.'

'Yes?'

'We need to look at what kind of work you're looking for.'

'Right.' She tried to look enthusiastic. Good dog. Boring job. Beg for boring job, get money. She wondered what he'd do if she barked at him and squashed down a laugh.

'Have you considered retraining at all?' he asked.

'I considered retraining as a soldier of fortune, but there's not much call for it around here.'

He blinked. Too late. They'd already performed the necessary sense-of-humour bypass. 'How about barwork?'

'Right. Anti-social hours and walking home late at night when the streets are full of drunken potential rapists and girls glassing one another? Would you do it?'

'Well, I work here.' Steven said with primary-school patience, tapping his desk.

'That was a hypothetical question,' Adele said, realising she was dealing with someone very stupid indeed. Deserved his fate. There was a reason Steven wasn't out getting pissed, stoned and laid like a normal nineteen-year-old. He obviously wasn't normal. 'OK, do you have any catering jobs?'

He brightened, faced with something he knew and understood. 'Yes.' He clicked his mouse. 'There's a position at the bowling alley.'

Shovelling chips in a stupid cardboard hat and having to dress up as a pirate to wait on children's parties. No way. 'I'm allergic to that stuff they spray the shoes with,' she lied.

'You wouldn't be near the shoes,' he said, clearly

getting impatient. 'OK, how about this one, kitchen preparation...'

'Peeling spuds?' This was a common trick of the Job-centre. Give a bad job a longer name and somehow people would accept it.

'It says general preparation.'

'Right. Peeling spuds and carrots.'

'I don't have that information.'

'Of course you don't, mate. They don't give you that information because no bugger would take the job if they knew what it actually entailed.' She sighed, realising she was knocking her head against a brick wall. 'OK. Next?'

'Assistant chef at family restaurant...'

'Stop!' Adele said. 'Think. Use your imagination. Family restaurant. You know what that is? That's *baked beans*. Children in restaurant equals vats of baked beans and trays of fish fingers. Would you really want to be defined by that? Baked-bean dispenser for boring children? Wouldn't you rather die?'

'It's a job.'

She sighed again, so heavily she thought she would suck the oxygen out of the room. 'Do you enjoy your job?'

'I'm afraid if you are not actively looking for work your benefits will be cut.'

'Bugger. *Now* I get the answering service.'

'Well, you're not exactly being co-operative.'

'I would be co-operative,' Adele said. 'I would be *completely* co-operative if someone could offer me something more than minimum wage for cooking baked beans and chips.'

'This is the typical wage bracket for this type of work.'

She shook her head, despairing. She wasn't talking about the wage so much as the gut-wrenching dullness. Not that he understood. There was no use trying to explain to people who saw themselves as bland cogs in the system and had no imagination whatsoever. 'OK. Next?'

He bashed out the details on his computer and handed them to her. 'I don't think your attitude will do you any favours.'

'I don't think yours will either.' Not unless he wanted a lifetime of being an angry, mouse-eyed nobody whose entire wardrobe was composed of polyester with sweat-patches under the arms, but that wasn't her problem, since her problems weren't his – even if it was his job to deal with them.

He moved his mouse over the screen. 'Head chef. Full time. Possible live-in position,' he droned.

'Thank you,' she said, in the voice she reserved for idiots, drunks and broken toasters. 'Sounds more like something I could make an actual *living* from. Details?'

'I'll just get those printed off for you,' Steven said, sounding as though he was glad to get away from her.

He came back with a computer print-out giving her a contact name and address and she signed on the dotted line, said she hadn't done any work for the past two weeks, as required, and strolled out into the sunlit street reading the piece of paper: Paul Eades, at Shipworths, it said. She knew the place. Shipworths had once been a jewellers, a handsome Victorian building with an elaborate faux classical style and a white painted front. It had been a place of magic and mystery to her on holidays here as a kid. When you stepped through the door it had polished wooden floors on which your heels clicked, like when you walked into a church. It had a long counter and all around expensive things – diamonds, pearls, sapphires and emeralds – glittered and shone. And then, in the middle of the silky smooth floor, *the* emerald.

In a glass case that had seemed gargantuan in her childhood was a huge rock shaped like a truncated cone but hollow inside. It lay on its side and, within, were hundreds and hundreds of emeralds. It had to be the most beautiful thing she had ever seen, shimmering green stones, growing inside what looked like an ordinary rock from another angle. She realised now that it must have been worth at least a six-figure sum, even a decade or more ago. Every night fine metal grilles were folded down behind the glass of the jewellery shop. Then one day they must have packed up and left, and taken away the metal grilles and the emerald rock, because the old jewellers was being refurbished and worked on, and presumably now being converted into a restaurant. Worth a shot. It beat playing mind-games with the Jobcentre clerks every fortnight. The trouble with unemployment was that the money was shit.

There were no longer emeralds from Brazil in Shipworths. It now stank of sawdust, plaster and a thick fug of male sweat. The builders were working steadily to the tinny sounds coming out of a radio – one of the local stations that played golden oldies and three-year-old dance hits as if the really popular stuff was too expensive and aspirational for their station. The DJs always sounded like Alan Partridge, saccharin sweet, devoid of irony and apparently unable to know when to shut the fuck up.

There were four men inside: a guy in a vest with a huge beer belly poking out from underneath like some peek-a-boo maternity outfit; a sullen-looking boy with a crop of very curly dark hair and an eyebrow ring, and one of those men Adele knew instinctively was trouble. He wore a beanie hat and a capped sleeved T-shirt and was sucking on a tight prison roll-up. The edges of his eyes were creased, as if from squinting in what he no doubt imagined to be a thoughtful manner while pretending to listen to people's opinions. Every knot and slump of his body language said 'bad attitude'. He checked her out openly and Adele had to fight to keep the sneer off her face. She knew men like these – rough overgrown kids who talked dirty at the bar but were babies in bed, wanting nothing but to bury their heads in a pair of big tits and whimper.

Then there was Jude. The first time she got a good look at him she imagined herself as a cartoon: eyes bugging out, pupils replaced with big pink hearts, tongue unravelled to her shoes, the sound of sirens screaming red alert. It was lust at first sight. He was bent over a plank that was balanced on a workbench, working a plane along the length of it. His arse was the first thing she noticed, a thing of beauty in loose, faded denims. Then he shifted his body on the outstroke of the plane, his torso twisting subtly like a cat's, his eyes fixing firmly on her. Blinding. He was dazzling, dusty, half-naked.

The tuft beneath his arm was dewed with sweat, his long flank pale as a pearl, right down to the mouth-watering jut of one pretty hip peeking over the waistband of his loose, skaterboy jeans. When he stood upright his jeans slipped further down, revealing his whole slender front almost down to the curls of his pubic hair.

'Hi,' he said.

'I'm looking for Paul Eades,' she said. Somehow.

'Ah, right. Yeah.' He nodded. He glanced over at the boy with the eyebrow ring who disappeared out back for a moment and returned with Paul.

Paul Eades wore leather trousers and an acid-green shirt. His longish dark hair curled at the nape of his neck and he had a mobile phone in one hand and a cigarette in the other. To free up his hand to shake hers, he put his cigarette in his mouth as if he was unwilling to put down his doubtless expensive little telephone.

'Hi, you must be Adele?' he said, his eyes slightly

screwed up against the smoke but managing to balance his cigarette on his lip in an effortless Hollywood cool-guy-type way. 'Glad you could make it.'

'No trouble,' Adele said, breathing in all the testosterone hanging in the air and trying not to stare at the carpenter. He brushed past her with a muttered 'scuse me', and her bare arm bumped against his side. His skin was hot and moist.

'Drink?' Paul asked, moving behind the unfinished bar. 'I'm afraid we only have beer – was a cooler here somewhere . . .'

Eyebrow-Ring stooped and pointed out the cooler. The carpenter leaned over, his rump in the air about six inches from Adele's left hand. An inch of butt-crack showed above his jeans, a junior version of the traditional cavernous, hairy builder's crevice.

'Yes. Thanks,' she said. Her mouth was dry. Probably sawdust in the air. This already wasn't going well. 'No trouble' wasn't exactly an intelligent, articulate greeting.

'Good.' Paul set about opening a bottle. Eyebrow-Ring whispered something to him that made him smile and whisper, 'Shut up', instantly setting her on edge.

'OK, I'll level with you,' Paul said. 'We're a little behind schedule.'

'I thought maybe you were going for the distressed look,' she said, hoping to lighten things with a joke.

'Distressed?' Paul raised his eyebrows. 'Distressed? Darling, it's fucking *panicked*.'

She smiled and took a careful, frothy sip from the top of her beer bottle. It tasted bad, but at least it was cold and wet.

'What I *can* do,' Paul continued, 'is show you around what we have so far in the kitchen. Oh, do you have a CV done, by the way?'

'Um, yeah,' Adele said, starting to feel more confident

again. So he was serious. Good. She fished the paper out of her bag, relieved to see it hadn't got too crumpled, and handed it to Paul. As he moved forwards to take it, Eyebrow-Ring moved with him, as if they were pasted together at the hip.

'Come on round,' he said, gesturing to the other side of the bar. He took a pair of steel-frame glasses from the shelf below him and popped them on to read, resting his elbows on the bar. Eyebrow-Ring slunk closer and rested his chin on Paul's shoulder.

'This is very impressive,' Paul muttered, examining her CV and raising his eyebrows. The glasses somehow made him look younger – a peek at the eager, nerdy public schoolboy he might once have been.

'Thanks,' she said. From her new position on the business side of the bar she had a panoramic view of the carpenter's peachy crack. It looked big enough to hook her thumb into – to literally pick him up by the scruff of his pants, spin his hips around in her hands and take his mouth by force. There was a movement of air near her hip and she noticed Eyebrow-Ring's hand straying to Paul's bottom.

Paul shook his head as if in disbelief. 'This is great,' he said. He slipped a hand behind him to prise away his admirer's fingers crawling suggestively over the base of his spine, as if Eyebrow-Ring was illustrating what he'd like to do to the exposed skin the carpenter was baring.

Paul's back, where his T-shirt had been pushed up, was smooth and tanned, two luscious dimples at the base of his spine. She tried not to stare, but if she looked forwards she was looking at the carpenter's butt and if she looked to her side she could see Eyebrow-Ring and Paul's fingers wrestling flirtatiously over special rights to that shallow valley low on Paul's back, just above where his arse began. She wished she could turn her head one-eighty like an owl, because this was altogether way too much man-butt for a job interview.

She happened to notice a flaw in the band of clear coppery skin exposed at the back of Paul's waist. It looked at first glance like a strawberry birthmark, but then she realised from the mottled texture and colour that it was a love bite. Someone had bitten him there, probably Eyebrow-Ring. He'd suckled on the spot until it fractured tiny capillaries and made them burst under the thin membrane of skin. He had caused a little pain and left a semi-permanent forget-me-not. She had a startling mental image of what they must look like together – Eyebrow-Ring on his knees like a supplicant, his hands cupping Paul's butt, his lips moulded to the base of Paul's spine. It was a tender slow-burn of an image, and Adele had a feeling it had already slipped too deep into her consciousness to forget about.

'Come on through,' Paul said, standing up straight and brushing away exploring hands. He turned to the carpenter. 'Jude, can I borrow you a moment?'

'Sure.' His name was Jude. Hey, Jude, she thought, smiling. He smiled back, wiping sweat from the back of his neck.

Paul added a 'by the way' introduction for Eyebrow-Ring, but he need not have bothered because Adele couldn't make out the name Paul said. It was 'Owen' or 'Ewan' but somehow neither of them. Adele wondered if he spoke English because he was so gypsy dark and had so far not said a word. Well, an audible word, anyway. She disliked people who whispered. It was rude and reminded her unpleasantly of being a schoolgirl.

The kitchen was a big, dusty shell still in the process of being assembled and she had no idea what she was supposed to say about it.

'What do you think?' Paul asked.

'To be honest it's a bit difficult to say at the moment,' she said. 'I mean, you never know how you'll get along with a particular kitchen until you've worked in it for a while.'

'Absolutely,' he said earnestly. 'I mean dimensions and stuff. Is it going to be big enough?'

'It depends. On what meals you want to serve, how many covers you predict, how many staff are manning the kitchen.'

'Right, yes,' Paul said, nodding. He seemed to be hanging on her every word and she got into her stride.

'I'd say you could probably serve about forty covers comfortably in there for a lunch,' she said. 'Unless you have seating room upstairs?'

He shook his head. 'No. Just downstairs.'

'Forty people. Hmm. I'd say you'd need about four kitchen staff at least. It depends on what you're serving. Bar snacks, meals, both. Are you expecting people to come here for a three-course lunch or dinner?'

'Lunch,' Paul said, leaning against a doorframe. Ewan, or whatever his name was, slid an arm around his waist. Jude made a soft sound like a thin hiss – maybe disapproving. Adele wondered at them flaunting their gayness so openly amongst a bunch of builders, a species of men who in general weren't known for their political correctness.

'It would have to be lunch,' he said. 'I'd think about bar snacks in the evenings but I think doing two meals a day would be a heavy workload.'

'You're not wrong.' Eyebrow-Ring spoke at last. His voice was rich and soft, with a singsong lilting, rolling accent that Adele recognised as Welsh. His strange-sounding name made sense now. 'Paul, can I have a word?'

'Of course,' Paul said. 'Jude ... would you mind showing Adele around?'

'Uh huh.' Jude nodded. He was standing at her elbow and had a resinous smell of sawdust about him. His hair was red-gold somewhere under the dust and grime that turned it khaki, and where his sweat had dripped it left barely noticeable clean trails where dust had turned his skin to matt. 'I'll show you the garden,' he said.

'Great.' Adele nodded. She thought it was possibly the stupidest single word she had ever uttered in her life. 'Great'. Paul slipped out into another room and she was sure as she followed Jude she heard the soft, wet sounds of people kissing, somewhere behind her. Too much testosterone in one enclosed space. God only knew, Paul and Boyfriend generated enough hormones between them.

Jude walked ahead of her down a narrow corridor. 'Ladies loo through there,' he said, jerking a thumb towards a door on their left. 'Haven't finished painting in there yet.'

'Right,' she said, stunned cold at the paucity of her vocabulary and wanting to bang her head against a wall.

'Through here.' Jude opened a door on 'the garden'. 'Thinking about getting a patio out here,' he said shortly. 'For people who like flies in their soup.'

He held the door open for her and she laughed too loudly at his joke and slipped past him outside. It never failed to disgust her how she could go from nought to moron in twenty seconds flat as soon as she fancied someone. She could feel the heat coming off his skin as she brushed past him to step into a small, weed-choked courtyard filled with old metal beer kegs, pigeon shit and, in the middle, a broken rotary clothesline. It bore an ancient J-cloth which hung limp and tattered like the flag of the *Marie Celeste*.

'It's nice,' she said lamely.

His eyebrows shot up incredulously, little tangerine Roman arches.

'OK, it's not,' she conceded.

'It's a shit-heap,' Jude said accurately, taking a packet of cigarettes out of his jeans' pocket. 'Do you mind? I can't smoke indoors.'

'No, go ahead. Please.' Adele could smell something sweet and heavy, almost rotten. The thought that it might be a nest of dead rats made her feel slightly queasy, and worried how this yard would go down with the health inspectors.

'You want one?' Jude offered her a cigarette.

'Thanks,' she said, taking one. His hands were rough and knuckly and he wore a bracelet made of braided silk thread around his wrist.

She glanced around and realised what the smell was. There was a huge, ancient wisteria crawling up the back of the building, in full flower. The beautiful creeper swarmed over and around the windows masking peeling white paint, so lush it looked as though it had choked every other plant in the garden and blossomed on their stolen life force. The dropping pale violet blossoms were so fragrant the smell was nearly sickening.

'That's nice though,' she said, blowing smoke up towards the flowers. 'Must have been growing for years.'

'Not bad.' Jude shrugged. She wondered how old he was. He had the closed manner of a teenager and she began to think he was just a pretty face and ass. 'Needs a ton of work doing out here.'

'Yes.'

He stared at her. 'Do you live round here?'

'I live nearby. Hoping to move.'

'Right. Yeah. Cool.'

Wow. Yeah. Right. Cool. Devastating repartee. She

wondered if she was in the wrong line of unemployment after all and, instead of looking for work as a chef, she should set up a class for men to teach them to make proper conversation with women. Surely they used to know how to do it, back in the days when social mores dictated they had to woo with their lips and not their hips. Or maybe that was the point of port and cigars after dinner – to take the strain off all the giant intellects of those poor gentlemen who had sprained a brain cell or two after five or six courses spent in the company of a bunch of vacuous young ladies. Of course, the ladies weren't born airheads. They'd been taught to be stupid, the better to keep them suitably decorative, but their menfolk had conveniently forgotten this fact.

What the hell was the point of being decorative if you had bugger all to say for yourself?

She impatiently blew out smoke. 'Well, this is nice,' she said, struggling to hide her sarcasm. She leaned back on her unaccustomed high heels and nearly swayed backwards to lean against the wall. Conscious that the wall was grubby and cobwebby, and that she was in her interview suit, she quickly kicked back with one heel to steady herself and keep her bottom off the wall, and was sure she almost pulled it off as a nonchalant pose. Almost. She wasn't used to either heels or short skirts, and her skirt had ridden up her thigh just enough to show where the thin, glossy coffee-cream nylon of her stocking was stitched to the shiny beige-brown border of lace, and flashed the tiny tab of ribbon that covered the suspender.

Jude was looking and trying not to. Well well.

Adele was high enough on the stink of working men and the titillating mystery of Paul and the Boyfriend to want to goad Jude further. It was absolutely the wrong time and place and that just made the thought of mischief seem more seductive. He smelled of sawdust, and his sweat had washed his skin clean in tempting streaks of pink and white where it had run in rivulets. He looked like a melting ice-cream, she thought, smiling at him. His eyelids, previously dipped in an expression of contrived cool, lifted and showed more of the blue iris, so that he looked even younger, and eager.

She smiled again, and crooked her knee further so that her skirt rode higher. She realised that there was an advantage to this ridiculous outfit. No matter how she loathed the discomfort of wearing it, he liked it and was paying close attention to the lace top of her stocking. She doubted he'd look twice at her if he passed her in the street while she was wearing a T-shirt and jeans, but she wouldn't turn down an opportunity purely out of feminist pique. He was too pretty to pass up. She nearly laughed. Seemed that both sexes had an equal capacity to be shallow.

He looked down at her thigh and drew a little closer. She moved away, back into the shelter of the wisteria, keeping her eyes on his to let him know he wasn't being rebuffed – far from it. Under the thick blossom of the purple creeper the scent was overpowering and made her head spin. Stupid, stupid idea. Paul was bound to come looking for her to finish the interview. She would completely blow her chance.

It only made her want to do it all the more.

Jude's hair looked all the redder against the wisteria, and the dappled pattern of light on his body made him look exotic, puckish.

'Cooler in the shade,' she said redundantly.

'Uh huh.' He nodded and drew on his cigarette.

God, another awful conversation. She was sure she was going to laugh this time and turned around, looking up and pretending to be fascinated by the stringy mauve-lipped daisies growing on top of the wall. She could feel him moving closer behind her, just behind her shoulder, and saw the butt of his cigarette hit the ground. She stubbed her own smoke out on the wall and glanced over her other shoulder to keep a look out. She could feel him breathing against her neck, smell his sweat and feel the heat of his body through the back of her stifling suit. Come on, then, she nearly muttered aloud, hot and impatient.

If she set out to fool around with a virtual stranger she wanted to fool around for real instead of tentatively sniffing around each other like a couple of dogs in the park. She leaned back an inch or so and smiled when she felt his hand on her bottom, touching too lightly for her liking, so she made a low sound of approval and was gratified when his hand squeezed and kneaded.

Adele listened for the sound of anyone approaching, but all she heard was the sound of traffic on the other side of the building and the buzz of a power tool from within. Any second now she'd be caught out; the thought made her heart beat faster and her clit throb. Jude pressed his fingers into the flesh of her buttock but made no attempt to lift her skirt. Shy? Even better. She wanted to shock him.

She grabbed hold of his hand and removed it from her arse, and felt him stiffen, obviously thinking she was calling time out on the fun. Instead, she pulled his arm around her waist and shifted her feet apart. He exhaled against the lobe of her ear and kissed the skin behind it as she pressed his hand against the inside of her thigh.

Slyly, she glanced at the door again and shivered, savouring the risk of discovery and wanting his fingers inside her right now. They were caught up in a tussle and tangle of knickers, sweat and hair for a moment, until she guided his hand to the entrance and felt the tip of his finger in there. Eagerly she ground her hips down to take the rest and felt his rough callused skin worm its way up inside her, a sensation almost like satisfaction.

Jude made a wordless moan behind her, and she could feel what had to be the stiff length of his dick pressing against her butt. She moved against it and he gasped and found her clit with his thumb, beginning to rub. Anyone walking out or looking down from a window would have been able to see exactly what they were doing. Her skirt was raised high enough to show her thighs and her crotch, knickers pulled to one side where Jude had his hand jammed inside them, getting the hang of it now and starting to fuck her with his fingers. His thumb pressed against the stem of her clit and she looked at the door again, relishing the terror of being caught. The fear alone was almost enough to get her off.

'Fuckin' hell,' he muttered, his other hand reaching round to squeeze her breast. His thumb slipped and when he replaced it it was lower, dipping under the hood and grinding against the very ends of her nerves so hard that she shuddered and clenched her muscles around his fingers. She tensed subtly and let him feel with his fingers what she would be able to do to his dick; how the inside of her body would ripple and suckle wetly around him when he fucked her; how her muscles would twitch eagerly with every thrust. He moved his fingers faster in response, far clumsier than her own practised touch, but it was just enough, with his fingers jabbing and jumping inside and his thumb seeming like it was trying to squash her clit up into her pubic bone. The thought that she was getting fingerfucked at a job interview sparked her climax. She thrust her hips convulsively into his touch, teasing herself all the more by imagining that someone might see their frantic movements and envy them.

As soon as the aftershocks ebbed away and his fingers slid out, she realised that she would have to turn around and look him in the eye. That seemed suddenly mortifying and hilarious all at once, given that she'd only just met him. Fortunately, she heard voices near the door. Jude would have to go without. He must be so hard in his jeans. She smoothed down her skirt and turned around. He looked as though he was burning up, his cheeks and throat flushed pink and the rivulets of sweat in the dust on his body broader and fresher. His eyes were so dilated that there was just a sliver of a blue rim around the black of the pupil and his lips were slightly bitten and slack, hanging a little open over his teeth. His mouth looked like a predator's, panting, all red flesh and white enamel, and he was looking at the hem of her skirt as if he wanted to devour what was under it. He flashed his dark-blue eyes up at her face and deliberately pushed his wet fingers into his mouth, sucking them clean with an expression of relish on his face.

She felt one last little needle of pleasure run through her as she watched him, but that was it for now, because Paul was coming out into the yard.

'Hi. Sorry about that,' he said. 'Had to take a phone call.'

'No problem,' Adele said, surprised at how cocky and relaxed she managed to sound. She didn't feel it. She was sure her knees were trembling and the intricacies of all that ludicrous underwear felt knotted uncomfortably around her arse-cheeks. She was sure she reeked of sex.

'Hope you didn't get bored,' Paul said. Jude went red.

Adele smiled. 'Oh no,' she said, shrugging. 'Not too deeply, anyway.'

3

The girls looked like Xeroxes of each other, the littler one a poorer copy of the original the elder was aping. They had fine blonde hair and pale-blue eyes and they both had a habit of sucking their thumbs. Karina felt sorry for them, because they weren't entirely wanted. Their father had moved beyond the age of childrearing years ago and, while their mother, Suki, had wanted them desperately, they had almost been treated as gifts to keep her from straying. If Suki wanted a sports car, Edward bought her a sports car. If she wanted to get pregnant, he got her pregnant because he couldn't stand the thought of any other man knocking her up. If Suki wanted a music teacher for the girls, she got a music teacher for the girls. Suki couldn't stand the thought of her babies suffering from her own frustrated ambition. When Edward had met Suki she had been promoting a minor dance hit she had had in 1993; a tune Karina remembered hearing as a teenager. It had popped into the butt end of the top 40 and popped out again while Suki turned her back on the music business and settled down to pop out babies.

The two girls, Elisa and Hannah, were no more musically gifted than average nine- and seven-year-olds. Elisa could pick out a tune on the piano, while Hannah tootled 'Frere Jacques' on a descant recorder until Karina felt like crying and pleading hysterically with her to stop. She knew if she did such a thing the girls would gaze dumbly at her and roll their eyes in confusion and disapproval. Little Hannah might cry, but Karina doubted it. The girls had Suki's looks, but in temperament they had Edward's stodgy respectability.

Karina disliked Edward's stuffiness. He always had something in his hand – some kind of status-bearing penis substitute: a golf club, a shooting stick, a rolled-up copy of the *Daily Express*. When he was home, which he rarely was, he sat around his awful house with an air of entitlement. Suki leaped up, dried her eyes and did his bidding as soon as he walked in the door, and Karina wanted to punch her for it. The same way she wanted to punch Edward for calling her Miss May and covertly staring at her tits when his children were in the room.

She didn't feel like teaching the girls. Hannah was more interested in her pet tortoise, trying to cram a slice of apricot into its mouth. It had sensibly and sullenly retreated into its shell and Hannah pushed it around the gruesome, puffy, fake Chinese rug like a Tonka truck while Elisa screamed at her to stop it.

'You're scaring him. Stop it!'

'He likes it. Come on, Turtle ... come out and eat your food.' Hannah pressed her cheek against the carpet, bum in the air, staring into the neck hole of the carapace where the tortoise lurked. 'Turrrrrtle ...'

'Hannah, leave Turtle alone,' Karina said wearily. 'He doesn't want to play.'

'*See?*' said Elisa, looking infuriatingly smug.

'He does!' Hannah stubbornly stuck her lower lip out. 'He's just playing at hiding.'

'He hates you.'

'He does not!'

'Does. He hates you because you torture him. He's my tortoise anyway.'

'He is not. Mummy said he belonged to both of us.'

'I look after him better and I don't torture him.'

Karina grimly stared at the piano keys and wondered why any woman wanted children. So far as she could see, they leeched calcium from your bones for nine months, were small bundles of screaming need for the first eighteen months and then you spent their entire childhood trying to temper the natural selfishness that evolution had built into them. It didn't seem to make any sense that these creatures had come out of Suki, who didn't seem far enough out of her own childhood to have produced them.

'All right. Enough, you two.' She hit a key on the piano. 'Get back here and give me a scale.'

They grumped and pouted and Kariiiiiinaaaaaahed as they sloped back over to the piano. Karina didn't have the heart to tell Suki she was wasting her time. Hannah just yelled the notes tunelessly and Elisa tended to lose the plot halfway up the scale. They liked to sing, but even Elisa would never have her mother's gift.

Karina took them through the vowel sounds – e to a, e to o, e to u – and threw in Hannah's favourite exercise – singing the words 'macaroni ravioli' over and over while moving slowly up and down the octaves. She was trying to teach them 'Windmills of Your Mind' as a good breathing exercise, but with Hannah it was useless. She shouted and gasped like any normal seven-year-old singing a song. If she concentrated on Elisa then Hannah would get bored and start shoving the tortoise around, and then Elisa would become distracted by her sister's treatment of their pet.

Karina was just going through the motions, for Suki's sake if not for her own. Suki was not permitted to pursue her music career lest someone figure out who she was and embarrass Edward. He wasn't pleased about being reminded he had married a bubblegum pop princess, but that hadn't stopped him lusting after Suki, nor divorcing his first wife to marry her. Suki was almost too trophy-wife, with her slight success of a single and her earnest and laughable desire to be a serious recording artist. Edward more or less told her to put a sock in it as soon as he had a ring on her finger. It embarrassed him and his friends when she mentioned, in a soft, wispy voice that did nothing to hinder the impression that she was an airhead, her ambitions to record a self-penned track.

So, like a good little Cinderella, Suki settled down into her required role of a rich man's toy. She had appeared in glossy magazine shoots with headlines like MRS SUZANNE NASMITH SHOWS US EXCLUSIVELY THE BEAUTIFUL HOME SHE HAS CREATED FOR HER HUSBAND. The beautiful home was actually the creation of interior designers, since Suki had no natural taste and, if left to her own devices, would have installed heartshaped pink beds and hot-tubs. The Robert Adam-style interiors were as stamped on Suki as her collection of sleek white trouser suits and carefully snipped bobbed hair. Karina understood this. She understood what it felt like to be someone you weren't and, while dragged to a party at Edward's home by a somethinginthecity boyfriend, she was privileged to meet the real Suki first time around.

'I'm afraid Suzanne has a migraine,' Edward had said, greeting Karina.

'They've had a row and she's refusing to come down,' Karina's boyfriend translated, *sotto voce*, as Edward moved on to greet the next guest.

The party was a grindingly dull affair of airkisses and talk of stocks and shares. Karina, fresh from one of her regular self-reinventions, had other ideas of what made a party swing. She had once smoked a big dose of hash and unwisely popped an Ecstasy tablet on top of it, and woke up wearing nothing but a coat of dried mud in the somewhat incongruous surroundings of Glastonbury

Abbey. On another occasion she had propositioned two male dancers in a Bangkok nightspot while on acid and spent the night in a beach hut taking Polaroids of the two guys penetrating each other every which way and claiming she felt like Toulouse Lautrec ... and the way the walls were melting was just ... like ... whoa, guys.

By the age of twenty-five, Karina had seen it, done it, sniffed it, popped it, fucked it. One afternoon she woke up, examined her eyebags critically in the mirror, and decided she was sporting a full set of Vuitton luggage under there. She packed up her collection of dirty Polaroids, dyed her pink hair back to its natural black and decided it was about time she had a change of direction, lest her septum drop out the next time she sneezed.

Since leaving home at eighteen, Karina had been largely broke, and had travelled, partied and imbibed on a wing and a prayer. She felt bad because she knew she owed a large amount of money, but she wished she could remember to whom and how many people she owed it. A kind of stoned amnesia had set in around 1996, and the fog hadn't entirely lifted until the twenty-first century.

She thought she needed at least some sort of fiscal security, so she bought a plaid skirt from an Oxfam shop, which, in the right light, could be faked as a Burberry. She purchased a collection of preppy little roll-necks and started hanging around the right bars and restaurants in Kensington and Sloane Square. She had gagged at paying three pounds a go for a small glass of fizzy water with a slice of lime floating in it, but looking the part was everything, so she would hang around nursing a Buxton water and trying to look as though she was posh-girlfriend material.

The types she met were not what she expected. A provincial girl, she thought London types still wore red braces and screamed 'buy, buy, sell, sell' into mobile phones day and night, and she was surprised by the scruffiness of the *uber* rich. Famous models dressed like bag ladies, and ludicrously wealthy boy popstars dressed like teenage skater boys. The people who gravitated towards Karina tended to be at least twenty-five years older than she was. They wore suits and shirts and liked to think of their style as 'classic'. Karina, with her Oxfam skirt and a set of cultured pearls she claimed to have inherited from her grandmother, was much more their scene. She reminded them of a schoolgirl, wearing her pleated plaid skirt and little black beret. She accepted with resignation that she would always be a curiosity, a piece of exotica you could never take home to meet Mummy and Daddy, but she slipped easily into the life of a courtesan. Men, like idiots, thought she was some kind of geisha, and she bought into the lie, wearing a kimono around the flat and inventing stories about the cherry blossoms in Kyoto. They loved it. She found she had inadvertently turned herself into an ageing business-man's wet dream. It was in such circles that she met Edward Nasmith, and was invited to the party where she met Suki.

Raymond, her boyfriend at the time (she said 'boy-friend' for the sake of convenience. He was actually forty-seven, said he was forty-three and was as far from boyhood as Karina herself) had been getting too close for comfort. He wanted full sex and Karina's latest incarna-tion involved being the Great Unattainable. She had no idea why he wanted to fuck her, seeing as he only lasted a matter of minutes whenever she blew him. They all did. It seemed to be some kind of problem common to men who wanted to marry nice girls but complained when their nice girls refused to be nasty.

'My wife will never do that. I asked her once but she said she thought it was disgusting.'

'Well, it's not a nice thing to ask your *wife* to do, is it?'

'Oh, she won't. She would never. I don't think she knows how.'

Karina had heard all these bedroom clichés and more. It seemed that men of a certain age and a certain class, when they stood up and said, 'With my body I thee worship' actually meant, 'missionary position and fucks on alternate Saturday nights' while they found prostitutes and lapdancers to take their dicks in their mouths. Odd kind of worship.

She had had enough cocks in her mouth and men gripping her hair, whispering dirty words while their balls emptied on her tongue, to wonder why the hell they didn't ask their wives to do it. Not only that, she burned to ask if any of them had ever gone down on their wives, because they never seemed inclined to do it to her.

Of course, even before she met Suki it was obvious Suki was a different breed of wife. She was the Second Wife, not the Nice Girl Edward had married, had kids with and unceremoniously dumped when the male menopause hit and he thought he deserved something better. Suki was leggy, blonde and featured in society pages in *OK* and *Hello!* magazines sporting a new set of highlights or a Valentino evening gown. In such photoshoots Edward posed with his Ferrari, and Suki posed with her children or her new couch. It was clear what her role was. 'Meet the new wife, guys. She's shinier than the old one AND she sucks cock.'

Edward wanted a newer, prettier, younger, more sexually adventurous wife, but probably wasn't prepared to change his own sexual repertoire. Karina felt sure of it.

Raymond was exactly the same. He wanted to fuck her, even asked nicely, but he had never offered to slip under the sheets and give her head, or varied from his ritual of sucking one nipple after the other and then lowering his fly with a hopeful smile on his face. Even if she planned on letting him, Karina was sure he would never be much of a lover.

Karina sometimes thought Edward had more balls than most. All his friends made fools of themselves over younger women, but kept it hidden. Edward had at least got it out in the open. Then again, Edward was a rich and influential man and, if people snickered at his male menopause around the offices, their careers would take subtle downturns, perceptible only to the paranoid.

Edward's house was huge and awful. It was new but built in a grand baronial manner with graceful Adam-style fireplaces made of plaster and chipboard; the fires that flickered under them were not real but regulated gas flames – cleaner and less smelly and messy than the real thing. There were family portraits on the cream walls of the reception room, the first Mrs Nasmith noticeable by her absence. Karina immediately classified the architecture as Kentucky Fried Manderley and wondered when Mrs Danvers would make her entrance.

She managed to extricate herself from Raymond and nosed around, sneaking up the stairwell – white painted wood and thickly carpeted in a gruesome shade of turquoise. Upstairs were guest bedrooms with four-poster beds and en-suite bathrooms with scented soaps, just like a hotel. She wondered where she might find Suki, as she had been looking forward to meeting a pop star, no matter how much her career had crashed and burned.

She heard a sort of wailing, which broke into a low, slightly off-key melody, a sound familiar from radio stations and MTV. It was extremely disconcerting to hear a voice she had heard so many times before in the unlikely setting of a boring party in Hampstead. Disconcerting and exciting. People who had had hits appeared on TV. Well, they were just more real than people who hadn't, weren't they? They lived in a kind of hyper-reality where their existence was constantly verified by being known, and Karina wanted a piece of it.

She followed the sound of Suki's voice and heard notes being picked out on a piano. Tentatively she approached the door where the music was coming from and heard Suki crooning convincingly through a classic Smokey Robinson number. Karina tuned into the song and listened critically. It was still the same sound Suki had once had, holding all of its old sweetness, but croakier and more world weary – a singer who had evolved and learned but was not permitted to be heard lest she embarrassed her husband.

When she peeked through the crack in the door it was obvious that Suki was stinking drunk. There was a bottle of Johnny Walker on the piano and she was in a world of her own. She wore a short, dark-blue dress with spaghetti straps, and her face was partially obscured by a thick flop of blonde hair and a gangster fedora. She looked like a little girl who has been raiding her dressing-up box and her performance was for nobody but herself.

It was probably about then that Karina's curiosity turned into downright worship. Oh, she knew this. She knew how it felt to burn to perform, to put on a show and impress and have no applause from anyone but the imaginary crowd. Suki had been visible but not striking in her brief pop career. Now she looked iconic, her feet in clumsily laced silver sandals working the pedals of her piano, tossing up her head as she reached the climax of 'Tracks of My Tears', her hat tumbling off and her voice broken, croaky sweet and wonderfully expressive.

A genuine diva. A big star Karina wanted to see shining the way she deserved to shine more than anything else in the world.

She broke into spontaneous applause at the end and Suki, drunk as a skunk, staggered to her feet and took a bow. She turned her ankle on one of her high-heeled sandals, wobbled and gripped on to the piano stool for support.

'Ooops . . . thank you . . .' she said, giggling.

Karina went over to help her up. Suki wrapped her arms around her neck and breathed boozily in her face.

'Hello. Who are you?'

'A big fan,' Karina said sincerely.

Suki's face had aged since she was last on *Top of The Pops*, but still had the same doll-like prettiness. Instead of the candy sweet colours of make-up she had worn back then, she had a different face painted on, huge smoky-violet-edged eyes, smudged from where she had rubbed them in a careless, drunken state, and her mouth was painted gold. She looked fucked, self-destructive and born to be sold.

'Darling, that's so sweet of you,' Suki said, hiccupping and settling down on the piano stool. 'Where's my hat?'

Karina picked up the blue fedora and placed it on Suki's head, pulling down a strand of hair to curl sweetly across a glitter-streaked cheek. 'Thanks,' Suki said. 'Supposed to be at a party . . . I think.'

'Edward said you had a migraine.'

Suki laughed. 'Um, no. Just pissed. Very pissed. Oops. When I get drunk I sing and make a fool of myself.' She scootched up on the piano stool and patted the seat beside her. 'Sit, sit . . . please. S'nice to have company.'

'You don't sound like a fool to me,' Karina said. 'You sound like a baby Janis Joplin.'

'Pfft. My voice is useless. I smoke too much.' Suki

sighed. 'Have you got a cigarette, honey? Gasping for a smoke here. Have a drink. Plenty there.'

Karina took her cigarettes out of her bag, and passed one to Suki. She lit it up for her, and Suki placed her fingers on her wrist, steadying her hand as she used the lighter. Suki's nails were long, curved and gold, like the expensive sugar almonds Karina had seen in wedding favours. Her big blue eyes flickered through a film of smoke as she exhaled and she smiled remotely, maybe seductively.

Karina had no idea. She rarely met any women who could outvamp her, and Suki was in the Bergman and Davis league, as far as she could see. The girl had got her head spinning and her guts fluttering and her heart thumping like a wild thing in her throat.

'Have a drink,' Suki said again, expansively offering the whisky bottle.

'Thanks.' Karina took the bottle. Before she tipped it enough for the strong liquor to wash against her lips, she could taste a faint fatty oiliness on the neck of the bottle – a taste she recognised as lipstick. Tasting Suki's mouth by proxy.

'What'd you say your name was again?' Suki asked.

'I didn't. It's Karina. Karina May.'

'Right.' Suki frowned, puzzled. 'Where do I know you from? Sorry ... don't mean to be rude. Eddy has so many friends. Can't keep track sometimes.'

'You don't know me,' Karina said.

'I do now!' Suki said, and laughed. 'I know you. You're Karina May.' She hiccupped and ran her thumb along the piano keys. 'You know what, Karina May?'

'What?'

Suki leaned in close, playful and teasing. She smelled of booze. 'Tell you a secret,' she whispered, right in Karina's ear. Her breath was wet and whiskied and her satin-covered boobs brushed against Karina's upper arm, sending goosebumps prickling all over Karina's skin. 'Wanna hear a secret?'

Karina deliberately leaned closer. She hadn't felt this way in over a year, since she started her career as a golddigger, and hadn't felt this way about a woman in so much longer. Suki's breasts crushed against her, soft and squashy, barely covered by the draped scoop neck of her midnight-blue dress. A woman was silky and secretive compared to a man; a closed pale-velvet jewel box she wanted to plunder like a greedy, curious child, to try on the bright, pretty things inside.

'Tell me,' Karina whispered.

Suki stiffened, dropped her cigarette on the polished beechwood floor and clumsily ground it out with the ball of a silver sandal, leaving it there to smoulder and mark the boards with a burn that would need expensive specialist restoration.

'OK,' she said, swinging one long leg over the piano stool so that she straddled it. The cut of her dress was of a classic fit and flare, like a Brazilian dancer's, and slid up over her thighs. Karina wanted to do the same but her own red evening gown hugged her body to the knees and she couldn't lift it. She settled for turning slightly to the side, in time to see Suki stretch her arms up and yawn, showing off the long slope from under her breasts to her crotch, sleek as a cat, wrapped like a gift in satin. Her thighs were showing, toned and tight from riding horses and working out, running on her little pink electronic treadmill like a hamster staving off the boredom of being caged by running miles on its plastic wheel. Karina coveted what lay just under the flower petal edge of her skirt: Edward's prize possession – a pussy he probably no more knew what to do with than the elegant Bechstein at which Suki had been seated.

Suki wound her arms around Karina's neck and sighed.

'OK . . . secret. I think . . . I think . . . and I may be right, and I may be wrong . . .'

'But you're perfectly willing to swear?'

Suki laughed and sang. 'That when you turned, and smiled at me, a nightingale sang in Berkley Square.'

She seemed so thrilled that Karina turned her body slightly back towards the piano and played the melody, singing the next line. 'The moon that lingered over London town . . .'

'Poor puzzled moon, he wore a frown,' Suki slurred happily, hugging her like a prize. 'Sing with me. Please.'

Karina played the piano, so Suki held the bottle of whisky to her lips for her, tipping it clumsily. Karina managed to get some in her mouth but a thin rivulet of Johnny Walker ran between her breasts, the spirit stinging and evaporating on her skin and pooling under her dress, where it would probably ruin the thin red velvet.

When Edward entered the room to check on his wife, the two women were smoking cigarettes, swigging whisky, laughing like drains and bouncing up and down in time with their duet, classical jazz having given way to 'Chopsticks'. Karina was quite drunk by now and remembered telling Edward he was a lucky, lucky man. Or a lucky, lucky bastard – she wasn't entirely sure.

She woke up in her flat with a head that felt as though it had been used as a latrine by an entire parachute regiment and the phone ringing angrily. She ignored it and pulled the pillow over her head, but just as she did she heard the answering machine click on and Raymond's pissed-off message.

'Hi, it's me . . . look . . . this is getting really difficult for me, Karina. I'm sure you can understand. My wife's getting suspicious ... I don't think we should see each other any more.'

'Suits me, Mr One-Shot,' Karina muttered to herself. She had nicknamed Raymond Mr Big-Shot in their early acquaintance and changed the nickname accordingly when she became familiar with his sexual technique.

Later that evening she spent far too much money ordering a wreath and a card saying 'With Sympathy' to Raymond's wife. Her bank balance was telling her a grave story of its own, and Karina cursed her own inability to manage her finances. She crawled back into bed with a bottle of Baileys, stared uncomprehendingly at *London Tonight* and wondered if she dared call Edward and Suki's house. She had no idea what to say because she had no idea what she had done the night before. She could have done about a billion things to Suki, all of them filthy, and hoped she hadn't, since she had a nasty, lurking, delectable suspicion that she might be in love. Not with a married man, for a change, but with a married man's wife.

It was Suki who made the call. They must have traded telephone numbers at some point during the night because Karina's mobile started doing its strange little fandango around 8.00 p.m., beeping out the first bars of 'Are Friends Electric?'

'Can I meet you somewhere?' asked Suki. 'I really need to talk to you.'

Karina felt her heart skip a beat, suppressed the urge to squeal like a teenager and said yes, anywhere. Just make it soon. Now. Whenever. She suggested the Embankment as a place to meet because there was no way she was inviting Suki to her place. Karina had been unimpressed with the flat in Balham when she first laid eyes on it and no amount of decorating could make it any less boxy and dingy.

She put on her make-up. Instead of reaching for her usual plum lipstick, she found herself drawn to red, a shade that lovers had told her made her look like a geisha. It annoyed her, but she let them carry on dreaming the dreams their white-boy geisha memoirs had planted in their heads, and neglected to mention she had been born in Brighton. It meant something else to her – a clear 'do not fuck with me' message, a sexual invitation, an assurance that she was still the alpha bitch and in control. Suki might daydream she was rendezvousing with a geisha girl, but Karina meant to set her straight. Suki was different and special, and would get to know the truth.

Karina thought she would faint on the Northern Line tube to Embankment. It was Sunday evening and the line was almost deserted. It smelled of dust and mice, as usual, but even the foul-smelling wind that whooshed down the tunnels seemed fragrant. She was so dizzy and more excited than a child at Christmas. She counted each stop on the way, each one bringing her closer to her destination. It was cold when she came up from the station into the shabby tiled hall. She wasn't sure where she should wait, and stared at the map of the Underground to figure out which direction Suki would come from. The map was reassuring in its familiarity, a collection of coloured arteries that ran through the heart of the city: black, brown, blue, yellow, red. She thought Suki would probably be on the Bakerloo line, if she hadn't chickened out, and Karina wondered if she should go down and wait on the platform or stay where she was.

She heard a rumble from the platform below and realised a southbound train was coming in. She wondered where to stand and how to look – smiling or serious? – watching the top of the escalator and the turnstile for a glimpse of Suki.

Suki came up from the deep guts of the station all dressed in black. Black trousers, high-heeled black boots, a fitted coat with a fur collar and a round black mink hat. She walked almost shyly over to her, smiled and said hello. Her cheeks were pink, and there were square-cut diamonds in her ears. She wore very little make-up, except for a touch of mascara and a light rosewood-coloured gloss on her lips, but it was clear she'd taken trouble to look pretty. In the cold, Karina thought she looked like a snow queen from a fairy tale, wrapped up in her furs with her diamonds sparkling like ice.

'I'm sorry if I'm late,' she said. 'I had trouble getting away.'

Sober, she seemed more formal, almost prim, nothing like the demonstrative vamp she had been the night before.

'You're not late by my watch,' Karina said.

'It's just difficult.' Suki sighed. 'I have two children, you know.'

'I know.' Karina nodded, meaning she didn't care. 'Shall we go for a walk?'

'Yes. That would be nice.'

They walked awkwardly along the Embankment, pearls of lights strung between the naked winter trees. Karina wanted to cry, tell her to stop being so stiff and be like she was last night.

'Don't you just love the Savoy?' Suki said, glancing towards the well-tended gardens and pale façade of the rear of the famous hotel. 'Have you ever had tea there? Oh, you must. So nice. Cream scones and petit fours.'

'I'm not really Savoy material,' Karina replied ruefully. She wondered if she could ever really be part of this girl's world. Over the river was the flashing hulk of the National Theatre, the ugly towers of Battersea, Chelsea Bridge gleaming with floodlight like a magic road to the fairyland of the wealthy. Karina's place was on the South Bank, amongst the drab sidings of Clapham Junction and the derelicts of Waterloo Bridge. Suki's world was north of the river, amongst the overpriced Monopoly board locations – shopping in Bond Street, taking the children for hamburgers in Piccadilly, buying houses in Mayfair.

Suki sniffed and sighed. 'Edward is so pissed off with me,' she said confidentially.

Karina paid attention again and stopped feeling sorry for herself.

'Is he?'

Suki stopped and leaned against the wall. 'Have you got a ciggie? Thanks.'

She lit up with difficulty in the wind and they leaned against the wall above the river and smoked.

'I'm not supposed to drink,' Suki said. 'We had the worst row after the party.'

'Oh dear.' Karina wished she could remember a little more, if only to have more interesting things to say than 'is he' or 'oh dear'.

'We have –' Suki blew smoke into the cold winter wind '– a total conflict of interests. He doesn't want me to sing or perform, or anything.'

'Why not? You're good. You're better than you used to be.' Karina was pleased for the chance to pay a compliment and Suki smiled, dropped her cigarette and, to Karina's delight, linked her arm with hers.

'Darling, it's so sweet of you to say, but I'm not what I used to be.'

'And that's what's good,' Karina enthused. 'You've evolved, developed. Come on leaps and bounds.'

'Stop it. You're flattering me.' Suki gave her arm a

squeeze as they walked past the Savoy. 'I'm a terrible egotist and need no help from you in that department.'

'You're wonderful.'

Suki laughed. 'And you're insane. I so miss crazy people –'

'Oh, so do I.' Karina took a chance and tucked her arm around Suki's waist. She didn't resist, and Karina prayed that it wasn't just girl-to-girl chumminess inculcated at the fancy single-sex boarding school that Suki's accent spoke of.

Suki laughed again and pressed her cheek against Karina's collar. 'You know this is insane, don't you?'

'Yes.'

'You know I have two daughters and a husband I'm bored of?'

'Uh huh.'

'And you know I'm an alcoholic?'

'I do now,' Karina said, stroking the back of Suki's waist. Suki's arm snaked around her waist and she felt her body stir and wake and her mouth fill with water at the prospect of more.

'I'm probably the worst person in the world you could have an affair with, Karina May,' Suki said quietly. 'I'm not even a lesbian.'

'That's handy,' Karina said, trying to be cheerful despite the doomsayer tone in Suki's voice. 'Neither am I.'

'You're not?' Suki pulled away, looking puzzled. She stopped walking.

'Not technically,' Karina said. 'Does it actually matter?'

'I don't know,' said Suki. 'It wouldn't matter to me. I'm just too busy working out how I can get you in my life. Silly, aren't I?'

Karina sighed and took her hands. 'Maybe. Don't care. Do you care that I'm not what I seem?'

Suki stepped closer. 'Right now, I don't.' She smiled and her teeth were white as a cat's. The wind blew her hair across her cheek, sticking a strand to her lips. She loosed one hand and brushed it away, looking shy and desperately sweet. 'May I kiss you?' she asked timidly.

'You may.' Then Karina found herself beaming like the Cheshire cat at how demure she was.

'I may, Miss May?' Suki giggled, leaning closer, so that their lips brushed.

When her mouth opened, Karina heard her heart pounding in her ears, kissed cold lips and felt a hot tongue slide into her mouth. Suki moaned deep in the back of her throat and Karina held her tight against the cold wind, Suki's mink collar brushing her cheek, soft as a whisper. She knew she was in for more trouble than she'd ever been in since she was eighteen years old, and she didn't especially care.

4

The morning noises started early down here, Paul noticed. There were rumbles of dustcarts, road sweepers, car doors opening and closing. The night noises finished late as people staggered home from the pubs, yelling, swearing and laughing. It was reassuring because he knew he hadn't wasted money. People pounding up and down the pavements all day and night meant customers, and customers meant success.

The smell of the sea and the early morning sun was wonderful, and he relished being able to sleep with the window open, the cool of sleepy early morning making him huddle deeper under the duvet, warming himself against the bundle of slim, tightly curled limbs beside him. There were few pleasures in life to compare with this – waking up cosy and naked with a lover. He spooned in hopefully, petting a silky, narrow bottom with his hand, getting a low grumble in response. His lips found the delicate nub of vertebrae at the nape of his lover's neck, imperceptible to someone else, maybe, but he'd taken time to memorise this body, find out all its secrets.

He opened his mouth and swirled his tongue around the bone, suckling on soft skin and tempted to suck until he drew the blood to the surface, leaving a little red brand in the shape of his lips which would hide sweetly under the collar of Ieuan's shirt. Only they would know it was there.

'Morning.'

'Middle o' the fucking night – piss off.'

'It's nearly six.'

He could forget about sleeping. The builders would be arriving downstairs in an hour or so, laying the new floor and hopefully finishing the bar. With the thump and bump of beechwood being hulked around and the thud of dance beats from their radios, there wouldn't be any sleep for either of them. Paul wanted to grab a little quality time before the mundanity of the day intruded on his pleasant drowse.

'You'll miss the best part of the day,' he said playfully, wriggling his sleep-erection against Ieuan's hairy upper thigh.

'Mmmm.'

Paul sprawled over Ieuan's naked back and nipped the back of his shoulder with his teeth. 'I want you,' he whispered, his mouth finding the patch of soft, soft skin beneath a pierced ear.

'Nnnrgh.'

Paul smiled and wriggled in closer so that his dick rested flush in the crease of Ieuan's butt. 'Hel-loooo? Guess what I've got?'

'A weight problem? You're heavy. Get off.'

'Trying to,' Paul said, rolling off him.

Ieuan rolled over and yawned – all bedhead and stinky armpits, raw, unwashed and sexy as fuck. He was dark and hairy against the white sheets, a glint of silver winking out from his right nipple, which was almost lost in a mass of dark hair. He squinted with slightly myopic blue eyes at the travel clock on the bedside table.

'You're a bastard,' he groaned, his rich voice throaty from sleep. 'It's too early.'

'Early bird catches the –' Paul peeked under the duvet. Ha! Not that early. Not so early that Ieuan's thick, warm cock wasn't poking up in all its morning glory. 'Ah.'

'Worm?' Ieuan wriggled his hips lazily. The coarse, tangy smell of man and pre-come drifted up to Paul's nose, making his own dick twitch eagerly. He loved the smell of him – a heavy musk composed of sweat, beer and cigarette smoke, unquestionably male. It was light and delicate in the hollows of his neck, and powerful and dirty in his groin and between the fuzzy cheeks of his arse. His belly was hairy too, hair curling up from the inverted V of his black pubic hair, guarding the dip of his navel. His hip-bones stuck up like pale tan islands, silky skin over hard bone. Paul kissed one hip and nuzzled his cheek against Ieuan's belly, rubbing like a cat. Ieuan arched his butt off the sheets and let Paul wind his arms around his waist and curl between his open legs. Obligingly slutty when stirred, Paul thought, burying his face in warm hair and skin.

He groaned happily. He had always been crazy about the surprising fragility of Ieuan's narrow waist in his arms. 'Mmmm ... nice.' He sighed, closing his eyes and breathing in the smell of him.

Ieuan made a soft, impatient sound and raised his hips again, pushing his dick against Paul's face so that a pinprick drop of moisture touched under Paul's chin like a tiny wet kiss. Paul squirmed lower down the bed so that he could run his tongue up the full length of him, licking from root to tip in a slow tease before raising his head to take him in his mouth.

He loved doing this, loved the down and dirty intimacy of it, and loved the control and power it gave him. Paul almost gagged but held the reflex off. He moaned around Ieuan's penis, his own stiffening further at the recognition of his lover's pleasure. Ieuan's fingers wound into his hair, stroking and tugging.

'Come here, c'mon ...'

A harder tug threatened to hurt his scalp, so Paul

crawled quickly up over him and offered his mouth to be kissed. When roused from his customary morning laziness, Ieuan was as hungry for him as if he'd just recognised his lust for the first time. Paul allowed himself to be rolled roughly onto his back and kissed with almost bruising force. He wrapped his legs around Ieuan's body like a girl, and mewed with need when he felt a hand grip his cock and start working it sweetly and cleverly. He was keenly aware of the sounds he was making – low moans in the back of his throat; gasps and grunts that were intermittently silenced by the firm crush of Ieuan's full, chapped lips and the wet push of his tongue.

Ieuan broke off and breathed hard in his ear, and Paul reached for the bolt screwed through Ieuan's nipple, twisting, pinching and getting more out of control as he listened to Ieuan's breathing catch and grow faster in his ear. Ieuan's hips were grinding against his thigh, humping firm and fast in time with the rapid pulls of his hand on Paul's cock. Paul moaned more loudly and pushed his thigh up against Ieuan's hardness, feeling the soft squash of his balls and the prickle of rough hair behind it. Ieuan groaned and pushed back harder, his hand whippingly sweet by now, so that Paul was at the point where he had to come.

One thing Ieuan had never been was a tease, and he breathed encouraging filth in Paul's ear – dirty, dirty things that Paul loved, calling him a slut, my slut, my hot, dirty, take-it-any-which-way slut.

Paul moaned, twisted underneath him, straining towards his climax. Ieuan was spitting words of lust in his ear, getting more vehement as he humped faster against his thigh. 'Come. Come now. Come for me, slut.'

He closed his eyes and let his body take over, his hips bucking as his balls emptied in slow, shivery spurts. Ieuan cried out and Paul felt come spill over his thigh, and he held him as he tumbled forwards into his arms, panting and sweating.

God, he loved morning sex.

Ieuan rolled off him and smiled. He looked flushed and satisfied and his eyes looked brilliant crystal blue under their fringe of jet eyelashes. His dark hair stuck up in messy spikes and his lips were red – so irresistible that Paul had to kiss him. His mouth was warm and pliant now, its earlier aggression dimmed.

'What was that in aid of?' Ieuan asked, nuzzling into his shoulder, kissing lightly, his stubble grazing the skin.

'Christening the new bed.'

'It's not a new bed,' Ieuan said, turning over and reaching for his cigarettes. 'This one's got some miles on the clock.'

'New flat then,' Paul said, sitting up and wiping himself off with the sheet. He liked the thought of the bed as well used, as it had been. Lots of feet in the air, knees in the mattress, springs shaking and creaking as they had fucked like bunnies in every position they could dream up and a few they'd borrowed from pornography. 'That was nice.'

Ieuan was coughing over his morning cigarette and nodded, lungs full of smoke and eyes full of tears.

'Coffee?'

'Coffee.'

'Have to be instant.'

'Whatever.'

Ieuan didn't place much importance on good coffee. Paul needed something powerfully caffeinated to wake himself up fully in the morning. He liked being shaken out of sleep by a good satisfying fuck and a hot, strong cup of coffee; going from drowsiness to a brain-vibrating, heart-pounding buzz was one of the best feelings in the world. He walked naked around the flat, still not quite sure which room was where, and found his new kitchen. Small but nicely fitted with marble surfaces, and painted white like the rest of the flat. It was full of boxes he had to step over to get to the kettle.

On the floor was a box parcel-taped up and with the words COFFEE MAKER! Magic-markered on the cardboard in his handwriting to denote its importance. He would have to sort it out later. Right now he needed coffee, instant if he had to. He went to the bathroom while he waited for the kettle to boil. The bathroom was twice the size of the kitchen. Typical Victorian conversion job – rooms all the wrong size.

The builders had left paint rollers and paint trays in the bath, and he resolved to say something about that later because he needed a shower and didn't appreciate having to wash out the bath and remove their mess on top of rummaging through boxes to find his shower gel and shampoo. He hated moving.

It was when he was standing in front of the toilet with his dick in his hand that he realised there was no fucking toilet paper and Ieuan hadn't bothered to look for it last night. No wonder he'd smelled particularly goatish this morning, resorting to the shake-off method in which no matter how much you shook it, the last drop always ran down your leg.

Paul went back to the kitchen to make the coffee. He grinned when he smelled a wisp of cigarette smoke and heard a creak of unfamiliar floorboards, which meant Ieuan was up and about. He leaned back at the touch of a hand on his bottom and felt Ieuan's solid, hairy body against his back, lips drifting smoky kisses over his bare shoulders.

'Hi.'

'Hel-lo.' Ieuan nipped his ear.

'The builders left their stuff in the bath.'

'I thought I could smell paint in there.'

Paul poured water over coffee granules. The smell floated up to his nose, a thin echo of the stronger, richer brew he usually enjoyed in the morning. 'They left the trays and rollers in the bloody bath. I'll have to see to them later.'

He sipped the foul-tasting instant coffee and felt the buzz of good sex wearing off already, replaced by the slightly pissed-off harassed feeling that came with having a half-finished bar and restaurant, a half-unpacked home and a half-divorced wife. She was supposed to have called him two days ago and Ieuan was antsy and possessive. Paul suspected 'issues' – he had probably been left for a woman at some point in his life. It happened a lot with the young and the bi-curious, who were gay one week and straight the next. Given the choice, Paul would have settled on being one or the other, as it no doubt led to less confusion. Less fun, probably, but a hell of a lot less chaos.

'You coming back to bed?' Ieuan asked.

'I can't.' Paul once again struggled to get the coffee past his tastebuds and winced. He tossed it down the sink. 'I'm seeing this woman about the chef's job at twelve.'

'How? The kitchen isn't finished.'

'Yes, I know. I did notice.' Paul sighed. 'Need to call the electricians. They still haven't fixed the fucking extractors.'

'So why are you interviewing a chef when you've got no bloody kitchen?'

Paul shook his head. 'Because I want the place up and running the second everything is ready,' he explained wearily. 'It's turning out to be a money pit as it is after arseing about with the sale for so long. I've completely missed the first half of the tourist season.' He leaned back against the kitchen worksurface, resting the back of his head against a cupboard door and closed his eyes. 'Why did I do this again?'

Ieuan draped himself reassuringly over him and kissed him on the mouth. 'Something about hating London?'

'Yes ... that was it...' Paul muttered, squeezing Ieuan's rear and returning the kiss.

'Wanted to get some fresh air...'

'Uh huh...'

'Less stressful...'

Paul laughed. 'Oh yes. What the fuck was I thinking?'

'Hey, you're the one waking up at six in the morning.'

'With a mind to some stress relief.'

'Doesn't seem like it's worked.'

'No, it doesn't, does it?'

'Probably God's way of telling you that you need to have more dirty sex.'

'That could be it.'

Ieuan would have gone for an encore right there in the kitchen if Paul hadn't insisted he didn't have time. Horny little bastard was twenty-three and indefatigable, Paul reflected, as he showered and shaved in the paint-scented bathroom. Forty was becoming a real and unpleasant inevitability in a world where people increasingly seemed to make their first million at about seventeen, the better to strut about blinding you with their dazzling square white teeth and shaking their minuscule airbrushed bottoms all over MTV.

He poked his tongue out at his reflection, scraped the fuzz off it with the bristles of his toothbrush, and set to work at a slightly discoloured premolar with a vengeance. He wondered why on earth he was fucking a twenty-three-year-old with whom he had nothing in common but a penchant for hot, nasty sex, then realised the stupidity of the question as it was summed up in the last three words. Hot, nasty and sex.

Ieuan had no interest in fine dining, or what consti-
tuted a decent cup of coffee, and Paul's one and only
attempt to make a gourmet of him had resulted in Ieuan
getting drunk and practically demonstrating fellatio on a
bottle of Chablis while fondling Paul's crotch with his
toes under the table. If dinner had been a manmade
disaster, then the sex afterwards had been distinctly
Vesuvian – hot, explosive and excessively destructive.
Paul accepted it because, even if he couldn't coax Ieuan
to comprehend that seafood did not begin and end with
cod and chips, he was so delighted to have achieved a
close encounter of the furniture-trashing kind that it
cancelled out Ieuan's revulsion at the idea of kalimari.

Paul finished brushing his teeth and decided that he
wasn't so badly off. He didn't look thirty-five; he could
get this business off the ground and even if this Western
woman didn't work out to be the perfect chef then maybe
he could tempt her with the tenancy of the flat upstairs
to generate a little extra income.

She was the perfect something, but he wasn't sure
what. Perfect way to make Ieuan act up, in any case.

Paul spent the morning on the phone arguing with the
electricians, demanding to know why Big Dave hadn't
grouted the tiles in the kitchen yet and clinging on to his
nerves and the phone for dear life. If Ieuan picked up the
expected call from ex-wife Sarah there would be hell to
pay. Ieuan had been jealous and playing up ever since he
found out Paul was in contact with her again. Miss Adele
Western's arrival didn't exactly help matters.

The phrase that immediately jumped into Paul's head
was 'a whole lotta woman' – a tall, well-padded girl of a
type that had gone out of fashion in the early 1960s. Men
had been on a similar starvation diet for decades,
deprived of the tits and arse they were naturally

attracted to, so, when she wobbled Monroe-style across the sawdusty floor on heels she looked distinctly unsure about, even Ieuan stared.

She looked like she'd made an effort, which made the state of the place all the more embarrassing. He apologised and took her CV, reminding himself that her first name was Adele. A French name. He decided he liked it and that it didn't suit her. She looked more Latin than French – a substantial, matriarchal woman, dark and vivid with her curly black hair and full red mouth. Should have been a Maria or a Carlotta or a Carmen.

She cooked Italian. She cooked Mexican. She cooked French, Thai, Chinese, Japanese, Traditional English, Creole and Middle Eastern. She cooked every damn thing going by the looks of it. 'This is great!' Paul exclaimed, trying to remove Ieuan's hand from his arse.

'Oh . . .' She smiled and glanced at the beer he handed her, as if reluctant to wrap her lips around the neck when surrounded by men. 'Um . . . yep.'

Ieuan wasn't helping to put her at ease, rummaging at the hem of Paul's shirt, trying to touch skin. 'For God's sake, I'm not going to try and fuck her,' he wanted to say.

Irritably, Paul swatted him away. He could do without this. It was obvious that, unless Adele Western was bluffing, she was an excellent chef, and, if he took her on, the last thing he needed was a jealous boyfriend crawling all over him every time he went down to the kitchen to check the menu. What did Ieuan think he was capable of? He didn't need another woman in his life. He was stuck with Sarah's constant procrastination anyway. The bloody woman probably enjoyed the bent-status symbol value of saying that her estranged husband was screwing other men now. It would only fuel her 'All Men Are Bastards' rant to the point where she could get women to swear off men so that she could make her way into their knickers.

'Come on through,' he said, standing up and tucking his shirt in. 'Jude, can I borrow you a second?'

'Sure,' Jude muttered.

Adele was looking at him like she'd just found God. As if the little bugger needed anything else to keep his mind off his work.

Ieuan insisted on following, so Paul introduced him anyway, but hands kept wandering as Paul attempted to gauge Adele's reaction to the state of the kitchen. When Ieuan requested a word, Paul wanted to give him several – all of them obscene. He left Adele in the less-than-capable hands of Jude and quickly hurried Ieuan into the half-finished Gents toilets.

'What?' Paul asked impatiently.

Ieuan pounced. Paul surrendered to the assault for a moment before turning his face away and sighing.

'Ieuan, could you ... no ... OK ... *no* ... leave that alone. Not *now*.'

'Why not now?' Ieuan asked, kissing the side of Paul's neck. 'Come on, it'd be hot.'

'It's not a good time.'

'Exactly my point.'

Paul shook his head and disengaged himself. 'No...' He bit his tongue when he wanted to say that this was about whatever insecurities Ieuan had about women backed up in his past. Saying it now would only lead to a row, and he had even less time for a fight than he had for a fuck.

He was saved by the phone finally ringing.

'Let the voicemail get it.'

'No,' Paul said, heading for the door. 'I can't. I've been expecting this call.'

Ieuan rolled his eyes. 'Oh God. It's *her*, isn't it?'

'None of your business,' Paul replied impatiently, and

shut himself in the cleaning cupboard to gain a moment's privacy while he answered his phone.

'Where the hell have you been?' Paul snapped, dislodging a mop handle that was poking him uncomfortably in the kidneys. 'You were supposed to call me two days ago.'

A carefully contrived yawn came down the phone. 'Yes, I know. Got tied up, unfortunately. Edward and Suki were having one of their dos. You know, the ones when she gets hideously pissed and refuses to come down?'

'Right,' Paul said, knowing that his aunt would chuck a screaming blue fit over this. He was sick of caring, or even pretending to care, about his incestuous, dysfunctional family and their not-so-delicate sensibilities. 'It took you two days to drink gin and tonics with a pack of golf club rejects and insipid town councillors?'

'No, but it took me that long to curb my homicidal impulses after being slapped on the arse and called a lovely filly by Uncle Ned's utterly cuntish friends and pitied for being *single* by their trophy wives.'

'Yes, about that –' Paul had to press her on the matter, since she conveniently forgot.

'Oh, don't you start. It was hideous. What on earth makes fifty-something men think that they can marry a twenty-one-year-old and be taken even remotely seriously anyway? I think I'll get myself an eighteen-year-old for my birthday.'

'Sarah!'

'Makes perfect sense. I'm officially at my statistical sexual peak, so it makes sense I should be screwing a nineteen-year-old at his sexual peak.' She sighed and he could hear the rasp of a cigarette lighter.

'How is the fucking boyfriend, by the way?' she asked nonchalantly.

'The fucking boyfriend is fine, thank you very much.'

'Still fucking, I suppose?'

'Very much so.'

'Still haven't worked out he's a moron?'

'He's not a moron.' Paul swallowed and tried to forget the blank look Ieuan had given him the other day when he used the word 'supercilious' in conversation. 'Not everyone has had the virtue of an expensive education.'

He could forgive Ieuan that. It helped that Ieuan could probably suck a golfball through a hosepipe if he ever had a mind to.

'Wonder what he's up to,' Sarah mused.

'Oh, you are horrible, do you know that? Not everyone in this world has sexual relationships because of what they might gain fiscally or otherwise. You can't measure everyone by your own benchmark ... just because your role model appears to be the Empress Messalina.'

'Dear me. Aren't we tetchy today, darling?'

'I have every right to be. You know how much I hate moving house. It's been four weeks and I still have things in boxes.' He didn't tell her he was in a cleaning cupboard. He really couldn't bear another round of 'closet' jokes.

'Well, I hope you cut him some airholes otherwise you're in for a nasty shock –'

'You sick bitch,' Paul snapped. He contemplated hanging up, but didn't. 'I know damn well why you're procrastinating – you only do it because you can't stand Ieuan.'

'I've never met him,' Sarah said smoothly. 'So how could I possibly loathe him the way you say I do? And I don't. I just expect a reciprocal agreement; we've always confided in one another, Paul, and then you insist you couldn't possibly tell me the details because you insist that you're in love and therefore he's somehow sacred. It's not fair.'

Paul kicked over a container of scouring powder in his frustration. He should have told her that this wasn't normal but, if he did, she'd stop telling him stories about her adventures and, whatever moral qualms his brain had about their exchanges, his dick didn't share them. 'Look. I'm supposed to be doing a job interview right now,' he said.

'Oh.' Sarah sounded disappointed. 'I turned down an extremely expensive lunch for you. One that I wouldn't have to pay for.'

'Best kind of expensive lunch,' Paul said. 'Don't be like that. If you'd called when we arranged, we wouldn't have this problem, would we?'

'Could you be any more condescending, Paul?'

He smirked. 'I could certainly try, but I wouldn't want you to worry your pretty little head about it.'

'Fuck off.'

'OK. I'll call you later.'

'No, wait.'

'Really, Sarah – when a lady tells me to fuck off, the gentlemanly course of action would be to fuck off.'

'Off you fuck then,' she said wearily.

'I will,' he said. 'Bye.'

He almost missed her as he left the cupboard and brushed scouring powder off his shoes with an old rag that looked suspiciously like half an underpant. He had always appreciated her nasty tongue and the ease with which he could bait her. It wasn't healthy, the way they worked their frustrations out on each other, but he had simply never met a better bitch than Sarah. Even the most hydrochloric of old queens couldn't hold a candle to her.

Ieuan was nowhere to be seen and Paul assumed he was sulking. He had been in a kind of low-grade sulk since discovering that the nightlife in this part of the world involved getting stoned to bejeezus in front of the television, drinking oneself unconscious at a pub with a late licence or an evening spent in the one and only nightclub in town. The place had a distinct *Phoenix Nights* vibe about it, only without being intentionally funny.

Paul looked for Adele and found her in the yard with Jude, apparently fascinated by the wisteria that was crawling all over the back of the building. Judging by the butts on the ground, far from showing her around, Jude had been instructing her in the noble Jude-art of Taking a Ciggie Break.

'Sorry about that,' Paul said. 'Had to take a phone call.'

She smiled, and looked for a moment like a woman who had been up to something. 'Oh, no problem,' she said airily, smoothing down her skirt.

Jude was looking studiously at the ground.

'Hope you didn't get bored,' said Paul, sensing atmosphere.

'Oh no. Well, not too deeply anyway,' she said.

Bored. He picked up on the double entendre as soon as he noticed Jude's face had turned redder than his hair. Paul struggled not to laugh. Jude had probably found he had bitten off more than he could chew, the hot little prick. He was surely about seventeen and strutted around women like a dick on legs, looking studiely nonchalant and masculine at the first whiff of guy-on-guy action. Paul found him amusing. He'd had enough boys like Jude to know that once you probed their sweet virgin arseholes with your tongue they were so damn grateful they'd spend the rest of the night wearing their knees out to show you the depth of their gratitude.

'Come on through,' Paul said. 'Thanks, Jude.'

Jude nodded a surly acknowledgement and went indoors, staring furtively at Adele as he did so. She looked torn between looking appropriately jumpy and pleased as fuck with herself. When they went indoors, away from the powerful smell of the wisteria, Paul caught a smell of something else clinging to her.

'Sorry to keep you waiting,' he said, ushering her into the small, untidy backroom that he was trying and failing to use as an office. 'Take a seat.'

'Thanks.' She sat down and crossed her legs. Her skirt rode up and flashed the lace top of her stocking. She didn't seem to notice. He wished he had the choice of *not* noticing, but he didn't. The sexual scent coming off her was intoxicating in the heat of the summer afternoon. He was glad of having at least found time to get a desk into the office so he could hide behind it.

'I'm really sorry about this,' Paul said. 'I've been having trouble getting the place finished. I don't mean to look as though I'm taking the piss, but well . . . the builders –'

'– are taking the piss,' she said, nodding. 'Yep. They do that. Used to be a jewellers, you know.'

'So I hear.'

'There was this emerald there,' she said, seeming to relax at last. 'When I was a kid – well, emeralds. Huge lump of rock from one angle and then when you walked around the case it was full of all these emeralds. It was from Brazil.'

'No. Nobody mentioned it. Jesus, that must have been worth a mint.'

'It was pretty,' she said simply, shrugging as if she didn't give a shit about the fiscal value of anything. Probably another victim of the ageing hippy culture around here. A bunch of folks who had apparently managed it across the Solent but otherwise never really found their way back from the Isle of Wight festival.

He tried to get his head back into interview mode. It wasn't easy considering he was distinctly sure she had just done something to Jude in the back yard. Sarah would love to hear the story and, if Sarah liked a story, Sarah generally reciprocated. And since Ieuan was off-limits ... What the hell. Her CV was impressive enough and all the other candidates had been adept at nothing but flipping burgers.

'OK,' he said, sighing. 'Do you want this job?'

'Well, yes,' she said. 'That's why I'm here.' She looked as uncomfortable with the charade of the interview as he was, and smiled.

'This is silly, isn't it?' Paul ventured.

'How do you mean?' she asked, in a tone like a psychiatrist.

'This. It's probably just easier if I hire you.'

She raised her eyebrows. 'I'm not going to argue with that.'

Paul sighed again, relieved. 'OK. When can you start?'

Adele smiled and tilted her head, as if considering it. 'Uh ... when you finish the kitchen?'

'Right. Of course.'

5

'Another rite of passage,' Kim pronounced. 'Done and dusted. Have we got time for a celebratory smoke before your Dad gets back?'

'Or before your parents send out a search party,' Adele said.

'Relax. They don't even know.'

'They don't know? How did you keep it secret from them?'

'I just did.' Kim leaned over to open a window. 'Have you got something I can use for a roach?'

She tore a small strip of cardboard from a hairpin packet on her bedside table. 'Here.' She handed it to him and seemed unable to take her eyes off her table – the mass of clutter that covered it. Alarm clock, sweet wrappers, a musical jewellery box that had belonged to her mother, filled with her own junk jewellery. A small mirror compact and a make-up brush. Useless crap. All stuff she had never even thought about long enough to contemplate either its fiscal or sentimental value and soon it would be gone from here, packed up and taken somewhere else, along with her and her life. It had felt like a massive, floating possibility for years and now it was heavy with reality, like an inflatable beachball that had suddenly turned into the weight of the world on her shoulders. It was scary, but she was young enough to think she could move mountains because her exam results said in black and white that she had pulled it off. In three weeks she would be leaving home and becoming a real student.

'It feels like an anticlimax,' Kim grumbled. He was methodically skinning up on the cheap brown envelope that had held the computer print-out of his exam results, as if to express his disdain for it.

'It is, kind of,' she agreed. 'It's like everything you waited for and then this big nothing. Nothing is really different, but then everything is different. At once. I can't describe it.'

'Doesn't look like much,' Kim said. 'Crappy slip of paper. After all that work.'

'I know. It's depressing. You can see the perforations where it's been torn off a strip, chucked out of a computer. Like everyone else's.'

'Like a train ticket,' Kim said. 'They look the same but how you use yours is up to you.'

'That's good,' she said, nodding. 'Very profound.'

'I'll stitch it on a sampler,' Kim muttered, sealing up the joint with his tongue. 'Between ballet classes.'

He pushed the window open a little way and lit up. 'Right, that's it,' he said. 'We are now officially *craaaaazee* university students, babydoll. We need to get completely pissed tonight and do lots of insane, stupid things we've never done before.'

She took the joint and inhaled, before Kim attached himself to it and smoked the lot. 'Such as?'

'Hey, I only had one drag on that!'

She took a deep pull of smoke and handed it back to him.

'*Thank* you,' Kim said sarcastically. He had a couple more tokes and announced that he was in the mood for some brazen debauchery.

'I've never tried magic mushrooms,' he declared. 'There was a guy offering them the other night. Think that's something I need to do.'

'Something I *don't* need to do is hold you up and drag

you away from the cops when you're laughing fit to piss yourself and screaming that they've all turned into Alsatians or something.'

He laughed. 'Oh, fucking hell. That would be funny as fuck. Could you imagine their faces?'

'That's what worries me. You couldn't handle it.'

'I could!'

'Could not! You can barely even hold your drink.'

'I can!'

'Hel-lo? Mr Ooo-Look-At-The-Underside-Of-The-Pretty-Pub-Table?' she teased.

Kim giggled and handed her the joint. 'OK,' he said, blowing out smoke. 'OK. I'm a sad, innocent little Chinese gay boy, OK? I've never even seen a pair of tits in real life.'

She sniggered, starting to feel pleasantly buzzed. 'What use would you have for tits?'

'I don't fucking know,' Kim said, shaking his head. 'I'd just like to see what they look like. What do they look like?'

'They look like ... tits.' She started laughing uncontrollably.

'Would you?' he asked, in a shy voice that was so unlike him she laughed even harder.

'Would I what? Show you my tits?' She sat up on the bed.

'Yes,' Kim said awkwardly, sitting up too and drawing his legs up to his chest. He was actually blushing. 'I'm gay anyway, so it's not like it's a big deal.'

'It is a big deal!' Adele said, snorting with outraged laughter and restraining the urge to pull her cardigan across the shelf of her breasts.

'Why?'

'Because they're mine,' she said, and found that funny for some reason. Her tits felt heavy in her bra and the lace made her nipples itch uncomfortably. She looked at his face and wondered what he would do if she actually did it. Would he look away, giggle or lean in and touch them, suck on them? Pretty unlikely, but she enjoyed seeing him off balance for a change. His lapse from perpetual brazen confidence made her feel closer to him than she'd ever been, because he was confiding in her, asking her for something only she could give him.

She really wanted to do it. It felt as dirty and thrilling as when she had first lowered a hand mirror between her legs and looked at what was between them, or tentatively pushed a finger inside herself for the first time.

'Fine,' Kim said, shrugging. 'I only asked.'

She pinched out the joint and made sure it was out before tucking it and the ashtray into a drawer.

'No. Wait . . . I'm thinking about it,' she said, taking off her cardigan. She was going to do it. Her breasts suddenly felt confined and she wanted them exposed. She smiled to herself behind the black cotton screen of her T-shirt as she lifted it over her head. Careful what you ask for. You may get it.

'You wouldn't,' Kim said, half laughing.

'I would,' she replied, trying to disguise the fact that her hands were shaking behind her back as she fiddled with the catch of her bra. Her thighs felt tense and hot under her skirt and between them she felt the dull, pleasant ache she still only dimly recognised as arousal. She imagined she could feel a kind of liquid core of heat building up deep inside her, somewhere in the depths of her pelvis, cradled by her bony hips. She was keenly aware of the vertical slash of her sex curved secretively between her legs, the lips folded and soft, guarding the wet heat inside. She hadn't realised her body could feel this way, so alight with excitement and trepidation, and wanted to fling aside her bra with a stripper-like flourish. Instead she slipped it off her shoulders and let it fall in her lap.

'There,' she said, presenting her naked chest. 'Tits.'

Kim stared and nodded. 'They're very nice,' he said politely.

He kept staring.

'You can touch them, you know,' Adele said impatiently.

'Um . . . thanks.'

His hands reached out uncertainly, cupping the shape of her breasts about an inch above them. He gasped when his fingers brushed skin, as if he'd been burned, and closed his eyes tight for a second as he squeezed. When he opened his eyes he looked pleasantly surprised and nervous as a cat. She felt like she had a sixth sense when she looked at him, some sense that could pick up the excitement which was seeping out of him like sweat. She didn't believe he was all that gay anyway.

He squeezed her boobs like they were made of glass. The lightness of his touch, nerves and cold air moving over her bare skin made her nipples stiffen and pucker.

'Oh my God,' Kim murmured, almost incredulously. He looked up at her face, his eyes round, asking what he couldn't get his mouth to ask as his fingers hovered over her nipple.

She nodded, breathless, and pushed her breasts closer. She thought he meant to touch them, but instead he cupped them in his hands and pressed his cheek into them. His lips touched the tip of her nipple and she held her breath, in case any sound or sigh she made be construed as no and frighten him off. When she thought she might make a sound, as his wet, wet mouth closed over her nipple, her breath stayed stuck in her throat and she only managed to let out a small croaking noise.

He sucked like a baby and she felt like all her nerve

endings were connected to that one point on her flesh where his mouth lapped and tasted. She moaned and touched his hair, wrapped an arm around him, then somehow they tumbled back on her bed and Kim seemed to surge up over and above her as he crawled up and kissed her full on the lips.

She had never kissed like this before, tangled up in a private parentless situation where anything could happen and skin was exposed. She had never had a boy suck on her nipple before. She had never kissed a boy who could make her inner thighs feel light and loose, make her brain reel and her cunt ache and itch deliciously. Not until now.

And he could kiss. His rough, smoky tongue felt soft and narrow inside her mouth, and his kiss felt the way screen kisses look – swooning into the sweep of his tongue against hers, pleasure making their mouths wetter and softer. She opened her legs under her long skirt, inviting him to touch. He didn't take the hint but she realised what was pressing against her thigh as he pushed his body forwards. His dick. His hard dick. Which should have felt like an embarrassment, the way it did when some boys humped your leg, but it didn't. She wondered what it would feel like to have it inside her, and the ache of need inside was so intense she clenched her internal muscles tight around the sensation. She could feel a spot of cooling moisture on the crotch of her knickers like her period starting, but she wasn't due. She was just wet.

Kim panted in her ear and started sucking at her nipples again. He took an experimental bite at one and Adele found herself crying out so hoarsely he pulled away for a second, thinking she was in pain.

'Do it again,' she said, unable to believe that horny, bedroom voice was coming out of her mouth or that her own body was doing these things. If he didn't put his hand between her legs soon, she was going to do it herself, and that excited her further. What would he do if she masturbated in front of him? She thought she could do it – for real this time – actually come. She wasn't sure if she had ever experienced an orgasm on her own, and with hindsight she thought she probably hadn't, if the way she felt now was any indication. She had never felt such single-minded purpose in her body, had no real idea it could conduct lust like electricity. Kim was moaning, squeezing her breasts and biting her nipples. She arched up into his touch and he thrust against her, his cock, still in his jeans, bumping her thigh.

'You want to see something else?' she asked, blushing furiously and amazed she even got the words out of her mouth. Her entire body was screaming 'fuck me' but she couldn't seem to articulate the sentiment.

'Yes,' he gasped. 'Please. Please . . .'

She sat up and removed her knickers under her skirt. Kim breathed hard and stared at the wisp of cloth as she pulled it down over her feet and off. Adele wondered if she could actually do this, but she was dizzy with her own new-found power and determined that this was going to be it – at last. She was finally going to lose it. She lay back, lifted her skirt and spread her legs for him.

'Oh my God,' Kim said again. 'Oh. My. God.'

His gaze on her exposed and open sex was almost palpable. She lifted her hips and spread her thighs wider, feeling herself stretch, then almost flew off the bed when she heard the familiar slam of the front door downstairs.

'Shit –' She panicked and pulled on her T-shirt without a bra. Kim stuffed her discarded bra down the side of the bed and kicked her knickers under it. She suddenly felt foolish and darted across the hall to lock herself in the bathroom and gather her wits about her.

She could hear footsteps coming up the stairs – her father's.

'Oh, all right. Where's Adele?'

'Gone to the loo,' she heard Kim say.

'That bad, eh?' her dad asked.

'No. She did well.'

She sat on the rim of the bath, scared by her dad's uncanny knowledge that she was hiding from him. She was hiding from him, just not because of a poor exam result, as he thought. She was hiding because she'd just let her best friend stare up her crack with the thought of fucking him in the bedroom she had grown up in.

Jesus Christ, what did I just do?

Her cunt had felt like a deep, soft ache of need when she was in the bedroom. Caught out in her misdemeanour she lurked in the bathroom with no underwear and her bottom feeling exposed under her skirt. Just to see what it was like, she slipped a hand up her skirt and felt between her legs. She was instantly amazed and aroused by how wet it was. Soaking, and slippery. Her index finger skidded over the bump of her clitoris, which felt almost swollen beyond recognition, and the dart of pleasure the touch sent through her was startling in its strength. She had barely touched it. She pressed and had to bite her lip to stifle a moan because it was good, but not good enough. She still needed more.

Her father and her best friend were discussing exam results in the next room. Couldn't have been a worse time or place or situation, but her fingers were straying. She clenched her teeth to stop herself from shouting aloud when she pushed two fingers inside, slowly and deliciously. If Kim knew what he was missing . . .

The inner walls of tissue were slick and smooth under her fingers and incredibly hot. She pushed her fingers deeper, pushing them up herself and rocking her hips on to them. It felt fantastic. When she moved her hips and hand, the friction was like nothing else, inexorable, something she couldn't stop doing even if she wanted to. She nearly cried out when she pressed and rubbed her clit with the fingers of her other hand. She rubbed and pushed, fucking herself with her fingers until suddenly she found an angle that felt even better; made her hips slam and pump into the rough strokes. Her cheeks felt red, her skin hot and her sex hurt the way a religious ecstasy must hurt – so good she could barely stand it. She bit her lips hard, sure she was going to scream as her hips moved of their own volition. Something seemed to melt and explode inside her belly and the slippery walls contracted wildly around her fingers.

She swallowed down the whimpering noises threatening to burst out of her throat. She left her fingers inside because it felt good, throbbing and warm, flesh rippling lazily under her touch, slowing down. That was it – the real thing. So many doors opening, so many new vistas of possibility and opportunity: the chance of leaving home, the realisation of what her own body could do and what it wanted to do to Kim.

Adele didn't have the chance to linger. She flushed the toilet to make it seem as though she had been putting the bathroom to its proper use, washed her hands and went to tell her father her results. She felt indecent, speaking to her dad with no knickers on and her crotch soaked from masturbating. She was sure she reeked of sex and was red in the face.

'Well done,' Dad was saying to Kim. 'Excellent stuff. Ah, here she is. Let's be having it then.'

She picked up her envelope from the dressing table and handed it to Dad. He opened it and read. 'Bloody hell, girl. You didn't muck about, did you?'

She smiled. 'Well, I did. You know I did . . .'

He grinned and kissed her cheek. 'You smartarse little cow. Just like your mother. She'd have been proud of you, you know.'

'I know.' She knew so little of her mother, a tough Irish socialist and academic who had had enough of intellectuals and fell in love with Adele's father – drawn to a man whose work was taming an uncontrollable force of nature. It had always been her ambition to live up to her mother's brilliance, and she really felt as though she could do it, step out of her shadow and better her parents. She could just live – unbound by school, knowing about sex. She could have her own flat, take lovers, attend lectures.

She wanted to jump up and down, squealing with joy, and was grateful for her father wrapping her in one of his bone-crushing embraces. She squeezed back, hoping she had washed the smell of her own flesh from her hands, but Dad's sense of smell was fucked anyway. He had breathed in so many fires that he would wake up and prowl around downstairs at night. And when she went down to see if he was OK he'd be roaming like a sleepwalker in his dressing gown, claiming he could smell burning – the fires in his dreams slipping into his consciousness. He pressed a kiss into her wiry hair and said, 'Proud of you, our kid', making her want to cry at the thought of him walking around alone at night, smelling fires that weren't there, without her there to drink sugary tea with at four in the morning.

'I'll see if your brother's at the station,' Dad said, heading downstairs. Chris, her elder brother, was also a fireman.

Kim quickly scrambled over the bed and opened the window wider. 'Jesus. It must stink of dope in here. Do you think he noticed?'

'You know he didn't,' Adele said. 'And don't be evasive.'

'All right,' Kim sat on the side of the bed and gave her a guilty, dirty, sexy smile. 'Do you know what we nearly did?'

'I know.' She bit her lip, trying to keep from laughing out loud at her own daring. 'You're supposed to be gay. That's the only reason you're allowed in my room.'

Kim shrugged. 'Perfect cover, don't you think?'

She thought of all the times he had stayed over, sometimes slipping into sleep on the bed with her. Sleepovers were about to get more interesting. Naked interesting. Fucking interesting. Biting on the pillow interesting. 'And we work this out three weeks before we're supposed to go to different universities?' she said. 'Sod's law.'

'We'd better make the most of it, then,' Kim said slyly.

'Yes, we had.'

Adele considered herself spoilt in that her first experience of sex had been everything first sexual experiences are supposed to be according to romantic novels. Almost. Perhaps. In romantic novels the hero was rarely previously sure that he was gay and didn't come after about two tentative thrusts, but she and Kim had always snickered over such novels and their mauve-tinted prose anyway.

'Why does he always address her by her full name when he sweeps her into her arms and tells her he loves her?' Kim mused, dropping cigarette ash between the pages of a rose-tinted tome they had bought for 10p at an Oxfam shop for the express purpose of mocking. 'It's always "I love you, Jonquil Elizabeth Markamthwaite Smythe, and I always have". Jesus –' He flipped back a few pages, checking the hero's name. 'I can only hope Clive's a long stayer 'cause that's one hell of a tongue-twisting handle to shout when you're coming.'

Adele frowned and rolled over in bed. 'I seriously don't think I could fuck a guy named Clive.'

'You couldn't?'

'Of course not. Imagine it ... oh God, yes ... oh yeah ... oh yes, yes, yes, YES, CLIIIIIIVE!'

Kim cackled approvingly. 'Yeah, but you don't call out anyone's name when you come. Except maybe Jesus. I don't know what he has to do with your clitoris exactly.'

'I know. It's odd,' she said. 'I always thought of myself as an agnostic.'

They had so little time that it was fortunate that they had the kind of energy that went with youth, cramming as much sex into their time as possible. They tried to keep up their pretence of absolute innocence, just good friends, but Adele found it difficult. She had always coveted Kim's beauty and, now that she could have a share of it for herself, she wanted to grab him and kiss him breathless with every sly, knowing little look he darted her way.

The day after they collected their exam results, he came round with a bottle of wine he had stolen from the restaurant. Neither of them liked wine much, but it was the effect they loved, not the taste. It wasn't even especially good wine, acid and vinegary, but she swallowed a glass to soothe her nerves before registering that she wasn't too keen on it. The moments before kisses and letting instinct run free were always awkward at first, until she took pity on him – all eager face and wide eyes – and made the first move.

Adele had kissed only a couple of boys and they had all been uncomfortable, messy affairs, with too many teeth and clumsy tongues. The first time she had been properly kissed she had almost wanted to draw back from the yawning cavern of his mouth drawing towards her like a predator. It was only when she felt the strange alien squirming of his too-wet tongue in her mouth and she realised that this was her first real kiss that she felt something like excitement. She had been seventeen at the time and pushed the boy's hands away from her crotch, although she allowed him to squeeze her tits through her T-shirt, and felt even more rebellious when she allowed him to put his fingers inside her bra. The second one was an older man – the barman at the local pub where she had gone for her first legal drink with her brothers. They had chatted a lot before, while she sipped her Coke and Tony drank his pint, but, on her eighteenth birthday, everyone bought her drinks. After three pints of strong cider she had gone to the toilet to puke, drunker than she would usually have been because of a birthday diet of chocolate gifts and ice-cream sundaes. When she came out of the toilets, Paddy the barman was there, murmuring, 'C'mere, you . . .' in seductive West Irish tones that had always made her melt. She protested, saying she had just chucked her guts up and was in no fit state to be kissed, but he said he didn't care. She thought it was rather disgusting that he didn't.

Kissing Kim was a completely different experience. His mouth was fresh and clean and his lips were soft. He had so little stubble that his kiss was silky smooth, his tongue narrow and flickery like a snake tasting the air. He made these noises when she did something that he liked, so that when she nipped gently at his lower lip with her teeth he made a low gaspy catch of breath in the back of his throat. The sound made her gut clench and flutter with some deep pulse of aroused response somewhere in the barely understood intricacies of her womb. Her hands shook when she reached down and tentatively rubbed at the front of his jeans with her palm, searching for that strange cylindrical bulge that told you were doing something right. He moaned quietly when she found his dick through the denim, hard and slender.

There was a quick flash of panic in the back of her mind when he reached down and unzipped his fly for her, because she thought of being penetrated, of no going back, but when he slid his jeans over his hips, taking down his shorts, she was fascinated. She didn't dare look, and kept her eyes closed while she kissed him. He had to guide her hand towards his cock, and gulped and whispered when she curled her fingers around it. It was warm, astonishingly hard, and yet the skin was amazingly fine and soft. She stroked it gently and made a decision to peek, just as his hand moved up over her thigh and started pushing her skirt higher. His hand moved higher, and she felt that ache of need inside again. When his fingers lifted her skirt high enough to expose her, she could feel cool air on the crotch of her knickers, cooling the wet fabric. His hand kneaded nervously through her underwear, her hand stroking the slim shaft of his cock back and forth, mouths joined, not daring to break off.

She decided she had better remove her underwear, since he had done the same, and swiftly slid down her knickers, catching a glimpse of him. He was sitting back on his elbows on the bed, his jeans around his knees and his hips bared, his cock poking up from a tangle of black hair. It looked smoother than she had expected, not knotted with veins like the comedy penises people drew on toilet walls. His eyes were round and black, his mouth wet from kissing. She was desperate to know how it felt to have it inside her.

Adele sat down on the bed once more, next to him. This time when they kissed they were both bolder and, as she reached for his dick, his hand darted up her skirt. Kim's fingertips tentatively stroked her pubic hair until she couldn't stand it any longer and lifted one foot onto the bed, spreading her legs and lips. She felt as though she was going to burst with excitement. His finger squirmed nervously at the top of the cleft and she flinched when he accidentally bumped the nub of her clit.

'Did I hurt you?'

'No, no. It's nice.'

'Can I put my fingers inside?' he asked shyly.

She nodded, heart thumping, relieved that he'd asked at last. She had never felt anything quite like it, not even while masturbating. Her cunt felt like a pulsing, living, sentient thing, a hungry mouth watering at the prospect of things being put into it. She directed his fingers to the entrance and shivered when he pushed one inside her. It didn't feel like enough.

She resumed her grip on his dick, stroking back and forth with her clenched hand, which was what she assumed he liked. He moaned and wriggled his finger inside her, making her gasp.

'Use two fingers,' she told him.

He was so nervous. 'I want . . . if you want, that is . . .'

Adele had a packet of condoms squirrelled in the bedside table. She assumed Kim had probably bought some too, but she handed him the pack. 'Do you know how to –?'

'Of course I do,' he interrupted a little testily, and took one from the packet. At school they had put condoms on cucumbers, to much hysterical giggling, but doing it for real seemed much more serious. She felt too nervous to take off her clothes, and his T-shirt had slid back down anyway so that his latex-covered cock poked out comically from under the hem. Instead she lay back on the bed, hitched her skirt up above her waist and opened her legs. The pose excited her and she wanted to indulge in the familiarity of her own fingers and come, because she was under no illusion that she was going to have an earth-shattering orgasm the first time – although she felt like she could when he leaned above her, bracing himself up on the palm of one hand, the other hand trying to position his dick against the hole.

She moaned when the narrow head of his cock found its way, and arched her back up, watching her own pale thighs spread wide around his slim hips, slotting them into place like pieces of a puzzle as he pushed, filling her cunt. When she looked up at him he looked so amazed, so aroused that her hips wanted to move of their own accord and find a rhythm that would take them to the peak.

'Oh God,' he panted. 'Oh God ... fucking hell ...'

He pulled back and pushed back in again, and she cried out at the sensation. Jesus. It was fucking beautiful, that in and out, sliding, thrusting motion that was the object of all those dirty jokes. She could feel her flesh giving way, wrapping around him and she could tell by his bitten-lipped, closed-eyed expression that this felt as good for him too. She had made him look like that.

'Ohhhh shiiit ...' Kim groaned; a low wail of disappointment that she knew was bad news. He pulled out, gasping.

'Fuck, fuck, fuck. I'm sorry.'

She laughed, feeling flattered.

'It's not funny!'

'No, of course not,' she said. 'Although I'm kind of impressed I make you feel that way.'

He turned back to her with a starved, intense look on his face that made her body move eagerly into his touch as he leaned over her again and kissed her on the mouth. 'Oh you –' he began to say, but broke off to push her T-shirt up and suckle on her breasts, his hand squeezing between her legs. When he pushed his fingers back into her she moved her hips, humping his hand eagerly, desperate to come.

'What's it feel like?' he asked.

'Oh God –' It almost hurt it was so intense. Not just the physical sensation but the mad, dizzy excitement caused by the sheer dirtiness and enormity of what they had just done. He had put his dick inside her and now he had his fingers where his dick had just been, and it only seemed to go some way towards satisfying her. She needed to come, but the very thought of reaching down and rubbing herself to climax in front of Kim made her hands shake and her cheeks burn.

'It feels good,' she said, realising it was a poor expression of *how* good and yet how frustrating it felt. He tentatively pushed his fingers in and out, and she realised she was going to have to show him how.

Without speaking, she reached for his wrist and removed his hand, guiding his sticky fingers to her clitoris. He looked wide eyed and surprised; she smiled at him, feeling like she knew it all for once.

'Is that...?' Kim murmured, giving it an experimental rub.

'Oh yes.' She stretched into the touch and bit her lip.

'Just here?'

'Just there.'

6

The trouble with married lovers, Karina thought, was that, as soon as your lover started getting that well-fucked spark in their eye again, their spouses got wise to it and started trying to reclaim what they thought was rightfully theirs. She was sure Edward was watching from the window as Suki made her way up the grass bank, bottom swaying with the air of a woman who knew what it was to come and come hard. He had been trying to cash in on Suki's freshly reawoken sexuality and Suki was pleading so many headaches that Edward wanted her to have a CAT-scan. Whenever he returned from his latest business trip, he was sniffing around Suki so much like a horny dog that Karina imagined him on his hands and knees, trying to poke his nose under her skirt.

Karina had disliked him before, but she now loathed him with a hot, sweet hate that made every aspect of him an object of disgust to her: the hairs on the backs of his hands; the way he ate a meal – stolid and functional as a cow – and, most of all, the thought of his pale, fish-like eyes roaming greedily over Suki's body.

They were at the country house in Suffolk. Edward owned two homes in a hopeless attempt to make the old money like him. The girls and Lotte, the German au pair girl, splashed happily in the pool like minnows while Karina sewed and sulked. It was like something from Jane Austen, she reflected – all these disparate women thrown together, mothers, daughters, servants, and

Karina acting the grumpy governess. Lotte was climbing out of the pool. Fair and freckled, with a snub nose, she could have been the girls' older sister. Her legs were unshaven, covered with fine blonde hairs, and her breasts, glossy in her tight black Speedo, were like two halves of a tennis ball. If Lotte hadn't been so fiercely obsessed with Enrique Iglesias then Karina might have considered her a threat, but there was no doubt about Lotte's sexuality. She played her Enrique CDs in her room and screamed whenever he appeared on MTV, to much derision from the children, who were still young enough to think that boys were yucky.

Suki had been riding. She came strutting up that bank like a feminine Mr Darcy in her tight jodhpurs and white silk shirt. Suki's passion for dressing up was not confined to the bedroom, so she would never dream of going riding in an old sweater and wellingtons like a real aristocrat. She liked to dress the way she imagined the rich dressed, so she wore a loose silk shirt and a plum waistcoat when sat astride a horse. On anyone else it would have looked absurd, but Suki had been dressed up as so many different fantasies that the outfit made her look unbearably sexy. It was masculine but emphasised every curve of her body. The sleeves of her shirt were soft and billowy and the cut of her waistcoat nipped in and showing off her still-tiny waist above the strong flare of her hips in the khaki riding pants. She wore tight leather riding boots to the knee and carried a crop, the sight of which made Karina shiver in pleasant recollection. She had fucked Suki with the leather handle of that crop – pushed it inside her soft, warm cunt and watched with rising excitement as it moved in and out of Suki's squirming body. Afterwards, Suki had heatedly said she would never be able to use a riding crop again without thinking of this. Karina knew what she meant. Every time Suki went riding, Karina thought dirty memories, gripping the leather of the crop which was infused with Suki's juices and pounding her clit down hard on the saddle with the rhythm of the horse's hooves.

'Good ride?'

'Not bad,' Suki said, wiggling across the pool terrace to dogged, noisy cries of 'Mummy! Mummy!' 'Must call the farrier though. I think one of her shoes is loose.'

'Mummy, Mummy! Watch me do a somersault, Mummy!' Hannah yelled from the water.

'In a minute, darling,' Suki called. 'Mummy just has to make a phone call.'

'I'll help,' Karina said lamely and hastily. She never understood why all mothers of young children tended to refer to themselves in a grammatical case that should have been called Third Person Maternal.

'I don't need any help lifting a phone on my own,' Suki said, teasing.

'I'm there if you need me.' Karina followed her into the house, where it was cool and dark compared to the poolside. Cool and dark like a hole in the ground or the underside of a rock, under which toads like Edward lurked. Fucking Edward. With distaste she imagined his penis, like a pale blind worm under the bedcovers, and wondered how Suki had ever stood that thing inside her. Edward, as Karina had guessed, was a lousy fuck, according to his beloved unfaithful wife. In ten years of marriage, he had never gone down on her once. Consequently, Suki's gratitude and pleasure had been almost earsplitting the first time Karina's tongue had teased apart the lips of her sex. It wasn't only behind a piano that Suki was vocal.

'Come upstairs,' Karina whispered conspiratorially.

'I can't. The children want me,' Suki said.

'They'll have forgotten you in a blink.' Karina inclined her head to the staircase. 'Come on.'

Suki darted her eyes back for a moment, towards where the sound of splashing, yelling little girls could be heard, then glanced back at Karina. She licked her lower lip and gave Karina a mock-reproachful look. 'You're terrible,' she said, smiling.

'No I'm not,' Karina said. 'I'm fabulous. Anyway, we need to talk.'

Suki frowned. 'Please –' she sighed.

'We need to talk,' said Karina, leading her up the stairs. She had never imagined anyone with more issues than herself until she met Suki. They reached the bedroom and Karina closed the door behind them. Suki sat down on her bed, a wide expanse of pale gold-beige satin. Karina burned to think of Edward sharing that bed with her.

'Last night –' Karina began.

'Headache,' said Suki. 'I had a headache.'

'And tonight?'

'I can't have my period again.' Suki looked distraught. 'Darling, he thinks I've got a brain tumour as it is. If I keep having two *periods* a month then Eddy will be calling my gynaecologist demanding to know what's going on.'

'Did he see you naked last night?'

'He's my husband.'

Karina glared. 'I don't think I can take it,' she said.

'You can't?' Suki stood up, a thin little line creased at the bridge of her nose by her frown. 'So, what? You're breaking it off?'

'No,' Karina said, deciding it was now or never. 'I'm asking you to leave him.'

Suki shook her head. 'Oh God, please, darling. Not that.

You know I can't do that. I have two children and we wouldn't stand a chance in the courts. The judge would fucking *eat* us.'

Karina stepped closer and ran her hands up and down Suki's silk-clad arms. She felt goosebumps under the material and pulled Suki into a hug to warm her.

'What if I ate you in the witness box? Any pervy old judge would find in favour.'

Suki snorted, giggled. 'You're wicked,' she murmured, lips brushing Karina's ear.

'You love me that way,' Karina said, pressing herself closer. Already she could feel the pressure of Suki's pubic bone against her thigh, beginning a slow, nearly imperceptible grind. Suki's hips were one of the sweetest parts of her body. Since they started their affair, Suki had begun to walk differently, move her hips differently. She used to walk with a cutesy Monroe wiggle, but now, whenever she moved, the fluid snakiness of her hips became apparent and made her old bouncy-star jiggle look skittish and contrived. Now she moved like a woman in some kind of Tantric harmony with the column of her spine and the centre of her womb. Her hips swayed as though suspended by threads from the rest of her body, and when they made love they did amazing things – grinding, rolling, lifting and falling, bouncing off the bedsheets.

When her hips shimmied, no matter how subtly, it was an arousing reminder of how she moved in bed, and, when she ground her hips gently and hungrily, Karina had to grip her butt tight and close, the better to feel her move.

Suki smelled of sweat and stables, and her face was still flushed from riding. She painted herself a different, fresher face in the country, leaving behind the golds and violets she favoured in London. While she played the role of pampered wife and doting fresh-air-fiend mother she applied only a light foundation, a touch of tan mascara on her moth-antennae luxuriant lashes and a soft gloss to her mouth. It made her look younger and fascinated Karina all the more, while confirming her initial impression that Suki was a kindred spirit. Like Karina, she was a chameleon, changing faces according to who-ever she needed to be at the time.

Karina liked to fix Suki's make-up for her, dressing her up like a doll in her beautiful, expensive clothes and taking pictures. Suki's London wardrobe was the size of a beach hut Karina had once lived in in Thailand. She had ribbons and laces, feathers and furs, scented silver card-board boxes filled with rustling coloured tissue paper for her hats and lingerie and high, painful shoes. Suki's shoes were like exquisite instruments of torture, some that looked at a distance like jewelled invisible platforms that lifted her feet into a Barbie-doll tiptoe position, until you got closer and saw they were made of transparent plastic, like a low-rent Cinderella shoe. There were others that were glittery chains of diamanté pushed between the first two painted toes and looped slut-style around the ankle, and sparkly pink jelly mules with fake daisies stuck to the heels – deliberately trailer trashy. Not a single pair looked comfortable, but Karina had long since become accustomed to the notion that beauty and dis-comfort went hand in hand. Nothing made a waist look prettier, made hips flare and breasts bulge like a corset. Nothing was more uncomfortable either but the pain became part of the pleasure; that and the sense of having your whole torso cruelly constricted with only your sex-ual organs free of the bones and satin.

Suki owned a couple of basques, but she didn't wear them, complaining that the lace itched. She liked soft, floaty baby-doll lingerie with tiny straps, which her breasts could fall out of easily. She would have her favourites, like the oyster silk slip she wore in the bedroom. The silk was so fine you could tell immediately what she was wearing underneath, or what she wasn't wearing, which was more often the case. Her nipples showed through the fabric and, when she moved a certain way, Karina could see the silk snagging slightly over the curls of her bush.

One night when Karina entered the room, Suki had been sat at her vanity table, wearing the slip and putting on mascara, deliberating over lipsticks. The lipstick palette was filled with shades of gold, cherry, red, silver, pink and buff. Suki had a separate brush for each colour, like a fine paintbrush. She had giggled over lipstick traces at first.

'Isn't it strange, tasting another woman's lipstick, getting it all over your mouth when you kiss? This must be what men feel like.'

There was a red lipstick that had a strong artificial smell and taste of morello cherries. Karina often borrowed it because, try as she might, she couldn't get away from the fact that red lipstick suited her and was lucky for her. Red was her colour. Suki was a Libran, and looked especially lovely in pastels. When she put on red lipstick her face became too hard, too old Hollywood, and only suitable for slightly kinky encounters.

As Suki rose from her dressing table that night, Karina had noticed that her slip didn't move the usual way over her thighs and crotch. It slithered where it usually snagged, and tumbled down smoothly to her neat, rosy knees. And when she turned around there was no shadow between her thighs, where her pubes would normally have showed as a dark smudge beneath the silk.

'What have you done?' asked Karina, initially feeling

bereft. She loved Suki's bush – soft fine tendrils like fair moss that decorated the fleshy outer lips of her sex and curled coyly over the root of her clit. Even the thought that the hair would grow back didn't assuage her.

'Want to see?' Suki lifted her skirt an inch or so, smiling mischievously.

'What did you *do*, Suki?'

'I thought I'd try that full bikini wax,' Suki said. 'It hurt like hell but now ... God, it's incredible. You can see *everything*.' Her voice chimed teasingly as she wriggled her arse, hands on her hips so that the slip moved higher up her thighs. It lifted slowly, like a theatre curtain before the main attraction, and Karina could feel her own heart-beat pounding in her ears, her throat constricted and her brain fogged and stupid with lust.

'Show me,' she said, hearing her own voice as if from far away; a pathetic mew of need.

Suki lifted her skirt higher. The tops of her thighs were perfectly smooth. Two children had left her with only fine snail-trail silver lines on her hips and lower belly, but had turned her cunt into a deep, smooth-walled maternal cave that could accommodate Karina's small fist when it was soaked and hungry.

Her skirt moved tantalisingly higher, the delicate, scalloped lace skimming like a decorative fringe above a more exciting shell-like curve, like the cusp of a cowrie.

'Oh my God.' It looked edible, lickable as candy, primly closed between Suki's thighs, but Karina knew instinctively that she was wet inside. Suki loved to display herself and her hand snaked down her body, demurely covering her shaven crotch with the slip for a moment, before lewdly cupping her sex through the silk. Tease.

'It feels amazing, 'Rina,' Suki whispered. 'It's so soft. All naked.'

She removed her hand and the slip slid down to her

knees again, a thin veil over her body. The silk was spotted with moisture from where she had pushed it against herself and the sight of that tiny wet stain made Karina's head reel and her hips move involuntarily, so that her tight panties squeezed her like a lover's hand.

Suki sat down on the little buff velvet boudoir stool and Karina could no longer keep her hands to herself. She pushed the slip up Suki's thighs and knelt on the floor to look more closely. Suki was blatantly aroused. She couldn't hide a thing, stripped of her hair. The wetness that would have usually dewed the inner curls of her pubic hair glistened on the outer lips, and the inner lips were just *wet* – shining flushed petals of swollen flesh. She was panting quietly and Karina could see her muscles, tense with excitement, relax for a second, making her cunt stir like a carnivorous hothouse flower. She even smelled different. Where a faint tang of female musk would inevitably linger on her pubic hair by the end of the day, the smell no longer had anywhere to cling. She smelled purely of sex, of salt. She whispered a soft mantra of 'please, please, please' under her breath as Karina peered up between her legs, letting her breath touch the open shell of Suki's cunt, but not her mouth – not yet.

She breathed in Suki's smell, teased her with a light touch of the tip of her tongue on the plump nub of her clit. Suki reacted as though she had been given an electric shock, tensing, jolting and crying out.

'Shh.' Karina took a tissue from the box on the dressing table. 'Don't wake the girls.'

Suki clapped a hand over her mouth and giggled breathlessly. 'Sorry ... noisy me. What are you doing now?'

Karina dabbed her dry with the tissue. 'You'll see.' She took the lipstick palette from the table and the brush stained with red. The cherry red, with the morello smell. It was awkward to reach on the edge of the stool so she made Suki lie down on the bed with her knees drawn right up, then she dipped the brush into the palette and began to paint. She started at the corners, painting into where the lips met and pressed together above the perineum and where they pouted above the clit. Then she carefully painted the outer lips, edging them in brilliant red. Suki moaned and muttered with lust and disbelief, and Karina had to tell her to keep still several times as her apparently autonomous hips moved of their own accord.

When Karina had finished, Suki had a vertical pair of lips painted between her legs. When she closed her legs they looked sweetly pouting, the smile half hidden between her thighs. When she opened them it looked bizarre, monstrous and exotic. It was like a toothless alien mouth where nothing was in the right place – a freak of nature hidden behind a pretty girl's red smile. The game was to make her come without smudging the lipstick but, in all the three times they had played it, it had never worked out that way. Karina always ended up drowning in the smell of morello cherries, spit and Suki's juices, and with her face and fingers stained like a greedy child that had stuck its whole face into a tub of pink candy floss.

They had played their game right there on the bed behind Suki, leaving stains on the sheets that they had giggled over when they tried to conceal them from the housekeeper. So much good old-fashioned dirty fun. Suki couldn't *not* leave Edward. She had to leave him.

'You will *die* if you don't get out of here,' Karina said firmly, the horsey smell of Suki's shirt bringing her sharply back to the discussion in hand.

'I can't think of myself.' Suki pulled away, her hips

stilled, annoyed that Karina was pushing the issue. 'You don't understand, 'Rina. You can't understand unless you have children.'

'Seeing as that's totally impossible I doubt I'll ever understand, then,' Karina said bitterly. 'Look ... I know you have to think of Hannah and Elisa, but do some thinking for yourself as well. Stop doing what you think you ought to do and do what you want to do, because that obviously makes you happy.'

'Does it?' Suki moaned, already starting with the tears. Distractedly she began to straighten the bed, as if emphasising that she was a wife and mother. Karina loved her but sometimes Suki's diva-ism was plain infuriating. The girl was all marshmallow and teary-eyed heartbreak when tough choices needed making.

'Yes, it does make you happy,' Karina said fiercely. 'Look at yourself. You haven't had a drink in four months. I am so proud of you, Su, and has he even noticed you're not half-pissed all the time? I don't think so.'

Suki beat a pillow into shape, even though the house-keeper had puffed it into perfect shape that very morning. 'I know,' she said, sighing.

'So stop lying to yourself, because it's fucking obvious to anyone with half a brain that, while you're pretending to be Mrs Stepford, you hit the bottle to kill yourself that little bit faster. Being a lesbian doesn't mean you're any less of a fit mother.'

'But I'm not a –' Suki stopped in mid-denial and pulled something from under a pillow. It was a new paperback copy of *The Joy of Sex*. 'Is this yours?' she said, staring at the book in puzzlement.

'No,' Karina said. 'I think I committed that book to memory before I'd even left school. Why? Is it yours?'

The door of the en suite bathroom opened. 'It's mine,' Edward said, standing there stony faced and shaking almost imperceptibly. He looked as though he had been crying, and Karina stared at him in horror, realising he had been in there all the time, hoping to spring a little whoopee on the wife and rekindle the spark with his tired sex manual.

'Oh fuck,' she said, looking at Edward's wet eyes and trembling shoulders. 'I know; you're about to tell me I'm *so* fired, aren't you?'

The girl arched her back and thrust too-big-to-be-real breasts into the shot. She mewled and panted softly as though the camera lens on her body felt like a lover's touch. Someone had obviously told her that she had that rare ability to 'make love to the camera'. That someone had probably had their hand on her tits or in her knickers when they'd said that to her. The old casting couch.

'Get off! You're fucking shite!' Karina heckled, tossing a potato chip at the TV screen for good measure. Naturally the girl didn't hear her, but Karina had had half a bottle of vodka and wasn't concerned about small matters like reality. She required alcohol, food, weed and a lot of bad softcore cable porn to pick apart, because she didn't care to think too hard about anything else in her life.

The actress wasn't even especially pretty. She just had the necessary requirements – an ability to make sex faces, little or no inhibitions about nudity, and a pair of silicone knockers that looked like they'd been tacked on as an afterthought to her skinny body. Karina had vaguely followed the vestigial plot. The girl was supposed to be the prey of a neighbourhood voyeur who had her house wired for visual and sound. She had shown no signs of being creeped out or any way disgusted by this guy bashing the bishop over her and had, in fact, gone and started picking up men and women in bars in order to enhance her friendly neighbourhood pervert's viewing pleasure. Karina had resigned herself to not understanding women as much as she should, but even in her craziest years she could never imagine herself being anything but disturbed by such a situation.

She squeezed frozen orange juice from the carton and added a healthy two fingers of vodka to the sticky glass. The juice was melting already. It had to be thirty degrees outside – a hot stinking London summer day, so thick with traffic fumes that she couldn't open the window to let in some air. She had to sit with the curtains shut and a fug of smoke that the fan couldn't disperse, sweating in her boxer shorts, which felt as though they were pasted to her arse.

The actress moaned and rubbed her nipples theatrically, feigning ecstasy. Karina frowned and gave one of her own nipples a rub, wondering if she had been missing something here, since the girl seemed to be enjoying herself so much. Nope. Nothing. Just the sensation of her own breast in her hand. A tit is just a tit – the fundamental things, and all that.

Karina wondered if she could find her old videotape of *Casablanca*, thinking she could use a good weepie, but she suspected that the tape had gone AWOL during one of her many moves. She loved *Casablanca*. It would be so easy if you could bring yourself to hate Lazlo, but he was so noble and so brave – the scene where they sang the 'Marsellaise' at Rick's always brought a tear to her eye. She felt like Bogart. Suki was Ingrid Bergman, of course, and the kids were like Lazlo. A good cause you couldn't question, the good of which tore you away from your love.

Love sucked. It couldn't suck any more than it already did if you attached a hose and a cyclone suction system. It sucked like a top-of-the-range Hoover, sucked like an orally fixated fluffer. It could suck a golfball through a hosepipe or a rock through a pipette, it sucked that much.

She had written 'LOVE BITES' across the mirror in lipstick in true slighted-starlet fashion, trashed her flat, got hideously drunk, rehearsed everything she should have said fifty thousand times, listened to a ringing telephone that nobody picked up at the other end and related to every sad song on the radio. It was different from her usual ways of ending relationships, and she found herself wallowing in the agony.

Suki had called only once. Once was enough. Karina knew the moment she heard her voice down the line that she was about to get dumped.

'It's complicated,' said Suki, sighing down the phone.

'You don't say.'

'There's no need to be like that. You knew I had to put the girls first, and you knew if Edward found out he'd take me to the cleaners and take the girls away from me. They're my children, Karina. I can't live without them and he's offering me a second chance.'

'You won't be happy,' Karina told her, like a gypsy delivering a curse.

'No, I probably won't,' Suki agreed, sighing again. 'But Hannah's wetting her bed again.'

'She knows something's up. Kids always do. They have a sixth sense for that. You owe it to them to be happy.'

'I can't. Not without leaving and Edward would never let me have custody.' Suki was crying. 'The bastard. He didn't even want them that much, but, if I want them, he wants them.'

Karina was disgusted at how weak she was, angry at being turned away. Blood, it seemed, really was thicker than water, or any other bodily fluid you cared to name. Maternal love was a frightening thing. Even when they were old enough not to nip at your nipples with their tiny new teeth, they never let up yanking at the heartstrings. Damned kids. It wouldn't matter what Suki did to try and be the perfect mother to them, they'd still grow up with their own set of issues. Children always did, no matter how good their upbringing.

It made Karina think of her own mother and wonder if she had ever been happy. She never looked it, heavy hipped and drooping over her chopping board, her face impassive and flat. Karina feared becoming like her mother, but she thought she looked more like her father, a small, bird-boned, soft-skinned man who took a week to cultivate even a minor growth of stubble. He had steadily diminished into a wrinkled child, dwarfed by his monumental wife, but his temper was quick and his words pointed and sharp – another thing Karina had inherited.

Between them they had somehow given their child beauty. One thing Karina could be sure of in herself was that she was beautiful. Her skin was flawless, her nose straight and small, cheekbones high and wide. Her dark eyes were heavy lidded and her lower lip was shorter than her upper lip, which made people say she reminded them of a doll when she wore red lipstick. Her mouth, painted and in repose, had a look of old Kyoto about it: demure, mysterious and expensive.

She rarely gained weight, being so fidgety and restless she could burn off the calories just thinking about it, and frequently forgot to eat anyway. She would have liked wider, curvier hips, but if she gained enough weight to pack on a few inches around her arse she got a double chin into the bargain, so she had to settle for being too thin.

Drink bloated her, and part of her wanted to toss the vodka down the sink. The other, self-destructive part wanted to drink herself to death. She had gone out looking for money and had found love, and in the process got burned.

'Have to get to the fucking root of this,' she muttered to herself, switching off the porn. Figure out why everything she touched turned to shit. It would be so much easier if she had some definition in her life, something she could definitely state that she was. Other than fabulous. Fabulous really didn't help at times like these.

Karina moved around a lot. It was easier to hop on a plane and put miles between her and a mistake, but throughout her travels she had always kept a diary of sorts – where she had been and what and who she had done. It wasn't a conventional diary. It was a battered, red leather suitcase shaped like a heart, starting to bulge and split with the letters, postcards, dirty Polaroids and other junk that it contained. None or little of it would mean anything to the casual observer, although some of her Polaroids were eyebrow raising. Drink swizzles, matchbooks, a sprig of lucky white heather, a pebble from a Corfiote beach with the head of a Greek warrior drawn on it with felt-tip pen, postcards from Bangkok, a voodoo doll made as a joke from tied-up ice-pole wrappers, love letters, hate mail, luggage labels, cigarettes that bore lipstick traces, even airline tickets to romantic places. Her life: a suitcase full of priceless trash.

She peered inside, a cigarette stuck out of the side of her mouth, making her screw up one eye wise-guy style against the smoke. The first thing her open eye hit on was a Polaroid from Bangkok – those two guys in the beach hut. She lifted the photo to check it out without the smoke in her eye, and smiled at the image. One blond, one black, locked together at the lips, a pink feather boa draped around their necks and bodies, and the blond's hand wrapped around his lover's large, stiff cock. She couldn't remember their names, but it had been one hell of a night.

Nice, obliging boys. They were so thrilled to have discovered a creature of such exquisite perversity as Karina that they'd done everything she asked them to: hands and tongues slipping and sliding over skin, between legs, into mouths, until it all got a little blurry and she couldn't recall who penetrated who or whose tongue had knowingly snaked down the crease of her arse and pushed inside.

There were pictures of herself in the suitcase – a magazine shoot she had done when money was tight. Nothing really sordid. Well, not for general viewing any-way. She had told the photographer that she didn't do open-leg shots and she didn't take her bottoms off. Tits only. She was pleased with the result. He had asked if she wanted to show a bit of arse through fishnet tights, peeking out from under a short leather skirt, and she had agreed. So she had put on the fishnets with nothing underneath. The picture showed her half leaning against a sink, her breasts visible as a reflection in the mirror over the sink, a chain dangling between her stiff plum-coloured nipples, attached by clips that had hurt like hell. Her butt was showing under the brief leather skirt and between her slightly splayed legs her hand was visible, squeezing and clutching at herself, her other hand non-chalantly painting her lips in the mirror.

The photographer had ripped the fishnets when he fucked her, so there were other pictures that hadn't made the magazine. One with the fishnet tights torn around her upper thighs, her lipstick smudged across her cheek, her arse held high and spread wide, exposing her freshly fucked arsehole. She hadn't minded. She had been so aroused by her own position and outfit, and the sting of pain in her nipples, that she was almost grateful when he announced he wanted to fuck her. Men always wanted to fuck her, probably so that they could tell their friends that they had.

She had had enough of being some kind of twisted arm candy. Even Suki had done it to a certain degree, revelling in her own wickedness but without the balls to admit that she was a lesbian. Karina rifled through the suitcase, searching through letters and photographs, until she found what she was looking for. A Polaroid of a friend – dark hair adrift in the sea breeze, red mouth sticky with seaside rock, the impression of her lips forming a lipstick kiss on the thick white photoframe. That was what she was after.

'Hello again, babydoll,' Karina said aloud, planting a kiss on the smudgy impression of lips on the photo.

7

Moving house was a pain at the best of times, but with a monster hangover and a sense of slight alcoholic remorse, it felt like hell itself. Adele staggered up the stairs carrying boxes, dashed back downstairs to pick up the next load and it didn't seem to ever be enough. The pile decreased, of course, with Jude's help, but she felt like a broken-down wreck watching him hop up and down stairs like a mountain goat. He was nimble, used to using his body, hammering home the embarrassing reality of her own tobacco-stained lungs and appalling state of fitness. She wouldn't join a gym. She didn't want to be one of those wholemeal bread bores who got their regular cardio and always seemed utterly smug about it, but it would make a change to get up and down stairs without breaking a sweat. She was sure she was sweating rum and Coke after last night.

Drunk didn't cover it. She had been sick twice already that morning. The booze hadn't seemed to bother Jude, but he was used to alcohol. She hadn't been drunk in two years. She let her knees hit the stairs halfway up, turned around and let her arse follow suit.

'Fuck it.'

That box was going nowhere unless someone, anyone, took it because she wasn't shifting the goddamn thing another inch. Her head was spinning and her skin felt sweaty and prickly – another rush of nausea coming on. She rode it out, determined not to puke down the stairs.

Jude came up the stairs, carrying a plant. 'You all right?'

'Yeah. Gimme a minute.'

He scooped up the box, tucking it effortlessly under a wiry, muscled arm and headed up to the flat. 'That's the lot anyway.'

'It is?' she asked, her spirits lifting.

'Yep.'

'Oh.' Adele got up carefully, worried that too much exertion too soon might prompt a quick dash to the bathroom. 'Thanks.'

'No problem,' Jude said, heading back down the stairs so that they were face to face halfway up. 'Hate to love you and leave you but I have to get back to work.'

'Yes,' she said, praying he wasn't going to try and kiss her because she had never felt less kissable in her life. 'Thanks for your help. I really appreciate it.'

Jude shrugged and raked a hand through his damp hair. The smell of his sweat was rank in her hangover-sensitised nostrils. 'That's cool. Thanks for last night. It was fun.'

'Mmm. Yes.' Beer, pool and watching his mates gob in the ashtrays. Thank *you*, Jude. What a blast.

She heard the door open downstairs and heard a cough that sounded like Paul.

'So, see you sometime?' Jude said, looking so much like a hopeful puppy that the eternal optimist part of her mind (which seemingly every woman possesses) thought she might be able to clean him up, educate him and pry him away from his disgusting friends. She stomped on the impulse. It was the same screwed-up optimism on which billions of incompatible partnerships were founded – that you'll change him. Yeah, right.

She found herself saying 'Sure' anyway, and accepted a kiss on the side of the mouth. Jude looked pleased, winked and darted off downstairs, grunting a blokey hello at Paul on the way down.

Paul glanced up the stairwell, his keys in his hand. 'Well well well. Night on the tiles, Ms Western?'

'Sort of,' she said coyly. 'And that was not what it looked like.'

Paul blinked. 'No? Why not? *I* would.'

'*He* wouldn't. Neither would I.' She realised how that sounded and laughed it off. 'I mean, you, I would. Hypothetically. Oh fuck.'

Paul sniggered and tossed his keys in the palm of his hand, looking infuriatingly ingenuous. 'No, please. Keep going. Nothing more entertaining than watching a lady dig herself deeper into it.'

She coughed and started again. 'I mean . . . I wouldn't. He's not my type.'

'What about me?' he said, lifting an eyebrow mischievously.

Adele applauded sarcastically. 'Finally – the Battle Cry of the Testicle Endowed.'

He smiled sweetly and raised his middle finger. 'You're a laugh a minute this morning. 'Fess up. Would you?'

'Paul!'

'Let me finish,' he said. 'Would you . . . care for a cup of coffee?'

She thought of the heap of crap stacked at the foot of her spiral staircase and decided that she'd cope better with it after getting some kind of a drink inside her. She was probably dehydrated. 'That *so* wasn't what you meant, but thanks. I will anyway.'

'Knew it,' he said, with a wicked grin.

'I'll be down in a minute. Let me lock up.'

'Too Freudian.'

She went upstairs and locked her front door, realising that they were flirting. In a whole evening in Jude's company there had been no such spark, but when she was with Paul they bounced as cheerfully off each other as if they'd known each other a lifetime. It was easy to flirt, she supposed, because there was no way anything was ever going to happen between them. He was, to all intents and purposes, gay – no question about that.

The sound of Patti La Belle singing 'Lady Marmalade' drifted up the stairs. 'Definitely gay,' she mouthed to herself and went downstairs, smiling.

Paul was firing up his elaborate-looking chrome coffee machine, his feet bare and his espadrilles tossed carelessly in the hall.

'Hey. Take a pew.'

'Thanks,' she said, perching on a kitchen stool.

'All moved in?'

'The bulk of it's out of the way. Just have to find a home for everything.'

Paul pulled a face. 'Ugh. That can take long enough on its own. I still don't know where to put Ieuan so as he doesn't clash with the couch.'

'Where's he got to?' she asked.

'Still looking for a job.'

'What does he do anyway?'

'You'd never guess from his appearance,' Paul said wryly. 'He's a piercer.'

'A what?'

'Professional piercer. He punches holes in people.'

'Interesting.'

Paul shook his head. 'It's positively gruesome. He keeps telling me to get my dick pierced. And I keep telling him to fuck off.'

She winced. 'Yeah. I can see why you wouldn't fancy it.'

'The results are intriguing,' he said, with a slightly dirty smile that made her wonder what else Ieuan had pierced besides his ears and eyebrow. 'But the pain . . . no way. He can't even talk me into a nipple.'

'Ow.'

'Very.' Paul turned around and leaned against the kitchen counter. He was wearing a short-sleeved blue shirt open to the heart and three-quarter-length khakis. His ankles were tanned and hairy but his chest looked smooth. He kept revealing, either by accident or on purpose, little scraps of his skin in a way that made Jude's full-on, arse- and chest-baring display look tacky. 'So, what's the story with Jude?' he asked.

'There is no story,' she said. 'We just went out for a drink last night.'

'Huh. Some girl-next-door you're turning out to be. I was hoping for at least some dirt.'

She laughed. 'Sorry. He's not my type.'

'Fuck type! He's gorgeous. Are you mad?'

'I'm not mad. I can see he's very attractive, but he's . . .' She wondered how to put it kindly and figured she couldn't. 'I shouldn't say. He did just help me move, which he didn't have to do.'

'Yes he did.' Paul curled his lip. 'He's trying to get into your pants. He'll do whatever he has to do. Trust me. Advice from the Testicle Endowed here.'

She shook her head. 'He's . . . not very bright.'

Paul nodded and took out his cigarettes. The coffee machine hissed and rumbled, filling the kitchen with a rich, tempting aroma. 'What's up with dumb and pretty?' he asked, offering her a cigarette which she thought would probably make her sick again. The smell of the coffee was so strong that her head spun.

'It's not what I go for,' she said, shaking her head. 'He likes jokes about tits and pool and his mates think spitting in ashtrays is hilarious.'

He smirked. 'Oh yes. Lads . . . lovely. The "backs to the wall" boys.'

'Something like that, yeah.'

Paul gave a nasty laugh. 'Oh, I love them. All that testosterone and so little brain. It's always fun when some mook who looks like King Kong's uglier brother thinks that because you shag men you have designs on *his* arse. Uh, *no*, honey. Not while I have a working pair of contact lenses and standards.'

She laughed, loving his bitchiness. It reminded her pleasantly of Kim.

'Why are all heterosexual men such pricks?' she asked. 'Come on, O Testicle Endowed One. I want to know.'

'Easy,' Paul said, blowing out smoke. 'They're not, but the ones who are are generally in need of a damn good ramming.'

'Oh please,' she said, starting to laugh so hard she was worried she might throw up.

'It's a fact. Or they've had one and can't deal with the fact that it made them come so hard they almost sustained a nosebleed. Denial ain't just a river in Egypt.' He sighed. 'I would *love* to put Jude in touch with his prostate.'

She laughed harder. 'Oh stop. He's thick as shit.'

Paul's mouth fell open in mock shock. 'Mi-aow!'

'He thought Billie Holiday was a *man*.'

Paul was giggling uncontrollably. 'So did Tallulah Bankhead, allegedly.'

'And he didn't realise she was dead.'

He howled. 'Oh, holy fuck. Please don't tell me he thought she was white as well. I don't think I could take it.'

'I did tell you he was no rocket scientist.'

'Like it makes a difference,' Paul said. 'Look, they don't

have to know the Gettysburg Address by heart or the significance of E=MC². If they can say three little words then that is *all* that matters.'

'I love you?'

'No! Harder, Faster, Deeper.'

They were laughing loudly when Ieuan came in, looking sulky and a little suspicious.

'Hello, baby!' Paul sang out happily, giving him a kiss. Not a polite kiss – a real kiss. Ieuan stiffened, but his arm slid around Paul's waist protectively.

'Any luck?' Paul asked.

'No. They want someone who does tattoos as well. Hi.' He gave Adele a quick smile and went to pour himself a glass of water.

'Oh. Well, have you considered ... retraining?'

'As a tattooist? Oh yeah, right. I'm crap at art.'

Paul shrugged. 'It's just tracing, isn't it?'

'Tell that to someone whose tattoo you just fucked up.'

He seemed to be in a bad mood and Adele thought she should give them some space. 'I think I'll go and tackle the flat,' she said.

'Oh? No coffee?'

'No, thanks. It'll probably make me ill anyway. Way too much to drink last night.'

Paul raised his eyebrows. 'He's driving you to drink already?'

She shrugged, laughed and went back upstairs to deal with the flat. She would rather have drunk tea anyway and unpacked the kettle. There was so much stuff to do that she blotted it out, lost track of time organising the rooms.

As soon as the bed was made she wanted to roll into it. It wasn't even dark yet, and barely ten o'clock, but the exertion of moving had taken it out of her. Odd phrase, she thought, it takes it out of you. What exactly? Energy or strength or both? There was no opposing phrase, puts it into you. She supposed that would be too rude, particularly for those men who Paul asserted had problems with things being put into them.

The smell of the wisteria climbing up the back of the house was sickly sweet and soporific. The heavy perfume mingled with the usual summer-night smells of the sea, the scent of smoke from barbeques and bonfires and overheated asphalt. She liked it. It was no one particular smell, but a reminder of many good times spent beside the sea and summer nights rolling with thunder and cool wine. She was certain she had landed on her feet. A new flat, a new job, new neighbours. What did it really matter if Jude's friends were gross and bratty and that he wasn't brilliant, or even especially clever? Paul was right – picky got you nowhere. It just left you embittered and antsy, with your body nothing but a container for your brain for all the use it got put to. May as well take what she could get like everyone else instead of holding out for the next great love of her life who might never show up, or even exist. Jude was young, sexy, obvious. His body was lovely – sleek, smooth and lean. If his breath was a little boozy and his sweat too strong then it was probably only her overcritical, oversensitive hungover self talking.

He looked good naked – hard and pale, except where the blood made his cock flush pink. Pink and white like an ice cream, lying back on his elbows with his legs slightly apart and his cock rising between them, his mouth a little open. She would have liked to open his legs right up, lift his thighs so high that his knees touched his nipples, and peer between his buttocks. Men never exposed themselves like that in her experience, and it would have been exciting to see it – a stiff cock lying flat against his belly, his balls bunched at the root and then that inch or so of fine skin above where his flesh puckered and pursed into the bud of his arsehole. She could push a fingertip against it, see what he would do. It might begin to give as she pushed and stroked, the way her own anus did as she pressed a spit-slicked finger against the narrow hole, rubbing her clit with the index finger of her other hand.

She was surprised by how awake and alert she suddenly felt when not half an hour ago her body had felt like a leaden weight of exhaustion. Her eyelids felt sandy but her fingers were touching wetness as she imagined penetrating a man with her fingers, fucking him with them until he came and had to admit that he loved it. He wanted it again, this time deeper, and to be stretched wider.

She drowsed and dreamed, breaths shallow and panting at the half-formed dirty thoughts in her head. It was a warm night and the heat felt as thought it was pooled and concentrated in her pores and glands, turning her armpits into coarse tufts of animal stink, oozing from the mouth of her sex, turning it into a hairy swamp of slick lubricity. In heat. She liked the idea.

Never mind being bought drinks and kissed and taken to the pub. Screw the mating dances. She thought of that song – something filthy and funny: 'You and me, baby, we ain't nothing but mammals, so let's do it like they do on the Discovery Channel'. Why the hell not? If you could spot someone you liked the look of, lift your skirt, flash your arse with your legs a little open so that the inflamed red lips sent out a signal as clear and obvious as a horny baboon's bright red butt. Come and get it: I want it, you want it, let's cut the crap.

She thought with a few deft rubs she could probably come, but she had an irresistible desire to call Jude. To cut the crap and get on with it. She didn't want to go out with him again. All that standing around leaning on a pool cue, sipping drinks and being given the once-over by his mates. It felt like a massive waste of time. She didn't like his friends and didn't care if they did think that she was a case of 'don't fancy yours much'. They were a post-nuclear case of 'if it were you, me and the cockroaches I'd fuck the cockroaches or wank myself to death'. It was Jude she was after. Or rather his dick.

Then they chose to start work downstairs. Adele hadn't really considered it, but when she did she realised that the chimney breast in her bedroom corresponded with the one in Paul's bedroom below. Her own fireplace was blocked over with a thin piece of hardboard, but the disused fireplaces in Paul's flat had been filled with potted plants and statues. Sound travelled up them.

The first moan was so heartwrenching a sound that she thought someone was being killed down there and froze, listened. Then another. It was a keening sound with the barely discernible words 'Oh God' in it. There was an answering noise – a growling groan – and she realised it was the sound of Paul and Ieuan going for the *coup de grâce*.

They must have been screwing against the fireplace, she thought, to make so much noise. But they couldn't have been. The rhythmic squeak of bedsprings travelled upwards. Paul was obviously fucking Ieuan, properly. Not just hands and mouths, but giving him the kind of dicking that made bedsprings creak. Adele was sure she shouldn't be listening to this but it was fascinating. She strained to hear over the pounding of her heart, intrigued to hear what sounds other people made when they were at it.

Another 'Oh God', this time loud enough to be unquestionably Paul's voice. 'Ohh ... fucking *hell* ...'

Her mouth went dry and she felt guilty, slightly perverted and madly aroused when she imagined him.

Drenched in sweat and licking pant-parched lips, Ieuan's hips in his hands from behind or spread wide underneath him, skewered on his cock, legs spread open like the wings of a butterfly spitted on a collector's pin.

Ieuan's voice was indistinct, softer – guttural moans and grunts. Paul was louder, making choked noises, exclamations. 'Oh God . . . oh yes . . . fuck . . . yeah . . . like that . . . harder, harder dammit . . . give it to me.'

He was the one taking it! That was a surprise. Surprising and a little disconcerting. It was strange and erotic to think of him being fucked – on the bottom but still very much in charge. Digging his heel into the small of Ieuan's back, spurring him on.

'Oh yes . . . oh *yes* . . . oh God . . . ohh my *God* . . .'

Paul's cries turned staccato, reaching crescendo as his last moans trailed off into an inarticulate, dry-throated scream. She heard Ieuan's voice, howling like an animal, a few moments afterwards and imagined Paul lying underneath his body, spent, oversensitive and robbed of speech and sound by the aftershocks of climax.

'Right,' she muttered aloud. 'Fuck it all.'

If you didn't ask, you didn't get. Those two were probably wrapped around each other, sweating, kissing and panting in their afterglow. Hearing them had whet her appetite still further and she was damned if she would lie there like some sad aural voyeur listening to the neighbours get some when she could take what she wanted right now.

She got out of bed, rummaged in a box for something to wear and yanked on the first thing she pulled out – a short, red satin shift dress she had bought for her brother's wedding three years before. Worn without a bra it looked blatantly slutty but she wasn't concerned. There would be girls on the street wearing much less and, anyway, Adele wasn't going out to attempt to attract someone. She was going out there to get him – making a booty call, as Kim would have said.

She felt a trickle of sweat run down the inside of her thigh and was once again reminded of how wet she was. She didn't want to put on knickers and blot the moisture, not when she could leave it there, juicy and in need of urgent attention. Walking down the stairs in a pair of wedge-heeled sandals with no underwear on at all was a buzz in itself. She used to do the same for Kim, taking off her knickers before going to meet him.

He would have loved this, little freakboy that he was, seeing her strut across the street to the phone box in nothing but shoes and a blazing red dress, still sweaty from her bed, her cunt soaked and predatory.

She shimmied her hips a little when she walked out of the front door into the night, conscious that if she bent over even slightly she'd be showing everything. Girls were wearing spaghetti straps and crotch-skimming skirts up and down the street as they rolled in and out of the pubs and clubs, but she didn't doubt that they were wearing thongs, bras or at least strategically placed toupee tape. Adele was pleased to be going one further. Under the red dress she was naked, body and soul.

She felt fantastic, spontaneous. The street had a bohemian flavour anyway at this hour on a summer night, packed and pulsing with the thump of bass, vibrating with shouts and laughter. She felt even more exotic, stomping to the phone like one of those psychotic, insatiable women from French arthouse movies, all body hair and defiant lust. Impatiently, she punched out Jude's number.

'Hello?' He was shouting over background noise.

'Hi. Where are you?' She was annoyed by how tentative her voice sounded.

'At the Clarry. You coming down?'

He probably thought she was making a nuisance of herself and could imagine the conversations he would have with his dogboy friends. Yeah, that bird, wants me to go up and look through *Brides* magazine already, neurotic cow. If she laid it on the line he'd probably tell all his friends she was desperate for it and feel like a big man keeping a lady waiting, but screw it. She wasn't interested in gaining his respect. She wanted his dick.

'Jude. I fucking *hate* the Clarendon.'

'Oh.' He sounded thrown off balance. 'So ... um ... last night?'

'Was terrible. Yes,' Adele said. 'It's my turn to pick the date.'

She could hear him laughing. Time of the month, love? Oh, he'd change his tune soon enough. 'Right,' he said. 'So what would you like to do?'

'Funnily enough I'd like you to walk the hundred yards up the street to my place so I can fuck your brains out. How does that sound?' It sounded filthy and she could barely believe she'd said it, but God it felt good!

Jude had gone quiet.

'Or you can carry on drinking and I'll just have to take matters into my own hands.'

The background had changed. He had left the pub. 'Umm –' He laughed. 'This is a turn up for the books.'

'I think it would save us both a lot of hassle,' she said, glancing down the street towards the Clarendon.

'You're not wrong.'

She laughed, elated. She could see him walking on the opposite side of the street towards her front door, cellphone clamped to his ear.

'Hey, Jude!' She knew eventually that she would have caved into her lame and burning desire to say that, and giggled.

'Yeah?'

'Turn around.'

'What?'

'I'm behind you.'

She steadied herself against the glass wall of the phone box, cold through the thin red satin. As he turned around, looking completely baffled, she laughed harder and waved. 'Hel-lo!'

He pointed, laughed and waved back. She hung up the phone to the clatter of descending coins and walked across the street towards him, sashaying on the sandals so that her body was a red rag to a bull, tits lifted to be looked at, belly held flat and sleek.

'Fancy meeting you here,' he said, looking shy and horny.

'I know. What a coincidence,' she said.

Jude leaned forwards and kissed her lightly on the lips. His breath was minty-sweet as if he'd just quickly stuffed a wedge of gum in his mouth. She nearly lost her nerve when she realised her own breath wasn't as impeccable, but his tongue pushed insistently at her lower lip and she opened her mouth for him, meeting his narrow, slippery tongue with her own. His hips pushed gently against hers and his hands were on her waist, threatening to edge her red skirt indecently high. She wanted to tell him to stop but he made a low growly noise in the back of his throat – a sound that made a spike of want penetrate her crotch, made her grind and tip her hips forwards into his hands.

'We should take this indoors,' Adele said, breaking off for a second and opening the front door. He stepped through the door and they shut it on the street, although it didn't yet have a lock. Semi-private, but good enough. In the half light, Jude's eyes looked lycanthropic, his teeth pale and sharp as he panted through open lips, close to her face. His eyes closed slowly, his lips going slack and greedy as he leaned in to kiss her again, and she leaned against the wall of the hallway at the foot of the stairs, plaster cold under her butt, Jude hot and hard against her front. A pulse beat slowly between her thighs and under the smell of sweat, plaster dust and mint, she was sure she could smell herself – a thick salt-musk.

He made that growling sound again and she pushed her tits against his squeezing hand, shifting her legs apart. Her legs felt long and light as a cat's in the high-heeled sandals, muscles straining in the unnatural posture fashion forced you into. Jude was polite, if nothing else, and she had to guide his hand to lift her skirt.

'Oh, God,' he groaned, sounding overwhelmed with grateful lust. 'No knickers.'

'No nothing,' she whispered, and only just stifled a cry as his fingers entered her roughly, satisfyingly. The stairwells echoed and she wondered if Paul would hear her upstairs, if he wasn't sleeping a deep, sated sleep right now, wrapped nude around his lover.

Jude moaned, whispered in her ear that she was soaked, so wet, and he pushed her dress higher as he half knelt, baring her naked from the nipples down. He sucked eagerly on her nipples, his callused fingers working deeper into the dark nest of her crotch. She wasn't sure how many fingers he had up her – two or three – but he was stretching her open, fucking her with his fingers, the rough ball of his thumb working over the slick nub of her clit. It made soft liquid noises that echoed off the walls and, although she was trying hard not to cry out, she could hear her ragged breaths, his suckling mouth.

The door wasn't locked. Out there was a busy street and it would just take a push from someone outside to open the door and reveal them, her with her dress bunched up under her armpits, tits, belly, hips, thighs, bush – everything on show. The thought made her head spin, the sight of her own body even more so; nearly naked and humping Jude's intruding fingers. She wanted to risk being caught impaled on his cock, being fucked up against a wall like a whore, and managed to whisper the words.

'Fuck me ... please. For God's sake ...'

Instead he withdrew his hand and she choked down a moan of loss as his fingers slipped out of her. He pushed her breasts together in his hands and flicked his hot tongue over her nipples, his hand smearing the scent of her cunt all over her right breast. She thought she smelled like an animal in heat. 'Please ...'

Jude shook his head, smiled and knelt. 'Wanna eat you out ...' he murmured, against her thigh.

His pointed little tongue darted over her clit like an electric shock, his fingers splaying her open. She gathered up her dress and tugged it back up, stuffing her mouth with the red satin because she was sure she was going to scream. He was making tiny satisfied grunting noises as though enjoying a good meal, gorging himself on it, stuffing his face with no table manners but plenty of hungry relish. She panted and bit down on the bunched cloth, her hips moving of their own accord, shoving her wide-open sex into his face. His fingers snaked down between her legs again, pushed back inside while he sucked and feasted on her clit and she heard herself making snuffling, sobbing sounds of need, desperate to come. He stopped to catch his breath, looked up at her, his chin wet and his eyes bright.

'Come on. Come on my face.'

Dirty little fuck. Her hips bucked and rocked as he buried his face between her legs again, lapping, kissing, eating, and then sucking – just there ... right there. Suckling the sensation to the surface while his fingers pounded away inside, triggering the point of no return. She could hear herself mewl into the fabric of her dress, squeezing her eyes shut and clenching her teeth. She felt sweat run into the cleft of her buttocks and came, silently, tensed limbs shaking against the convulsions pulsing through them.

'No more ... please ... easy ... shhh.' She pressed her fingers into his hair and detached him from her hyper-sensitive flesh. He was laughing softly and kissing the inside of her thigh.

'You like that?'

She licked her lips and nodded, breathless. *'Duh.'*

8

Adele watched Jude sleep next to her, his wiry red hair tousled and flattened on one side. His arm, resting above the covers, was perfectly pale with a dusting of freckles. His skin fascinated her. She loved red hair and the fine pale complexion that usually accompanied such a genetic trick. His skin was so white over his hips and thighs, beautiful and vulnerable where his hard little belly curved down into the fork of his crotch, into the cluster of mahogany curls – 'Ginger pubes. Don't laugh,' he had said with a self-deprecating grin as he took his clothes off for the first time – at the root of his slender cock. He had the second most beautiful dick she had ever seen, slim and uncircumcised, the head dusky pink and heartshaped. When he was crawling over her in bed or standing nude beside the bed, he looked like a Greek youth from an erotic figure vase with his arrow-straight penis and sculpted belly.

He lay half on his side with his knee pressed into the mattress and his thigh demurely covering his cock, denying her access. She nudged him tentatively and he stirred in his sleep, his hands automatically reaching for her breasts, his mouth following suit. He sucked on her nipples again and his fingers crawled down between her legs, rubbing at her uncomfortably swollen clit in a way that he clearly thought denoted his sexual finesse, but which was beginning to annoy her. He wouldn't fuck her. The chance was there, but he wouldn't wear a condom. He claimed he couldn't stand them and, when she had tried to roll one onto him, his dick curled up like a frightened hedgehog.

'I'm sorry. They turn me off. Can't help it. Mind of its own.'

At least he'd been good enough not to suggest that he wouldn't come inside her, which, in her opinion, ranked right up there with 'the cheque's in the post' and 'of course I won't invade Czechoslovakia' as one of the biggest lies in human history. Such things were the quickest ways to get kicked out of Adele's bed. It annoyed her that he couldn't seem to get past his problem. She hadn't had a dick inside her for over three years, and no amount of fingerfucking and oral sex could scratch that itch. I think I can only stand him when I'm so horny I don't care or when he's unconscious. Oh fuck.

She had stubble burn on the inside of her thighs and right the way into her pussy. She was reluctant for him to go down on her again, because, while his technique was aggressively exciting in small doses, after a while it made her sore. Jude seemed to think he was good at it. 'I love eating pussy, fuckin' love it. Nothing like hearing a woman scream like that.'

You could have too much of a good thing. She wanted to be fucked, the way she'd heard Paul and Ieuan fucking. Savouring every stroke, legs in the air, headboard banging against the wall, hair getting tangled. Really and truly pounded. It felt like an insult that he wouldn't do that. Didn't every man want to do that?

Someone was knocking on her front door.

'Leave it,' Jude said, buried between her breasts. 'You're busy.'

'I can't leave it,' she said, reaching for something to wear. The only thing at hand was the red dress, and it looked absurd in the light of day and sanity. 'It might be Paul.'

'Hmm.' Jude burrowed under the covers and watched her pull a pair of leggings and a T-shirt from a box. 'Want me to go?'

'It's OK,' she said, although she did. It would be embarrassing to witness Paul's 'told you so' expression when he found out she had slept with Jude. 'Just ... um ... stay here. I'll be back.'

'Cool.' He was so blah. *Shit.* What had she done?

The knocking got louder.

'OK! I'm coming!' Yanking up her leggings she opened the door and promptly, involuntarily, opened her mouth.

There she was, hand poised in mid-knock, still beautiful enough to break hearts, looking nervous as a cat. 'Hi, honey, I'm home,' she said weakly, trying the joke on for size.

Adele struggled to speak. 'Jesus –'

'No. Me. Remember?'

'What the hell are you doing here?'

'Passing through. Can I come in?'

Adele shook her head. 'Oh God ... this isn't a good time.'

'There was never going to be a good time,' Karina said, and ducked under her outstretched arm and into the flat. Adele knew she could easily have stopped her gaining access, but she didn't. She let her in.

'You're not an easy woman to get hold of, you know,' Karina said, dumping her bags on the stairs. 'Nice place. I thought you were living in some kind of commune or something?'

'I just moved in.' Adele stared sullenly at her. She was still so tiny, effortlessly thin, dressed in a pink PVC skirt and a tight black T-shirt that showed her breasts. High heeled, her mop of silky black hair streaked with red and wearing a punky studded-leather choker around her neck, she looked like something from a pop video.

'What do you want?'

Karina pouted, pushing out her scarlet underlip and drawing her perfect soft black eyebrows into a frown. Annoyed and annoying, she still managed to look charming. 'I thought it would be fun to see you.'

Adele held her arms out and offered herself for viewing. 'You can see me. Here I am.' Like what you see? Her hair was tangled, her breasts dangling sluttishly under the T-shirt, the seam of her leggings rubbing like a file on her crotch. She had never felt more like the embodiment of all that was disappointing and ugly about being a woman, and she wanted to rub it in Karina's face. Karina thought being female was so damn good. Take a reality check; it occasionally made you shrewish, spiteful and sore.

'Fun for both of us, or for you?' Adele added, feeling a small tingle of primitive pleasure at the thought that soon she might be able to scream, let out every angry word and feeling and damn the consequences because this thing was already broken.

Karina shook her head. 'Look, I promise, I'll explain why I'm here. Just let me get settled.'

Adele looked at the suitcases and burst into an incredulous laugh. 'Are you taking the piss? You expect me to put you up?'

'The problem,' Karina said acidly, 'is yours, sweetie. Not mine.'

Adele stared in disbelief. Typical Karina. No conscience, no idea of consequences, responsibility, nothing. She swore Karina had to have one of the most disordered personalities she had ever encountered, and she was no stranger to fuck-ups. 'Right,' she said. 'That's it already. Get out of my house.'

Jude chose that moment to emerge from the bedroom, obviously having overheard and deciding to act the protective male. All the better to spray his scent on her like a cat, the way he'd left his spit and sweat all over her sheets last night. 'Are you ... oh.' He did a double-take when he saw Karina.

'Ooops,' Karina said, smiling knowingly. 'You should have told me it was a bad time.'

'Like that would have stopped you,' Adele snapped.

'Is there a problem here, Adele?' Jude asked, pulling on his T-shirt and muscling in. She wanted to tell him to sod off.

'No. No problem,' she said, brittle and airy, struggling to keep her voice light. 'I'll go and make us a cup of tea, shall I?'

Jude nodded. 'Lovely.'

Karina followed her into the kitchen. 'Who's that?' she asked, sounding impressed, girlish. 'Spill the beans, sweetie.'

'Jude. And none of your business.'

'So how long . . .?'

'I told you,' she said, pushing Karina out of the way to reach a fresh carton of long-life milk. 'None of your fucking business.'

Karina raised both palms and stepped back. 'Okaaaay. I get the impression you're not delighted to see me.'

'Someone give that woman a medal.'

'Hear me out,' Karina said, laying a small hand on her wrist. Perfect fake fingernails with white shiny tips. Adele glanced up, into dark, heavy-lidded eyes. She had no right to look so beautiful.

'Please?' Karina asked, her eyes bringing back too many memories, too many good times that a fight had put a stop to, and the thought of getting them back made Adele want to cry.

'OK,' she said. 'All right.'

'Thank you,' Karina mouthed.

Adele stared at the teaspoon in her hand. 'Oh, fucking hell.'

'What?'

'I don't know how many sugars he has in his tea.'

Karina gaped, then giggled. 'You minx!'

'Shut up. You don't have to make people a cup of tea before you sleep with them, for God's sake. Do I look like Madame Butterfly?'

'Ha ha.' Karina rolled her eyes.

Adele found herself smiling, thinking how weird it was that they could pick up like they'd never quit in the first place. That was the trouble when you knew someone so well you could finish each other's sentences. No amount of time, distance or resentment was going to remove that knowledge. Old friends stamped their personalities on one another, anticipated every quirk and kneejerk reaction.

'Go and ask him.'

'I'm not asking him! He's your . . . whatever.'

'No, go on,' she said. 'I want to see if you fooled him.'

Karina sniffed. 'It's not a question of fooling people. What they see is what they get.'

'With added attachments?' Adele asked archly.

'That's none of your business,' Karina snapped.

'Isn't it?'

'No.'

'I think you'll find it is. I told you to stay away from Casablanca.'

'I haven't been near Casablanca,' Karina said, then laughed wryly. 'Couldn't even find the videotape, actually.'

'What?'

Karina stirred the tea and sang softly to herself. 'You must remember this . . . a kiss is still a kiss . . .'

Adele sighed, determined not to follow one of their old

conversations complete with strange mental associations and musical interludes. She peeked out of the kitchen doorway. Jude was still standing there, looking confused and totally male – lacking Karina's brassy confidence.

'Milk? Sugar?'

'Yeah. Please. Two sugars.' He glanced at his watch. 'Look, I'm going to have to run in a minute. I'm late.'

'No problem.'

'. . . the fundamental things apply, as time goes by.' Karina swayed out of the kitchen and handed him a mug of tea. 'There you go.'

'Thanks,' he said, looking even more confused. 'Is everything OK?'

'Everything's fine,' Adele said. She didn't want his protection. She didn't especially want him around. She could see him checking Karina out, eyes furtively darting over her hips, legs and breasts, probably wanting to push his nose up under the hem of her slutty, shiny, pink mini-skirt like a dog sniffing.

'I . . . have to go, actually,' he said.

'OK.' Adele nodded, and accepted a quick kiss. 'Call me.'

'I will. Bye.' Jude headed down the stairs.

'No you won't,' Adele singsonged softly after him, once he was out of earshot.

'No. He won't,' Karina agreed. 'You haven't got a phone.'

Paul knew instinctively that he was headed for trouble the first time he laid eyes on her. Some women you just knew. You knew right away that they had a battery of issues, that they could turn on the tears like a tap, crawl into your affections, kick you out, take you in. Chaos. It wasn't a physical thing, although beauty helped. It wasn't the curve of a cheekbone or the length of leg that made a woman some kind of angel of chaos and heartbreak. Some of them were superficially unattractive at first glance, but they had it; that certain something that allowed them to haunt you, get under your skin.

That was why he liked Adele. She seemed sane, dependable, intelligent – not given to attention-seeking tears and manipulative displays of flesh. She was a different breed to the creature he found roaming his stairwell. When he opened the front door he was confronted with a heart-shaped arse clad in a pink leather skirt, a pair of slender tan legs and a small scarlet diamond of knicker underneath the hem of the sleazy skirt. His eyes were instantly drawn to the flash of underwear and he could see a slight bulge there, that way a woman's sex pouted when she bent right over.

He didn't know what to expect when the girl straightened up from her tussle with her shopping bag. The skirt spoke volumes, of the kind of middle-aged tart who looked OK from behind but like an ageing Bette Davis from the front, complete with blonde ringlets and misguided ribbons. Her thighs were silky from behind, offering a glimpse of the inner thigh. A ludicrous way to meet someone, and a head-spinning pose – flashing crotch, showing thighs that any man would want to spread open, and revealing panties that would have looked better tangled around ankles.

And then she stood up. Paul realised that she was dark, bobbed jet hair streaked with scarlet, but that was all he really registered because she crossed her arms at her waist and took her T-shirt off. She turned around, tiny, beautiful and irritable, small perfect breasts resting sweetly in the lace cups of a black bra.

'I don't mean to be rude,' she said, her accent familiar somehow. 'But you could help, you know? I'm sweating here.'

'Right. Yes. Of course. You're ... sweating.'

She was sweating, a thin, human-smelling film over her skin. She clearly had Eurasian blood and her skin had that fragile, oriental clarity – pale copper and almost poreless. Her breasts looked delicate, defenceless, her face feline and beautiful. Paul picked up the shopping bags, compliant and stupid as he mentally stripped off her remaining few fragments of clothes. Her nipples looked to be a shade of pale tan plum. Her arse would be boyish; her hips neat, her vagina small, tight and wet.

'That's better,' she said, and gestured him upstairs with a toss of her streaked hair.

He followed like an idiot, already knowing that he may as well give in now. She was one of those women – the troublesome ones. The ones you would sell your soul for a taste of. The ones who knew it damn well. Sarah all over again. It didn't seem of any concern to his body that it had been well fucked the night before. If anything, it had whetted his appetite, an appetite he would have done better keeping under wraps. The girl high-heeled the final stretch of the stairs up to Adele's flat, pushed open the door and took the carrier bag from him. 'Thank you,' she said, and closed the door, nearly hitting him in the nose.

Paul blinked and clutched the narrow stair rail for support. This wasn't right. Surely she'd felt some connection between them? She had to have done. He'd been panting for her. Only he wasn't, of course, because he had a lover he adored in bed downstairs. And what the hell was she doing in Adele's flat anyway? He knocked, secure now that he had legitimate questions as a landlord that needed asking.

Adele opened the door. She looked puffy and tired, and her face looked strange and pale, denuded of its usual scarlet lipstick. Her lips were still pinkish, as though her mouth was permanently stained by the daily application. 'Hi,' she said, not opening the door all the way.

'Morning. I just couldn't help noticing that, er ... friend of yours?'

Adele pursed her lips. 'Ye-es. Karina. Is there a problem?'

'No, no.' Paul furtively peered over her shoulder. 'If I could ... er ... I might need to speak with you about her.'

'What's she done now?' Adele asked, in an angry, resigned voice, as though Karina made a habit of doing things.

'Nothing.'

'I didn't do anything!' Karina yelled from within.

'It's just ...'

Adele stiffened. 'Look, you needn't worry. I'm not going to turn your top floor into some kind of commune, if that's what you're worried about. I won't be holding a rave on the roof any time soon.'

'No.' Paul shook his head. 'No. Of course you wouldn't.'

'This is just ... complicated. OK?' she said.

'OK,' Paul said. He knew she was in there somewhere. Maybe removing more sweaty clothing.

'Private too. Personal.'

'Oh. Sorry.' He realised he was staring right over Adele's shoulder. 'I'll go.'

'Thank you. I'll give you a knock later.'

'Right.'

Paul went back downstairs, realising he had made an idiot of himself yet again. He had always had a problem with women, to the point where he thought developing a problem with men would be an adequate solution. He came out of that realising that he was bisexual and now had the other previously neglected half of the human race to make a fucking fool of himself over. He was that very special English breed – a guilty middle-class deviant.

He knew perfectly well that the values of his class were false, stupid and hypocritical, but, in railing against them, there was still a measure of guilt that he couldn't marry a nice girl and settle down. He'd tried that, but she hadn't been especially nice and his family had completely disapproved.

Ieuan was still in bed, sleeping deeply and peacefully. For once Paul felt like staying in bed and letting the builders wreck the place. He stripped off, tossed his clothes on the floor and crawled back into bed. It smelled like sex under the sheets, of sweat and come and the lingering, slightly spicy, earthy scent of penetrated flesh. His penis twitched and stirred against the back of Ieuan's warm thigh at the smell and he wriggled closer, snaking his fingertips into that soft little hollow where the juncture of thighs met the cleft of Ieuan's arse. Open sesame, Paul thought to himself, smiling when – true to form – Ieuan's legs opened wide and he sprawled on his belly, hips tilted to lift his buttocks to a tempting angle.

Paul pushed back the covers and trailed his tongue slowly up the length of Ieuan's back, the taste of his skin and sweat an antidote to further trouble and straying. He could stay faithful. He *would* stay faithful. Never mind the girl upstairs – she was probably a dyke anyway. Ieuan was all he needed; sexy, uninhibited and here for the taking.

He slicked his fingers with lubricant and gently pushed a finger past the tight circle of Ieuan's arse, intent on returning the favour from last night. Ieuan was silky smooth inside, arching back into his touch. Paul pushed in a second finger, stretching his flesh carefully. Ieuan moaned and thrust back harder against him, screwing himself deeper. Paul teased, not yet letting his weight rest on Ieuan's back, dusting the lightest of kisses over his skin, deliberately scraping his stubble against where the skin was softest. He moved his fingers slowly, slipping in and out at a carefully calculated pace. It was like wet velvet inside him, the grip of muscle as tight as a fist. Some contraction from deep inside Ieuan's body tightened the flesh further around his fingers and squeezed them. Paul gasped and pushed harder against the resistance, knowing how good that was going to feel when he gave in and fucked him. He pushed three fingers up him. Ieuan uttered a half-muffled gasp and spread his legs even wider, digging his knees into the mattress. Paul opened his mouth against the back of Ieuan's shoulder and licked, bit and suckled on the skin. He gripped Ieuan's hip with his free hand and pulled his arse up against his aching, leaking dick.

'You want this?' he asked, blowing lightly on the skin he had just soaked with his tongue.

Ieuan buried his head in his arms and moaned. Not good enough.

Paul increased the pace of his fingers and fucked him harder with them; he asked again, 'You want it?'

Ieuan cried out, a harsh animal sound, and raised his head. 'Yes ... oh fuck ... do it ...'

'Do what?' Paul asked mildly. He reached for a condom and carefully tore the corner of the wrapper with his teeth, spitting out the fragment of foil that stuck to his tongue.

'Fuck me.'

'Are you sure?'

'*Yes!*'

Paul was satisfied that he was sufficiently worked up and slid his fingers loose to roll on the condom. Ieuan was soft when he pushed inside, soft inside, hard and hairy on the outside. He wiped his slippery hand on Ieuan's hip and held him firm as he started to thrust. He watched Ieuan's back move and twist, listened to him moan, watched himself breaching his lover's flesh.

'What you wanted?' he whispered, heat flaring through his veins, pooling in his balls.

'Yessss.' Ieuan's voice sounded like something sizzling.

'You like that?' Paul asked, giving his hips a sharp twist, screwing him with a deep circular push then pulling back to thrust with hard staccato motions. Ieuan arched his back and made a choked, almost-sobbing sound, kneeling on all fours like an animal. Paul gripped his hips tighter and started to fuck him harder. Enough teasing. He wanted to come.

It was easy to get Ieuan off. Hitch his hips higher and his legs wider, slip a hand under him and grasp his hard, hard cock, and success. Ieuan came wildly with the second or third squeeze of Paul's hand, crying out hoarsely and gripping the head of the bed with both hands. His inner muscles rippled and squeezed, triggering Paul's climax as he thrust hard into the tight, animate sleeve of flesh.

He held Ieuan there a little longer, screwing his spent cock into him and teasing him by stroking the wet, hypersensitive head of his dick. Ieuan slumped and moaned, wincing at the touch and softly murmuring that it was enough, it was too much. Paul relented and let him go, slipping out of him and wrapping the used condom in a tissue for the time being. He felt pleasantly, lazily tired once more and wondered if they should make a day of it, napping, cuddling and screwing in bed.

Ieuan rolled over, sticky and sweaty, the tangle of dark hair on his belly decorated with splashes of come. He was shaking and his face was flushed, so that Paul couldn't resist going down to tease him, lick his cock clean and hold it in his mouth as it softened and wilted. Ieuan closed his legs and wriggled free.

'Stop . . . God . . . are you trying to *kill* me?'

Paul laughed and crawled over him for a kiss. 'Can you think of a more pleasant way to go?'

Ieuan moaned under his mouth as he kissed him. Paul had discovered early that it was a little kink of Ieuan's – tasting dick on Paul's tongue. Ieuan broke the kiss, still panting from his orgasm. 'You *will* fuck me to death if you keep this up,' he said. 'What's got into you?'

Paul stretched out on his back beside him, yawning. 'No idea. Must be all this fresh sea air.'

'Poisoning me would be quicker, you know,' Ieuan said, lighting a cigarette.

Paul leaned over and kissed his shoulder, his neck, his smoky lips. 'You're doing that to yourself.'

'Yeah yeah.' Ieuan got up and retrieved a pair of shorts from the bedroom floor.

'Where are you going?'

'Need a shower. I stink.'

'I love you when you're stinky.' Paul tried to coax him back, stroking his spine and nipping his earlobe. 'Come back here and cuddle. I thought we had an afterglow thing going on here.'

Ieuan dropped back onto the bed with a sigh and sucked on his cigarette. 'OK.'

'Don't strain yourself or anything,' Paul said, irritated by his reluctance.

'I'm just tired . . . pissed off,' Ieuan admitted.

'With me?'

'No.' Ieuan sighed and smoked.

'Then what?' Paul asked solicitously, stroking his belly. 'What's up?'

'Dunno – this place.'

'You want to go back to London?' Paul couldn't understand why anyone would want to go back. He already loved this town, the clean air, the easy pace of life. Older, he supposed. That was it. He was older. Ieuan could deal with pollution, stress, road rage, tube delays, all of that blood pressure-inducing shit, because he was younger. He liked drug-fuelled nights out, rejecting anything that didn't fit his idea of cool.

'Oh, come on . . . you've seen the nightlife around here. It's shite.'

'Yeah,' Paul said testily. 'And London's a toilet with good nightclubs and nice museums. What's your fucking point?'

'It's just . . . boring,' he replied. 'Going for a shower. You need the bathroom?'

'No,' Paul said, and watched him go, his arse pale and firm.

The bathroom door closed too heavily and made the walls shake, so that a rain of ageing plaster trickled down the back of the chimney breast. Ageing, fucked old property. Plenty of period charm but short on the mod cons. Apparently.

9

Seeing Adele again was harder than she had realised. As a show of good faith, Karina had gone out to get a few groceries from the shop across the road – bagels and cream cheese. Something edible. Adele had nothing in. She was half expecting not to be let back in the door, and so nervous that, when the gormless guy from downstairs appeared to stare up the back of her skirt, she was ruder than she meant to be.

Karina realised for the first time in years that she was probably coming across as overconfident, but it was as though she couldn't stop herself. Couldn't apply the behavioural brakes that had got rusty from years of disuse. Too much time spent doing what the hell she liked so that the once attractive veneer of confidence had become caked and thick, like layers of cheap make-up which ruined the complexion beneath. How hard was it to say sorry? I love you? Hard. Harder when Adele entered the equation. Little macho-girl. She'd got so angry, so mad that the sweetness was in danger of leaving her eyes and lips for good.

Karina put away the groceries and found a place for her red suitcase behind the chimney breast in Adele's bedroom and changed into a more comfortable T-shirt and combat pants. She needed them, waiting for the fight ahead. Adele was talking to the guy from downstairs at the door, just as Karina came out of the bedroom.

'What's she done now?' Adele asked, in a tone that hurt like fuck.

'I didn't do anything!' Karina yelled defiantly, and walked into the small, untidy living room. It contained a brown two-seater sofa, a few potted plants and boxes not yet unpacked. Sticking out of a box, rolled up, was something she recognised – an old poster of Kurt Cobain. No idea how it had survived all this time, but it had.

Adele came back into the room, looking like she was spoiling for a fight. Karina moved up on the couch to make room for her. Adele sat down on an unopened box opposite.

'You still have Kurt.'

'Yeah.' Adele pushed her hair out of her face and scratched her nose.

Could have given her something to work with.

'It's nice to see you.'

'Wish I could say the same,' Adele said. 'Where have you been?'

'Where *haven't* I been?' she said, attempting to be charming.

Adele shook her head. 'Forget it. Spare me the old crap. I'm tired, I'm busy and I didn't need this today.'

'I know,' Karina said. She had to ask. 'Who was that guy?'

'If you mean, what does he mean to me, I don't know.' Adele shrugged, and spitefully added, 'Yet.' Twisting the knife. 'You said you wanted to talk. So talk.'

'OK,' Karina said. 'I can understand you not wanting to see me, so thanks.'

'You got that right.'

She bit her lip. 'I'm sorry.'

'Sorry?' Adele stared at her. 'You're *sorry*?'

'Yes. I am.'

'Well, that makes it all perfectly acceptable, doesn't it?' Adele folded her arms across her breasts, a characteristic posture of defence, shutting her out. 'We needn't have a problem about anything because you're *sorry*. Congratulations. You correctly experienced and identified an emotion. What do you want? A fucking medal?'

Karina sighed, wishing it wouldn't hurt so much. 'I was hoping I could explain a few things to you. Never gonna happen, I suppose.'

Adele shook her head. 'I've been trying to explain this to myself for the past eight years and haven't reached any satisfactory answers, so go ahead, spill.'

Taking a deep breath and swallowing down the ache in her throat, Karina started. 'I know I hurt you ... and I'm sorry for that. I wish there was something I could do to make it better, I really do. I've ... I've come to realise I've spent my entire life treating people like shit, and it's about time I started cleaning up some of the mess.'

'What happened?' Adele asked, with painful percipience. 'Someone treat you to some of your own crap for a change?'

Karina winced, thinking of Suki and lashing out in her own pain. 'Yeah, well, you try it!' she yelled. 'You try having my family, my life, and see if you don't come out an emotional cripple.'

'Oh save it!' Adele screamed back at her. '"My parents never loved me", what-*ever*. Spare me the victim psychobabble. You know what? I missed out on my share of love too. My mother died of cancer when I was six years old. Do you see me pulling the weeping willow bullshit over it?'

'No,' Karina spat. 'But I've seen you hide every fucking tear you thought you were about to shed your entire life and turn into a tight-arsed bitter bitch.'

Adele stood up, red in the face, and really let loose. 'Yeah? Well, maybe I *am* a bitch. You have no idea. All you do is fake it. You think dressing up like a cheap slag and slapping on some make-up gives you a first-class ticket to be treated like a lady? Well, let me tell you something, Karina, you don't know half of what it means to be a woman. You don't have to put up with hormones making you want to rip your hair out, you don't have to put up with pain, you don't have to put up with all this shit inside of you that can turn cancerous on you for no good reason. You're playing some stupid little game of let's pretend. You want all the perks and none of the flip side.'

'Oh cry me a river!' Karina yelled, furious. 'You try being a called a freakshow.'

'Hel-lo? School? Remember Miss Goldfish?'

'Boo hoo. You got some crap. Don't carry it around with you for the rest of your life.'

'Yeah, and you added to the crap. Substantially.' Adele was snarling, finger pointed, no question of who she was accusing. Her coarse, untidy hair seemed to crackle with static and anger, her grey eyes black. She looked witchy, the kind of woman that men used to drown or hang for speaking or acting out of turn.

'It wasn't my fault you couldn't get past stupid labels,' Karina counter accused.

'Labels?' Adele snorted. 'It wasn't about labels!'

'Yes it is! It's always about labels. Gay, straight, bi, whatever. Everything has to be all boxed and pigeon-holed, doesn't it?'

Adele looked as though she was on the verge of tears. 'You stupid fucking cow!' she shrieked. 'You kept a secret from me. Not just a little secret. A fucking huge secret! Like ... life-defining stuff. You never told me shit, and you were supposed to love me!'

The floodgates opened. She started to cry and dropped down onto the nearest cardboard box. It buckled under her weight and she angrily swatted the thing across the room, scattering posters, diaries and dried flowers over the floor. She sat on the floor to cry, sobs like Karina had never heard before – because, when she had cried like that in the past, Adele would always lock herself out of reach in the girls' toilets.

Amazed and appalled, Karina went to hold her, soothe her. Adele's entire body was shaking and her hands knotted in fists, which she didn't hesitate to use in resigned angry thumps with no real muscle behind them. Just as an expression of her frustration.

'I'm sorry,' Karina said ineffectually. 'I'm so sorry.'

'You fucking bitch.'

'I know. I know, sweetie.'

'You could have told me!' Adele wailed in desperation, her hands still bunched in fists but returning the embrace. Her hair still smelled the same, of incense and spices.

'And what?' Karina asked. 'And lost you? Why do you think I didn't tell you? I couldn't.'

'You could!'

'And you would have understood?'

Adele pushed her away and looked up at her, tears streaming. 'Well, I could have tried. Instead of just being pushed away.'

'I didn't mean it to work out that way,' Karina pleaded. 'I didn't mean any of it to go wrong. I never do.'

'No, because you don't think.'

'I do! I'm just never given a chance to state my fucking case because I'm either some twisted status symbol or I get the shit beaten out of me.'

Adele's eyes were wide. 'Oh God . . . you didn't?'

Vindicated, Karina nodded. 'Yeah. Several times. You don't get an opportunity to explain because guys, being guys, they're on autocock mode – then when hands go a-roaming, all fucking hell breaks loose because they think their manhood has been insulted.'

'I'm sorry.' Adele looked fraught. 'I didn't realise.'

Karina sat back on the floor and sighed. 'No. Just like I didn't realise how much I'd hurt you. I was only trying to spare you more hurt, I swear.'

Adele shook her head. 'You stupid cunt. Come here.'

Karina gratefully snuggled into the embrace, feeling the soft crush of Adele's big, beautiful tits against her. She was so relieved to have had this out, so pleased to see her again. Being called a stupid cunt was Adelespeak for 'good to see you'.

'I swear, I never ever meant to hurt you,' Karina said.

'I know...' Adele sighed. 'I get it now.' Her hand descended on Karina's back in another thump. 'I'm still pissed off with you, though.'

'Yeah, well. You have every right to be.'

'I'll get over it,' Adele said. '*Tout comprendre c'est tout pardonnez* and all that.'

'Oooo, parlez that sexy franglais, baby.'

Adele shook with muted laughter at the weak joke. 'Oh, fuck off. It's been years since I had any reason to speak French.'

She sat back on the carpet again. Her eyes were red and her face flushed and blotchy, but she looked softer, purged. She exhaled slowly, the action pushing her lush, cushiony lips into an even richer pout. 'You know what I want?' she said, pushing her dark curls away from her face.

'To win the lottery?'

'Yeah, well apart from the obvious,' Adele said. 'No. This is going to sound so stuffy, but I really need a nice cup of tea.'

Karina laughed. 'You haven't changed.'

'*You* have.'

'I think that goes without saying,' Karina said, cupping her breasts in both hands and holding them up for inspection.

Adele shook her head in disbelief. 'Can't really miss them.'

'They're not as big as yours.'

'Yeah, but you're too tiny for a double C cup. You'd look ridiculous.'

They stood up, as if by mutual agreement, and Karina followed Adele through to the kitchen. She liked this kind of talk. It was feminine, companionable.

'What size are you?' Adele asked, filling the kettle. Her kitchen was small and cramped, untidy with half-unpacked boxes.

'Thirty-six B,' Karina said. 'Didn't want to go any bigger.'

'Did it hurt?'

'Like hell. It was so sore. When I came around they were massive and I thought they'd gone bigger than I wanted, but it was fine when the swelling had gone down.'

Adele shook her head. 'You're insane. How much did it set you back?'

'Two grand a tit,' Karina said, making Adele laugh.

'Four-thousand-pound boobs?'

'Worth every penny.'

Adele leaned against the kitchen windowsill and appraised Karina's chest with a critical eye, her head tilted. 'They don't look bad. Have you got scars?'

'Not so you'd notice. They were huge and red and gross afterwards, under my arms, but they healed nicely.' She laughed at the memory. 'I was the surgeon's pet. He said I had perfect skin. Apparently the skin from Asian races is stronger than white – heals better.'

'Really? I didn't know that.'

'Yup,' Karina said. 'Do you want to see?'

Adele gave a non-committal shrug, meaning that she

probably didn't, but she would anyway if a peek was offered. 'Sure.'

Karina peeled off her T-shirt and stood there in her bra. 'There.'

'Wow,' Adele said, raising her eyebrows. 'They're –'

'Boobs.'

Adele laughed nervously. 'So they are. Fucking hell.'

Karina stuck her tits out. 'Wanna feel?' she asked, teasing.

'Can I?' Adele said eagerly, then checked herself. 'Because ... you know. Silicone. I've always wondered ... do they feel ... real?'

'Come and see,' Karina beckoned.

Adele giggled a little, breathlessly, her palm cupped over Karina's left breast. Gently she pressed her fingers to the exposed part above the bra, not really cupping it, just feeling very tentatively. 'Oh, my God,' she said. 'Not that I have much experience of feeling other women's tits, but that feels like the real deal.'

'Give it a proper squeeze.' Karina sighed. 'What are you trying to do? Take my pulse?'

'OK.' Adele breathed in, reached down and squeezed. 'Wow! They're ...'

'Yeah.' Karina beamed. 'Squishy!'

'Breasty!'

They both laughed. Adele withdrew her hand. 'Well, that's a new one for me. I've never squeezed a breast aside from my own, and I've certainly never squeezed a silicone breast.'

'Good, aren't they?' Karina said, bouncing on the tips of her toes and watching them jiggle.

'Should I get them done too, you think?' Adele joked.

'Er ... no. I think you're ample enough there, honey,' Karina said. She couldn't stand when women went over the top. She'd seen so many bad tit jobs – huge independently moving grapefruit-sized things squirming around over bony rib cages. 'Unless you want to make a living as a pole dancer in the bar.'

'Well, I would,' said Adele, 'if I didn't already have my hands full with the chef's job. What about you?'

'Me?'

'Yes, you. If you want to stick around, you're going to need some money because I'm broke, and if Paul's business doesn't work out –'

'Paul?'

'The boss. Downstairs. You were hassling him on the stairs.'

'I was not hassling him. He was staring up my skirt.'

'He's *gay*.'

'For staring up my skirt? Not technically.'

'No.' Adele sighed. 'He has a *boyfriend*. They have *sex*. I think that's pretty gay.'

'How do you know? They could be just good friends.'

'Believe me,' Adele said, with a glint in her eye. 'They're not just good friends.'

10

Little Miss Trouble was on the loose again. She swayed downstairs in combat pants and a tight, cropped black T-shirt and announced that she would be delighted to help out. Paul could think of about a dozen ways he'd like her to help out – mainly ways in which she stuck her small hand down the front of his pants and then knelt to take his dick in her red-painted mouth. She'd leave lipstick on him, he thought. Something to taunt Ieuan with.

'I'm afraid I'm not hiring any more staff at present,' Paul said, hoping she wasn't after money.

'Oh no, that's fine.' Karina leaned back against the bar, distracting the builders. Not least Jude who was looking at her tight, tan midriff with appreciative lust. Paul gave him a dirty look. Little prick on wheels. He was probably angling for some kind of ménage with Adele and her friend. Jude glanced back and half shrugged, but Paul held his gaze. There were advantages to being older. Paul was confident he was a better lover than baby heteroboy over there. Given the opportunity he could have reduced Jude to a mewling wreck.

Paul shivered at a mental image of Jude that flashed into his mind suddenly – lips forming a perfect round o of need, hands tied behind his back, cheeks streaming with tears of shame even as his cock strained outwards for attention. I could take you, Paul thought. No problem.

Same type as Ieuan. A tough boy with a lot of wiry-limbed aggression to expend. Jude was the first to look away. He pulled the sanding mask back over his face and went back to the skirting board he was finishing.

'Anything you want doing?' Karina asked. She stretched her arms up and laced her hands behind the nape of her neck. For a second, as she stretched, Paul caught a glimpse of cinnamon-coloured nipple and the underside of a small, rounded breast. He caught his breath and struggled to keep his hands to himself.

'You really don't have to do anything,' he said.

'I'd like to help,' she said.

He shrugged. 'You could help clear up the kitchen if you want.'

'Cool.' She bounced eagerly on the balls of her feet and the underside of her breasts peeked out from under the hem of her cropped top again. 'Through here? Thanks.'

Paul watched her go and sighed. This was bad. He had that itch again – the restless desire to throw away an old relationship and start again. He was sick of having his age shoved down his throat by Ieuan. Ieuan probably wanted some tightarsed nineteen-year-old who was interested in clothes, clubs, drugs and piercings. Some dumb slut he could teach all Paul's bedroom tricks to. Never mind that Paul could fuck him more skilfully than a kid. It was youth and hedonism Ieuan was attracted to, the same as all the others.

He sat behind the bar and drank a cup of coffee, then peeked into the kitchen. Were they lovers? Adele had never given anything like that away about herself. Some people had a real problem with admitting to bisexuality. Paul knew that. It was such a big thing to face if you were unsure about yourself and who you were, and if anyone he had ever met conveyed uncertainty it was Adele.

Until now. She looked different. Brighter. Happier.

Something about this girl Karina made her light up like nothing else, and it was wondrous to behold. Before she had moved as though her curves were an encumbrance, weighing her down. Now, shaking it around the kitchen to Nickelback as she cleaned, she looked like someone else.

'. . . *are we having fun yet?*'

'Oh yes. Most definitely.'

During the slower verses her hips swayed in time with Karina's smaller bottom, scrubbing hard over the work-surfaces in time with the angry chorus. But she was smiling, laughing, flicking suds at Karina. Her lips moved as she sang along – pouting and curving – yeah, yeah, yeah, no, no.

So that was who she really was. Not as buttoned up and sensible as she made out, shimmying her arse and writhing on down to that loud, dirty rock guitar, with her arms in the air and soap suds spattering her irrepressible hair.

Karina spotted him watching and laughed. 'Oh fuuuuuuck!'

'Afternoon, ladies.'

Adele abruptly stopped poledancing around the mop handle and collapsed in embarrassed laughter. 'Oh shit! How long have you been there?'

'Long enough to wonder if your mother ever met Mick Jagger. Day-um girl!'

Karina laughed. 'Oh God, Del, have you got any Stones upstairs? I could so do with hearing some.'

'Will you dance some more?' Paul asked, leaning against the door frame.

'Only if you start stuffing tenners down my knickers,' Karina said, blowing him a kiss across the worktops.

'Don't tempt me,' Paul said. He meant it.

'You're evil,' Adele told her, tying up her hair again. 'Genuinely twisted.'

Her hair refused to comply and Karina sighed. 'Oh, come here you . . .'

She went over to Adele and gathered up the thick tangle of Adele's curls, pulling out the bandana and pins that had failed to hold. The two of them were close enough for Paul to touch, exuding a heady smell of female sweat. Karina stood on tiptoe to reach her friend's hair, glancing slyly at Paul as she pinned it up. Her mouth was full of hairpins as she fussed. Adele stood acquiescent, darting Paul a shyer look, her tongue wetting her scarlet upper lip. He caught Karina's eyes again. Dark, dark eyes, smooth lids. He couldn't make her out, but there was just something, everything about her that was so damn sexy. There was no jealousy, no warning to back off in her eyes. She was just an open invitation. All of her. Had Adele ever taken up the invitation?

'Bad as your mother,' Adele said.

'Hygiene, darling, hygiene.'

'I'm not even cooking in here yet.'

Karina picked the last hairpin out of her mouth and stuck it into Adele's hair. Her lips were the same bright red as Adele's – that mouth you couldn't miss; a bright peony-red pout. Karina's lips were narrower and so finely shaped that they reminded him of the delicate bow lips of geishas, painted the same brilliant shade.

'What's with you two and red lipstick?' Paul asked.

Both women smiled and looked infuriatingly mysterious. 'It's a thing' was all Adele would say, shrugging.

'A thing?'

'A *thing*,' Karina said. 'Just a thing.'

They had shut him out, back in their comfortable world of female intimacy. He went back up to the flat.

Ieuan was out, looking for a job. Paul settled on the couch and decided that a phone call was long overdue. He had to call her work number. Ugh. Her secretary picked up, making life difficult as usual.

'I'm afraid Ms Forrester is busy at present.'

'You mean she's not in the mood to take calls?' Paul said.

'I'm afraid she's busy. Can I take a message? Who shall I say is calling?'

'Paul Eades. And tell her to get a move on.'

'Yes, Mr Eades,' said the secretary, managing to distil into his name the same cadence she might have said 'horsefucker' or 'needledick'. Good. She would complain.

Predictably, within three minutes, the phone rang.

'Hello?'

'Don't hello me, you fucker. How dare you be so rude to Cheri?'

'Matter of expediency, my darling. I was working on the premise that women talk. I love that you're so predictable.'

She snorted. 'Who's predictable? I had a feeling you'd call. How's the poor brainless slut?'

'I'll have you know you're talking about the poor brainless slut I love.'

Sarah laughed. 'Oh, it's love now, is it? Or is that just what you're hanging on to now the initial lust has worn off?'

'I don't know why I called you.' Paul sighed, settling back on the couch. In truth he knew damn well why he had called her. His dick was thickening and filling in his jeans at the very sound of her voice – rich, well bred, hissy on her sibilants. She had apparently lisped when she was a gap-toothed little girl and never managed to shuck the habit completely.

'I do,' Sarah said. 'You're bored. Same reason you

always call.' She coughed, and Paul imagined her settling back in her office chair, slipping down her knickers – if she was wearing them. 'Fortunately for you, I'm bored to tears as well. What have you been up to?'

'Fucking Ieuan, mostly,' Paul replied, and couldn't hold back the sigh. 'OK, I admit it – it's not working out.'

'Oh, my poor baby,' she crooned, clearly trying hard to keep the amusement and *I told you so* out of her voice. 'And what now? You want a woman again?'

'I want you,' Paul said, deciding to cut straight to the chase. 'I miss you.'

Sarah sighed. 'Darling, you know it's impossible right now. Anyway, I miss you telling me your stories and how am I supposed to hear anything new if you're not gathering any new material?'

'Oh, don't worry about that. I have a very vivid imagination.'

She chuckled down the phone. 'Yes, you do. You always did have your head in the clouds.'

'What about you?' Paul pressed. 'Are you seeing anyone?'

'Only on a professional basis,' Sarah said, infuriatingly coy.

'Who?'

'I can't tell you that,' she said. 'I may take advantage of my position now and again but you know I can't reveal legal details.'

Paul sighed, becoming impatient. 'What about the intimate details? Spill.'

'Ah, but will *you*?' she murmured, her voice getting lower and more redolent of bedtime fun and games. He imagined her raising her skirt over her thighs and toying with the uppermost tip of her clit. He hadn't been lying when he said he missed her.

'Very probably.' He undid his jeans, easing the pressure

on his cock. It sprung up against the loose fabric of his boxers and he unfastened the small fly button to free it fully.

'Will you come for me?' Sarah asked, cajoling him.

'You know I will. What about you? Where are you and what are you doing?'

'In my office,' she said. 'I should close the blinds, but I don't think anyone can see – except maybe if the window cleaner comes by on that little cage contraption of his. Then he'll get an eyeful.'

'Tell me.'

'I wasn't wearing knickers today anyway. I had an appointment at the London Mayor's building ... you know? That godawful glass carbuncle of a thing, but it has all those glass walkways and I thought I'd amuse myself by walking around there and seeing who tried to peep up my skirt.'

Paul gasped. 'Oh, God ... Sarah. Did anyone look?'

'I'm not sure. I was distracted, but it got me wet. It was a good thing I'd gone Brazilian or I would have stunk of sex.'

'Brazilian,' he groaned, and squeezed the base of his cock, trying to forestall his pleasure for as long as possible, but Sarah was in fine form today. He would have given anything to have been on one of the floors below, watching her walk up the stairs above his head and catching tantalising glimpses of her waxed crotch as her thighs moved. 'All off?'

'Everything,' she confirmed. 'So if the window cleaner comes by, he'll have an extra nice view. I have one leg over the arm of my chair and my skirt unbuttoned. You'd love this skirt, Paul. It looks perfectly decent – a row of prim little buttons up the side, but they all unfasten for ease of access.'

Paul shivered and stretched out on the couch, making

himself comfortable and looking forward to a very pleasant conversation indeed. There was nobody to compare to Sarah. The only drawback was that she didn't have a dick as well, although she was happy to remedy that with a strap on if he asked her to.

'You are *disgusting* ... in the most wonderful way.'

'I know,' she said breezily.

'And are you wet now?'

'Drenched. Wet and desperate for it. Just the way you love me. If you were here now I'd have you under my desk licking me out.'

'I'd like that,' Paul said, aware that he was seriously understating the matter. He would love it. When she shaved, her cunt had the fine texture of the flesh of one of those white arum lilies – silky and rich as vellum. Much as he loved the prickle of her pubic hair on his cock as he pushed inside her, not feeling it was equally exciting. Licking her was easy and delicious without the tangle of hair under his tongue. He wanted so much to be under her desk in her office, tonguing her clit and pushing his fingers inside to draw out the salt moisture.

'I can be there in two hours,' he said.

'No you don't,' Sarah told him firmly. 'I've told you time and time again we're bad for one another.'

'Please,' he moaned. 'We can work something out.'

'No we can't. We always go too far. You need a nice steady influence. A good girl.'

'I'd die of boredom, Sarah!'

'Which is why you need a bad girl too. Which is why you're impossible. Now don't you want to hear about my latest client?'

Slighted, Paul sulked. 'Oh, if you must.'

'Don't be petulant.'

'I'm not.'

'You are. You probably have your lower lip stuck out the way you do –'

He bit his lower lip.

'There's no use pouting, darling. It doesn't wash with me. You know I won't stand for it.'

She wouldn't either. When she was pissed off she had always been quick to slap him down. Round the face, across the arse, wherever she could. She left marks on his skin and wasn't afraid to use her fingernails.

'Anyway,' Sarah said, as if trying to begin the conversation again. It was no use. His irritation had taken the edge off his hunger and, if he came for her the way she wanted him to, she would have won. He pushed his cock back inside his shorts and buttoned his jeans. He was annoyed at himself for still allowing her to lead him around by the dick after all these years. Years and years of screwing as many men as he could lay hands on because there wasn't a woman who could compare to Sarah, and then when he wanted a woman she turned him down.

'So who's this client, then?' he asked testily, wanting to go back downstairs. Adele was down there, her presence soothing and steady.

'Well, I can't tell you that,' she said. 'But strictly confidentially, anonymously, I can tell you that you will just adore this. My client inspired the Brazilian, actually.'

'Oh?' Paul asked, his interest sparking once again despite his bad mood.

'Yes. She came in looking to fight what looks like a very messy custody battle. Hubby is divorcing her on the grounds that he thinks she's a lesbian.'

'Really? And is she?'

'I'm not sure. When she went down on me I would have sworn she'd never eaten pussy before in her life.'

Paul sighed. 'You're a bitch. Do you know that?'

'Absolutely. You think I got where I am today by being nice? Anyway, it gets better. She admitted she didn't know how to give head because her last girlfriend had a penis.'

'Right. Her girlfriend had a penis? Not so girl-friend then?'

'It was one of those she-males from Bangkok or something. Can you imagine?'

'It has crossed my mind once or twice, yes,' Paul said.

'You'd love that, wouldn't you?' Sarah purred, once again riffing on the intimation of one of his long-held sexual fantasies. 'A beautiful girl with a long thick cock she could fuck you up the arse with?'

Paul was glad he had buttoned his fly again. He heard steps up the stairs and the front door open, the sound of Ieuan coughing. He clenched the muscles of his arse and thighs back against the couch, squirming back against the cushions with anticipation and imagining pushing back against a slender, female body, with one difference – a cock crammed inside him. Sarah couldn't fuck him for real that way, but Ieuan could, would and did.

Ieuan looked in. Paul brazened it out. If he hung up the phone and looked guilty, Ieuan would immediately know it was Sarah and go insane.

'I'll get back to you,' Paul said, adopting a businesslike tone of voice. 'I'll price check with our regular suppliers and see what comparable rates we can negotiate, OK?'

'You little bastard!' Sarah snarled down the phone, clearly savvy to the fact that she was being fobbed off. '*You* called *me*.'

Ieuan raised his eyebrows. He looked hot, sweaty and appetising. Paul beckoned to him across the room, then with his free hand he unbuttoned his shirt, teasing his own nipples with his fingertips, before sliding his hand down his torso to unfasten the uppermost button of his jeans. He watched Ieuan's eyes darken and his penis swell the front of his jeans as Ieuan prowled across the room to come get him.

'Come here,' he mouthed silently, then cheerfully ended the phone call.

'Thank you so much for calling.' Then the final insult – an American-style 'have a nice day!' delivered complete with shit-eating grin. He hung up and pulled Ieuan astride his lap, rejoicing in the knowledge that, in London, Sarah would be hissing like a pressure cooker that was about to explode.

Ieuan's tongue flicked over the lobes of Paul's ears, his neck, his nipples, his lips. His mouth tasted of peppermint chewing gum and was delectably slippery-wet inside, in contrast to his slightly chapped lips.

'Who was that?' he asked, squirming like a lapdancer, hips swaying against Paul's grip.

'Cold caller,' Paul said, smiling at the aptness of it. He looked up at Ieuan. 'And how are you? Still bored?'

'Hmm . . .' Ieuan inclined his head to one side and licked his lower lip. 'Still suffering from all that sea air?'

'It's gone to my head,' Paul said ingenuously.

'It's gone to your *cock*.'

'Exactly. Whichever way you look at it it's gone to the place where I do *all* my thinking.'

'That or you get turned on by cold callers,' Ieuan said. 'What were they selling?'

'Double glazing.' Paul was amazed at how easily the lie fell out of his mouth. He kissed Ieuan again to stop him asking more awkward questions. If Ieuan thought he was getting old and boring, then Ieuan had another think coming. There was nothing like a little afternoon whoopee to assure your lover you still had what it took. 'Come to bed.'

'Now?'

'No. Next Saturday.' Paul sat up and pulled off his shirt, tugged off Ieuan's shirt too and devoted his attention to Ieuan's nipple bar. Ieuan wriggled free and climbed off him.

'Back in a minute,' he said. 'I need a piss first.'

Paul nodded, got up and went to the bedroom. He undressed and crawled under the duvet, his dick already stiff with anticipation. Maybe it was some early midlife crisis – revisiting his sexual past in the shape of Sarah, lusting after the girl upstairs, speculating as to whether they were engaged in some Sapphic moaning and groaning, screwing a multi-pierced twenty-three-year-old. Pathetic really.

He sighed and stretched impatiently, wanting Ieuan.

He didn't want what he got. Ieuan flung open the bedroom door and hurled the phone at him – receiver, holder, cord, the works.

'Ow! Jesus!'

'Double glazing?' Ieuan yelled. 'What kind of fucking *idiot* do you take me for?'

'Oh, for God's sake.' Paul tossed the disconnected phone to one side. 'I was only keeping it quiet because I knew you'd do this. She's still my wife.'

Ieuan stared at him, eyes suddenly impossibly blue, fists clenched. 'Yeah? And why was she calling? Custody arrangements for the big dildo you bought together?'

'It's perfectly reasonable for me to keep things amicable while we're going through the divorce,' Paul said, although he knew Ieuan would never buy it. Ieuan had met Sarah. He knew just how amicable she could get. 'Anyway, did you 1471?' he asked, pleased that it had occurred to him. 'Well, thank you for your trust, baby.'

'Please! I wouldn't trust Mother Teresa to keep her knickers on with that fucking woman around.'

'Well, given that she died in 1997 I think your mistrust is ill founded. Sarah may be many things, but she's not a necrophile.'

'I'll tell you what she is,' Ieuan snarled, storming to the chest of drawers for a clean shirt. 'She's a one-woman black hole. It's like her fanny is exerting some kind of gravitational pull and she won't stop until she's sucked the entire world into it.'

'For your information, this is one of the many bloody reasons I'm divorcing her.'

'Right!' Ieuan snorted. 'Which is why you look all hot and bothered when she phones? Look, if you want to fuck a woman, go ahead, but count me out of your life if you do.'

'It would be my fucking pleasure!' Paul shouted, sick of trying to reason with him. 'All you ever do is criticise anyway and moan that you're bored!'

'Because this place is boring!'

'No, sweetheart. What makes it boring is the massive empty space between your ears! I wondered how you endured the pain of having all those piercings and now I now why – you haven't reached a level of sentience in which you can feel pain!'

Ieuan looked at him as if he was the lowest kind of lifeform on the planet, and maybe he was, but it was all going to come out sooner or later. It was nearly a relief to say it out loud.

With a scream of 'fuck you', Ieuan turned on his heel, slammed the bedroom door, slammed the front door and stomped downstairs. Another rain of plaster descended down the back of the chimney. Shaking with anger, Paul huddled on the bed and cursed himself for a fool. He was starting to wonder about that chimney. He'd been assured by the sellers and the surveyors that it was sound; now it appeared to be coming down in front of his eyes. He quickly pulled on some clothes, realising that, however pissed off he was at Ieuan, he didn't want to be there if God decided to add to his problems by dropping an elderly Victorian chimney through the roof.

'You see, this is what I have to put up with?' he told no one in particular, although he aimed most of the vitriol at the recently departed Ieuan. 'Builders, chimneys, dancing chefs, fucking horny carpenters.' He peered cautiously up the chimney, now that the plaster appeared to have stopped falling. 'And what the fuck do you know? All you have to think about is what part of your body you're going to get pierced next.'

Paul cleared away a potted plant, shaking the dust off the leaves, and moved an African statue, allowing himself a clear field to get a better look up the chimney. 'What kind of job is that anyway?' he muttered to himself. 'Try being me, babycakes – kneeling on the floor with my head up a fucking chimney . . . Jesus Christ . . .'

It smelled musty and sooty. Paul had a nasty feeling that there were probably a couple of dead birds up there. He was still talking angrily to himself when something rattled and rumbled inside the chimney. Hearing the noise he pulled back sharply, bumped his head on the top of the chimney and sprawled back against the side of the bed.

Not a moment too late. Something creaked, strained, and then gave way, and brick, soot, plaster and metal cascaded down the chimney in a noisy shower of dust and evil smells. The dust billowed into the room and, judging by the stink, Paul was in no doubt about the presence of at least a couple of dead seagulls.

This had to be it. The day couldn't get any worse from here-on in.

There was dust everywhere. His bedroom hadn't been exactly tidy before, but it now looked as though it belonged in Beirut. 'Fucking hell,' he said quietly, as if speaking too loudly might literally bring the house down. The dust was settling slowly on the bed, encrusting the bedsheets and smothering the carpet like some ancient and fatal case of dandruff. It was going to take days to clean up. He had to sleep in here tonight. Well, unless he graciously took the couch, true to post-row etiquette between couples. You take the bed, darling. I'll sleep on the couch like the bastard I am.

He smiled at the thought, reminding him that he could. It was strange, but he'd had a sense that it wasn't going to work with Ieuan for so long that it felt good to fight, brawl and burn those bridges good and proper.

Boring. This place wasn't boring. It was insane. Girls appearing out of nowhere to flash their knickers on the stairs, chefs who poledanced around mop handles, the house coming down the chimney. He had to laugh. The dust entered his lungs and he crawled up onto the bed to get above it and open the window wider. He looked down at the carnage.

It looked as though Santa had come five months early with a rocket launcher. Stuff was scattered all over the floor, radiating out from the chimney breast. He realised that the floor of this fireplace might be as unstable as the one upstairs had clearly been, and that it might cascade through with the extra weight.

He shook the dust from a T-shirt and covered his nose and mouth with it, before descending into the dust to remove the heavy wrought-iron fire grate that had fallen from above. Then stared. Amongst the rubble was a picture – distinctly seedy in its depiction of flesh, even through the film of dirt that caked it. He wiped it on the T-shirt and stared.

It was her. Karina. On her hands and knees, naked, with a young blond man's dick jammed inside her from behind. Her thigh and the man's hand obscured her crotch, but her breasts were visible, hanging like fruit between her upper arms. Her mouth was open, her eyes closed, skin white in the flash of the Polaroid camera.

It wasn't like any hardcore porn shot Paul had ever seen, simply because it didn't look like porn. It wasn't a silicone girl with a cutesy 'stage name' like Cherry Redd or Candy Walls pulling faces for the camera while she thought distastefully of the enema she'd need to take before the big anal scene. It was just a picture of two people fucking, and as such it was more arousing than any pornography.

Wondering where on earth it had come from, he wrestled the metal grate loose and a battered red leather suitcase spilled open into the fireplace. Letters, pictures, dried flowers. Stuff that was obviously so precious and personal that Paul's immediate worry was that it would be spoilt in the dust, dirt and ancient ashes. There were more pictures – of Karina leaning against a washbasin in a grubby-looking toilet, her fishnet tights torn open, her arse looking as though it had been recently penetrated. Karina in a classic soft-porn shot, pearls draped over her bare breasts and a sheet gathered demurely over her fanny. Paul gathered everything up and put it back in the case as best he could, pausing to glance at the erotic Polaroids. One of them especially made him do a double take – a picture of a woman's shaved crotch, on which had been carefully painted a pair of red lips. He shivered, fiercely aroused despite the dust. They were doing that. Upstairs.

He scrabbled amongst the rubble for more, and found a picture that was threatening to slide between a crack in the brickwork, quickly retrieving it before it could be lost forever. He had to return this stuff in the state he found it. It would be embarrassing enough as it was to have to go upstairs, face them and hand back such intimate pictures.

His embarrassment turned to shock and anger as he recognised the blonde in the Polaroid. She was smiling, lying topless on a bed, her hair tumbled and her face flushed and satisfied. The woman in the picture was commonly referred to in his family as That Little Tart, Miss Midlife Crisis or simply The Bitch. Paul recognised her, but anyone who had kept track of popular music in the last ten years or so would have recognised her.

This had to be Sarah's doing.

11

'He was checking you out.'

'I don't think he could check me out more than he has already.'

'You dirty slapper!'

'I learned from the best,' Adele said, raising her middle finger. 'It's not like a big love thing or anything,' she continued, waving her hand dismissively in the general direction of the back door.

'No?'

'Yeah.' Adele nodded and pushed the mop under the table. 'He's OK, but not really my type.'

'So what is your type?' Karina asked. 'I didn't even know you *had* a type.'

'I don't *know*,' Adele said, in an exasperated voice. 'I just know *he* isn't it. Now stop getting possessive. If you want to do the girl thing you can't be possessive.'

'I am not getting possessive!' Karina said, although she was. Jude had no business being in Adele's bed. He was too boyish – not in touch with his feminine side. Adele wasn't into men who acted like testosterone-crazed dogs on heat. In that respect, she did have a type, and short of pissing on the floor the other morning Jude couldn't have acted more like he owned the place.

'You forget how well I know you. Look, he's just . . . a bit of fun, OK?'

'Yeah. He's a regular laugh a minute, that one.'

'He can be funny.'

'And I'm Nancy Reagan,' Karina said. 'I know you. I

know you need someone who makes you laugh, isn't all alpha-male and is preferably toilet trained.'

'You don't know him!'

'And you do?'

'I don't *need* to know him,' said Adele defensively. 'It's not serious.'

Karina felt perversely pleased that it wasn't. In spite of herself, she was possessive. She'd learned to be possessive with Suki; when it made her breath catch in her throat and her fingers clench around a table knife whenever she saw Edward so much as touching Suki.

It seemed like it was her fate to hang around telling the women in her life that the men they were with weren't good enough for them.

Jude sloped into the kitchen, jeans halfway down his arse, and eyed her up and down. Karina stared back at him, challenging him to come closer. Adele turned and, to Karina's consternation, she said 'Hi', in a silly, girly voice that Karina didn't know she had.

'All right?' said Jude. 'You busy?'

'Nearly finished,' Adele said, clearing away the brooms and buckets. 'Why?'

'Fancy a pint?'

Say no, say no, say no . . .

'Yeah. OK.'

Shit.

Karina glared. Adele looked at her, shook her head and sighed. Jude, sensing an atmosphere, stayed right where he was. Stupid bastard. He had the look of a caged animal and she wondered what was going on in that head of his, if anything. He was about twelve, surely.

He wandered over to Adele and said something quietly to her, compounding Karina's dislike. Right. Fuck him. She didn't have to be here and, since her presence was irrelevant to him anyway, she'd go.

'I'll be upstairs,' she said, and walked through the bar, out the front door, into the street, through the side door and up the stairs. Then she remembered she didn't have a key. Adele had it. She waited on the stairs, pissed off and resentful. Bloody men. It was the same as Suki. Shackle yourself to an arsehole for ever by bearing his children.

Adele came up the stairs.

'So?'

'So what?' Adele asked. 'Why didn't you get the key?'

'Because I didn't want to get in the way,' Karina said. 'I thought you were going out?'

'I am.' Adele opened the front door and they walked in. 'I just needed to get my purse.'

'If he was a gentleman you wouldn't need your purse,' Karina argued.

Adele huffed and sighed. 'Yeah, well. He's saying we need to talk, so I'm going to dump *him* first.'

Karina offered her phone. 'Call him then.'

'I can't leave him hanging on. I owe it to him to at least dump him face to face.'

'Why?'

'Because I'm a nice person.' Adele unpinned her hair and shook it out.

'No, you're not. You're a magnificent bitch. Know thyself. Socrates said that.'

'Yeah. That was exactly why they poisoned the bastard,' Adele said. 'See you later.'

'Yeah. Good luck.'

Sighing, Karina watched her go, wondering what it was about the best women in the world that always seemed to make them end up with the worst men. She was sick of losing out to people who didn't deserve good fortune. She had tried so hard to put Suki out of her mind, but it was impossible. There were some lovers who stamped themselves so indelibly on your heart and mind that you would never forget the sound of their voice or the sense memory of their skin next to your own.

She couldn't just let go, not now that she had learned the meaning of real love, after all those years of running away from it. Seeing Adele again was a stark reminder of what an idiot she had been. What a hopeless emotional cripple. What a man.

The intro to 'Are Friends Electric' beeped out from her bag on the couch and she answered the phone, frowning at the unrecognised number flashing up on the display; a landline, from somewhere in central London.

'Hello?'

'Good afternoon. I'm trying to reach Karina May,' said an upper-crust female voice.

'Speaking.'

'Ah, Ms May. My name is Sarah Forrester. I'm calling on behalf of my client, Mrs Suzanne Nasmith . . .'

Karina gulped. Fuck. What now? 'Yes?' she said nervously.

'I'm calling to ask if you would be willing to be named in Mrs Nasmith's divorce, which I am in the process of handling.'

'Divorce?' Karina croaked, her throat dry. Her heart was hammering and the sudden thrill of optimism was dizzying. Finally, Suki had come round to the idea of ditching that twat Edward. Good news whatever way Karina looked at it, but huge with the dazzling possibility of having Suki back again. 'When did this happen?'

'Well, *obviously* you know that the Nasmiths' marriage has been . . . under strain for some time.'

Karina gulped at the accent the woman placed on the words. Edward was probably writing her name on clay pigeons before blasting them into the air and screaming PULL! 'Uh, yeah. Of course.'

'It's a delicate situation, naturally, and we are aiming to make the matter as painless as possible for the sake of the children, but I'm afraid Mr Nasmith is being rather difficult and I'm contacting you because it's really only a matter of time before his barrister demands that you be present in court.'

'Right.' Karina reached for her cigarettes and lit one. 'Shit.'

'Am I to take that to mean that I can count on you, Ms May?'

Sniffy little bitch, Karina thought, but said yes, sure. No problem. She didn't mean it. As she hung up the phone she realised she could be facing Edward across a fucking crowded courtroom and wondered when the next flight to Bangkok left Gatwick.

No. That was then. This was now. She was supposed to be facing up to all the crap she'd left behind her in her life so far. Adele was part of it, and it wasn't as hard as she had imagined it would be. You're gonna reap just what you sow, as Lou Reed would have it, and there was always the chance that Suki still loved her. Karina had to know that much. She had erased Suki's number from her phone in a temper, but she knew she still had it written down in her suitcase somewhere.

Except that, when she tried to fetch her suitcase, it was gone. There was an odd dusty smell in the bedroom and Karina's initial thoughts were that her case had been stolen, when she noticed that the floor of the fireplace had fallen right through. The suitcase was gone, the grate was gone, and only a few fragments of brick and board indicated there had ever been a floor to the fireplace at all. It must have fallen into the fireplace below. Frantic for her prized possessions, Karina ran down to knock on the door of the flat downstairs. Behind her, the front door slammed shut, locking her out. She swore and prayed someone was home.

Paul opened the door. At least, she thought it was Paul. Paul as she knew him was posh in an annoying way, too well scrubbed to be considered attractive and had very bad taste in shirts. He looked nothing like that. He was filthy, shirtless, sweaty and pissed off. Karina stared, sure she was experiencing some appropriately Damascene conversion regarding Paul. She was definitely not a lesbian. This was all man, and it was all good. His naked torso was beautiful, gently sculpted and rising and falling softly with his panting breaths. His dark curling hair was greyish with dust, and the dust had mingled with his sweat to cover his bare, tanned skin with smudgy, sexy patches of grime.

She drew in a breath, filling her lungs with the animal stink of him. The movement of her chest made her breasts lift, like her body was subconsciously sticking her tits forwards for his attention. Her throat was dry, but somehow she managed to speak.

'Hi. Is there something up with the chimney?'

'Something *up*?' he said, wiping his face with the back of his forearm. The hair under his arm was black, soft and wet with his sweat.

'Yes.'

'Gravity being what it is, I think it would be more accurate to say that something is down.'

'Well, yeah. Down,' she said dumbly, aware that her blood supply was also now subject to gravity. Heat was pooling in her groin and belly at the sound of his voice, that posh, snippy voice coming out of the mouth of this smoking hot male animal that the heat and the dirt had turned him into. 'The fireplace ... has ... er ... something ... dropped out ...'

'Yes, I know,' he said, spreading his arms to present the state he was in. 'Do you think I got like this cleaning the bath? I think you'd better come in.'

'Thanks.' Karina followed him in. The flat was obviously bigger than Adele's and less cluttered. Its decor appeared to have been thought out rather than accumulated over years of occupancy. The kitchen was all pale marble and polished chrome.

'Coffee?' Paul said, in a tone of voice that suggested he would rather have given her cyanide. 'Would you like a cup of coffee?'

'Um, thanks,' she said, suddenly aware that his hostility was nothing to do with the mess. She would have to ask about her suitcase, but the words stuck in her throat. If he'd looked inside the case, she was in trouble. She had had this so many times before – men freaking out when they found out that she was not what she seemed, their masculinity so threatened by the thought that they'd had a hard on for what they perceived to be a man that they lashed out. But then Paul had a boyfriend, so what was his problem?

He appeared to be having as much difficulty cutting to the chase on the matter of the suitcase as she did. He was preoccupied with the huge chrome coffee maker on his kitchen worksurface. 'Cream? Sugar?'

'Just sugar,' she said, feeling as though she needed it. Karina had never been that interested in food and often forgot to eat, so she attributed her jitters to low blood sugar. She'd be fine. She'd stop shaking and feeling cold to the gut as soon as she had something sweet inside her. She wanted a cigarette, but she had left her cigarettes upstairs, behind Adele's locked door.

Paul put the coffee down in front of her and sat down opposite her, arms folded defensively across his bare chest. 'The floor of the fireplace must have fallen through,' he said.

'Yes. I just found out.' Karina's head spun from the smell of the coffee. It was strong, dark and richly scented. 'We didn't know; we were downstairs in the kitchen. I'm sorry if it made a mess.'

His eyes were a very unusual colour. Green wasn't an unusual eye colour, but his eyes looked the colour of unripe apples in the evening sun. His eyelashes were long and dark, spiked and tangled together where he must have rubbed his eyes against the dust. Taken together with his flat feline nose and sensual mouth it produced such an effect that Karina didn't care how pissed off he was for a moment, because he was so damn pretty.

He nodded. 'Yes. I know. I did find something of yours, I think –'

'Oh!' She jumped on the subject. 'Yes?'

'At least, I assume it's yours.'

'My suitcase, yeah.'

She could have sworn Paul was flushing underneath the dirt on his face. Embarrassed? Had he looked at her photographs, stuffed his hand down the front of his jeans and made himself come with her image stuck on his retinas? She realised that she wished he had, and that he'd let her watch. Beneath the table, her legs parted instinctively. Under the baggy combat pants she could feel her tight underwear riding up, squeezing and gripping her sex and chafing pleasantly at her anus.

She hid her nose in the cup of coffee, taking a swallow of the searing, sweet, strong liquid. It was excellent coffee, and she found herself gulping more greedily than she meant to.

'The locks must have broken,' he said. 'I put everything back the way I found it.'

'Did you get a good look?' she asked, her head already beginning to spin with the caffeine.

'I know what you are,' Paul said simply, with an edge of confrontation in his voice.

'Do you really?'

'Yes. I know what I need to know.'

'Then why the fuck does it bother you?' Karina countered. 'Not like you've never sucked dick in your life.'

'Excuse me?' Paul frowned, but Karina was angry and determined to make her point. She ignored him and ploughed on regardless.

'What is wrong with you people? Everything has to have a label, doesn't it? One thing or the other – can't be both. If I dressed and lived as a man, would you get down on your knees and suck my dick? I know you fucking well would. But since I'm not either/or you all get so bloody hung up about it. Women are all, "oh, does this make me a lesbian?" and men are like, "you fucking freak, I'm not gay".'

'I'm sorry . . . I don't . . .' Paul looked completely baffled.

'What don't you get?' Karina snapped. 'You saw the pictures, didn't you? You said you knew I wasn't a woman. Well, let me tell you something, pal – I am a woman. I just happen to have a penis. I didn't choose to come out this way.'

He stared at her. 'You . . . oh my God . . . you're . . .'

'A chick with a dick,' she said. 'Yes. Deal with it.' She sighed, realising she was screwed. 'And at this point I would normally flounce out but I've locked myself out of the flat and have nowhere to flounce to. Fuck.'

'Oh.' Paul shook his head. 'Sorry. I don't have a spare set of keys. And you had me totally fooled, if that's any consolation.'

'I did?' Karina sat down again, flattered.

'Completely. I would never have guessed. You make
... I mean, you *are* such a beautiful woman.'

Some wicked little voice in the back of her head
whispered that she could have him. Maybe Suki wanted
commitment. That was fine, but Karina was going to
have her last fling first – if anything to avenge all those
nights Suki had spent with Edward in the line of wifely
duty. 'Oh really?' she said, leaning forwards and folding
her arms on the tabletop so that Paul got a good view of
her breasts crushed together in her skimpy tank top.

'Well, I'd say it was a fairly common male fantasy,'
Paul said awkwardly. 'Not all the strap-ons sold in the
world are sold to lesbians, surely.'

'Don't need a strap-on,' Karina told him glibly. 'I've got
the real thing.'

She had him. His eyes were hungry and his tongue
wet his full bottom lip. 'Does it –' he began to ask.

'Work? Oh yes. Very much so. I don't need to eat a
whole bunch of hormones every day, being as I looked
pretty feminine to begin with. I'm all man from the waist
down, sweetie.'

He leaned forwards, so that their elbows were touching across the tabletop. 'Incredible,' he whispered.

'What about you?' Karina asked, boldly reaching out
to trace delicate swirls in the dusty dark hair on his
forearm. 'Is it a fantasy of yours? Ever wanted to be
fucked by a girl?'

Paul nodded, not taking his eyes off her. His gaze was
steady and intense, pupils widening with arousal so that
his eyes seemed to shade from apple green to jade. He
closed his fingers over her hand and lifted her fingertips
to his lips. His eyes closed for a moment as he held her
fingers and ran the smooth surfaces of her nails across
his lips, his breath warmly fanning her knuckles. She had

her own breath stuck in her throat, because what he was doing to her hand was so unbelievably erotic. He was gently nipping at the tips of her fingernails with his teeth, teasing the fingertip beneath with tiny touches of his tongue, holding her fingers as carefully as if he were holding some delicacy Adele had constructed of spun and scorched sugar, something he was determined to savour. Karina was startled at the way her body responded to his tease. She had had her hands kissed before, had her fingertips suckled like fruit, but it was the way he took his time, took care. It was a challenge, daring her to make him lose control. They could have fallen on one another any time they liked. They were all alone, intentions spoken, but not yet. Not just yet. She wanted his mind and body to snap first.

She loved that moment of suspended animation, when you realised you wanted someone and they wanted you – and suddenly it was like a door swinging open in front of you. As if you'd discovered a password and wanted a while to savour your own cleverness before speaking the right word and stepping irrevocably into that realm of secrets and treasures that was a new lover's flesh. She thought Paul knew it too, because he was making no further move, other than rubbing his cheek against the back of her fingers. She felt the warmth coming off his face, the tip of his nose, the mothlike flutter of his lashes. She flexed her fingers, brushing them over his eyelids and the bridge of his nose, and let them find their own way down his cheek, to his lips and chin. Her thumb trailed over his lower lip and his mouth pursed to kiss as she held his chin up. His eyes looked drugged and hungry, his lips slack and pouting. She knew if she took his mouth now that would be it – no more control, because she would have to yank those jeans off him, grab his cock and suck on it until he begged her to let him come.

Her lips were already tingling in anticipation of the kiss she hadn't yet taken.

'Do you want that?' she asked quietly. 'Do you want me to fuck you?'

He nodded again. 'Please ... please ... I want to see ...'

'All in good time,' Karina said, lying. She couldn't hold off for much longer. Her dick was aching inside her knickers and she was eager to show it to him, push him onto his knees so that he could get a good look at eyelevel, shove it in his face and push it into his mouth, because she wanted to see her come decorating his pretty, pouting lips.

She trailed her fingers down his chest and pinched one of his nipples, squeezing and deliberately scratching the sensitive skin with a fingernail. Paul closed his eyes and moaned. When he opened his eyes again they were incandescent and overheated, like she had pushed him too far and he wasn't going to take no for an answer any longer.

'Come here,' he said, gripping her top across the table and pulling her towards him. His hand bunched up her brief top until it was a thin rope of twisted cloth over her breasts, and he pulled back again to stare. She took it off, offering her tits to his gaze and his hands.

'You're joking,' Paul said, shaking his head. 'You have got to be joking. You're a woman.'

'With a difference.' She climbed onto the tabletop and slithered across it on her arse, so that she sat in front of him on the table, legs dangling either side of his lap, her bum squarely planted where dinner would be if the table were being put to its proper use.

He could have grabbed her crotch and let curiosity get the better of him immediately, but Paul seemed fairly sophisticated in that respect, able to tease out the desperate urge. Paul wanted his kiss before anything else happened, so she complied. His full lips were sumptuously soft and squashy. At first it was just a firm press of half-open mouths, with the experimental push of his tongue between her lips and a strong whiff of coffee-breath coming from them both. While Karina was sat on the table, he had to tip his head up to meet her mouth, and in this irresistible, suppliant posture his jaw went slack and he moaned deep in the back of his throat. She echoed his moan back into his mouth. He was one of those gorgeous, abandoned kissers, the kind who just had to taste a hint of tongue to turn into a complete and utter slut.

'Oh God,' he whispered, breaking off to breathe for a moment. He was panting deeply already, his dusty lips now pink and swollen with kisses and shiny with spit. She wound her fingers in his dirty, tangled dark curls and went back for more. His tongue tasted so strongly of coffee that she imagined she could get a caffeine rush just from kissing him. Her head was already spinning from that intense cup of coffee he had made her and the buzz was making her want to laugh at the insanity of it all. Go downstairs, have coffee with the neighbour – have the neighbour while you're at it.

She wanted to lie back and get down to business. Enough dancing around and teasing one another, she wanted to get off. She leaned back, tugging on his hair to make him take the hint and follow the lead, but the table was too high and too narrow to fuck comfortably or safely on. 'Floor,' Paul gasped, helping her down off the table, his mouth nuzzling for her nipples, his teeth biting gently and making her cry out.

'Floor,' she repeated, nodding, and subsiding down onto the lino. The floor was good – perfect venue to get crazy. She knew she wouldn't get as far as fucking him, much as she wanted to. She could have come from the friction of his cock against hers through his jeans and her trousers. It had been so long since she'd had a young, sexy, desirable man and she wasn't sure if she had ever had one in her life while she was sober enough to really savour it.

She latched onto his mouth again, wrapping her legs around him, the better to feel the weight of his body. She loved this; being pressed so close to someone they could have been trying to crawl inside of one another's skin. He smelled delicious – a rank masculine musk she had missed like hell. His body was hard and solid above her, planes of hairless chest and silky back that hands glided over with such perfect ease that it made her ache and bite gently at his lips. He was breathing hard and his hands reached for her arse. She arched to grant him access and he gasped as he felt her hips brush against his and felt the hardness there.

'Oh my God,' he whispered, laughing incredulously as his hand cupped her crotch. 'You weren't joking, were you?'

'Why would I joke about a thing like that?' she asked, unfastening her trousers. It was starting to hurt, and not pleasantly.

He helped her with the trousers, yanking them down to her thighs, tussled with the tight underwear and stared. Karina breathed an audible sigh of relief as the pressure was released and her dick sprang up into the open. The poor thing looked so pleased to be free of confinement that she imagined it might jump up and lick someone's face, and she wanted to laugh at the thought.

Paul wasn't laughing. He was staring idiotically, mouth hanging open in such a lush, wet circle that his lips looked tailor-made for sucking cock. She wanted to push it inside and arched her hips for attention. Clever boy. He went straight down.

She moaned noisily at the intense wet heat of his mouth. It seemed to encourage him and he took it deeper, his tongue moving swiftly and expertly in a way that made her squirm and reach out and grasp one of the table legs as if she was about to drown or somehow fall through the floor. He was making low, greedy noises in the back of his throat as he sucked and licked and moved his body awkwardly, curled as it was between her thighs. She glanced down. He was struggling to pull his jeans down without looking up from what he was doing. She caught a glimpse of tanned flesh as he tussled with his belt and fly. A flash of black hair and a peek at the swollen, rosy head of his cock and his hand clenched over it, his own caress making him moan around it and stirring a similar sound out of Karina's own lungs.

Paul looked up for a second, his mouth full and his eyes bright. Karina cried out and buried her fingers in his dusty hair, thrusting up into his mouth. Oh God ... he didn't even gag. She had completely forgotten how phe-nomenally *good* gay men were at giving head. She was grateful for the reminder. His mouth was soaking wet, smooth lips wrapped around at just the right tension, his head bobbing up and down in time with the strokes he was delivering to his own cock. Karina threw back her head, the lino hard on the back of her scalp and her arse, the world contracting to a fine point of pleasure centred in Paul's sweet, hungry mouth. It wouldn't take long – she knew that – but she hadn't banked on him being this damn good. As she lifted her hips for more, he cunningly insinuated a wet finger between the cheeks of her butt and found her arsehole. The sensation was almost enough to make her come, but he had another trick up his sleeve, the gloriously dirty bastard. His finger slid up her arse, unerringly found the spot and wrung a wail of ecstasy from her throat.

She was coming – no way could she reign it back. As her hips began to move of their own volition, his finger sleekly fucked her arsehole, a smooth fine distilled ache of pleasure inside, expertly teasing the climax out of the very depths of her balls. He moaned as she filled his mouth and she heard herself making incoherent animal noises when she felt his throat work as he swallowed.

Karina lay back, gasping and staring at the underside of the kitchen table. Paul crawled up over her, wiping his mouth on the back of his hand, and kissed her deeply, letting her taste herself in his mouth before he slumped down flat on his back beside her. She glanced down at his dick, softening and sticky with come. A good time had been had by all, apparently.

'Fuck . . .' she moaned, dazed.

'Yep.' Paul exhaled. 'Oh God.'

'Uh huh.'

'Well . . .'

'Post-coital conversation not your thing, then?'

Paul laughed. 'What were you expecting? An elaborate Wildean epigram?'

'Fair point,' Karina said, staring up at the underside of the table again and fuzzily wondering what it was that she was doing here. Something about a chimney, and did they have time to do that again?

'And I have to admit that was, well –' Paul propped himself on one elbow and shook his head. 'That was unlike any kind of sex I've ever had before.'

'Thanks, I think.'

'Extraordinary,' he said, running his hand over her body. He stared down at her breasts and she saw his eyes travel in synch with his hand over her nipples, belly, hips and down to her dick. He fondled the softening organ he had just sucked off so skilfully and leaned down to kiss the carefully trimmed patch of pubic hair. 'I wouldn't believe it unless I had seen it for myself,' he said, his breath tickling her navel.

'No,' she said, feeling suddenly tired. She remembered her suitcase and was impatient to get it back, and she now viewed Paul as a pleasing but unhelpful distraction and something she wasn't looking forward to having to explain to Suki.

He glanced up, her hips in his hands, and smiled ruefully. 'So, uhm –'

'Hmm. Yes. So –'

He crawled up over her and kissed her on the mouth. She kissed him back reflexively. He moaned and wound his arms tight around her as his silky tongue pushed into her mouth and reminded her that, yes, OK, she should play fair and admit that it had been good. Better than good.

He spoke first. 'Look, I'm really sorry –'

Karina wanted to laugh at his predictability. 'Yeah, OK. I get it. You want me to leave before your boyfriend gets home.'

'No.' Paul frowned and caressed her cheek. His voice was too emphatically whiny for comfort. Liar liar pants on fire, she taunted, in her head.

'No, it's not that,' he said, digging himself in deeper. 'I don't know if he is coming home, and it's over. It's been over for ages. I just hadn't admitted it to myself.'

Karina blinked. 'Wow. You are so full of shit your eyes should be brown. You do know that, right?'

He laughed and kissed her, refusing to be rebuffed. 'Yeah. I kind of had a clue, actually. Look, let's get out of here. Get a room somewhere. Make a night of it. It doesn't have to be complicated. Doesn't have to be anything you don't want it to be.'

'Meaning it doesn't have to be anything you don't want it to be, natch.'

Paul sighed. 'You're as cynical as Adele when it comes to men.'

'Taught her everything she knows,' Karina said, retrieving her top and pulling up her trousers. Paul looked suddenly abashed and pulled up his own jeans. As he stood up the evening light caught his skin and silvered a little snail-trail of dried semen on his belly. He ran a hand through his hair and looked frustrated, obviously confused that his usual clichéd sweet talk wasn't having the desired effect.

'I came here for my suitcase,' Karina told him flatly, standing up and straightening her clothes.

'I know that,' he said, his hand resting on her arm. 'And we'll go get it. Right now. But hear me out, OK?'

'Ri-ght?'

He was trying on the charm again and she couldn't help messing with him, so she listened and waited for him to spin the right line.

'I think you're amazing. You're just . . . incredible. I've never been so turned on in my life. And I . . . I really need you to . . . give me more. Because that was extraordinary, and I want –' He sighed and looked heartfelt. 'I want more, Karina.'

She leaned closer and curled her hand around the nape of his neck, amused, and enjoying being back in her stride so much that she could squash down the regret long enough to run with it. 'Do you?' she asked, gently brushing her lips against his bare shoulder. 'What do you want?'

'More,' he whispered, trying to capture her mouth again. She pulled away, teasing.

'You'll have to be more specific than that,' Karina taunted. 'What is it that you want?'

He was a bright boy, this one. He caught on nicely to the game, nipping her earlobe and fanning the wet mark with a long, slow breath. 'Fuck me,' he whispered, his voice cracked.

'There,' she said softly. 'All you had to do was ask.'

12

Adele had told Jude she hated the bloody Clarendon, but he would not be swayed from his watering hole of choice. As a pub it had seen better days. As a nightspot, it could barely have seen worse. The toilets were squalid, with empty baggies and wraps, and the clientele tended to be about fifteen, sporting fake ID, strange-coloured hair, full-body fishnets, spikes and piercings that made Adele wonder what the hell their mummies and daddies were thinking. She saw them out on the streets during the day in school uniforms that stated clearly that they went to the very best private schools in the area. Little rebels without applause. Karina would have had them for breakfast. She may have faked a hell of a lot of things, but rebellion wasn't one of them.

Pissy nu-metal slacker music reverberated off the walls already, and Adele knew that as the night wore on it was going to get louder. It made her feel old, that she craved a place where she could have a drink and a quiet conversation rather than have to scream every damn word directly into someone's ear to make herself heard. She sipped a rum and coke dispassionately and wondered at what point in the evening to break the news to Jude.

He was doing that irritating thing that soon-to-be-exes always seemed to do when you'd mentally consolidated the decision to give them the chop. He was being nice. Instead of propping up the bar with his mates and expecting her to stand there with him, he had shown some consideration for the fact that she'd been on her feet all day and led the way to a table. The table might have been beer soaked and the seedy threadbare banquette littered with fag ash at even that early hour of the evening, but it was a seat. Infinitely better than standing at the bar and listening to his obnoxious friends pore over tabloid papers and offer what they clearly believed was a profound critique of the knockers on display, or the ongoing debate as to which footballer's wife was dirty enough to take it up the arse.

'I don't see how she could,' Adele had said. 'Doesn't look as though she owns a digestive system, never mind an arsehole.'

Jude's mates had looked her up and down, which was a start, she supposed. Usually they failed to even acknowledge her.

'Yes, that's right, boys,' she said sarcastically. 'I'm just jealous.'

Jude had laughed, which was good to hear, or would have been if he wasn't supposed to be being a prick so that she could dump him without a pang of conscience.

She watched the usual Clarendon wildlife roam by and wondered why it was that men and women didn't seem to like one another very much outside the bedroom. If she was in a group of men and said something funny, they responded in much the same way as they would if a monkey had suddenly sauntered up and started chatting. If she was in a group of women and a man came over to say something, they were either instantly defensive or flirtatious, depending on whether they wanted a girls' night out or they were out on the pull. The boundaries of gender seemed so rigidly drawn and ranks so tightly closed that sex, or, worse, marriage, seemed impossible and unnatural. She was sure it was a mistake that anyone should be born heterosexual.

Then again, she was sure she had seen some sex study

that said all women were potentially bisexual, while men were more rigid in their sexual orientation. So many women in the public eye were hopping in and out of the closet at their own whims these days that she couldn't be sure if it was a fad or just the way it had always been and it was just being done because it was allowed.

She couldn't talk to Jude. It was too loud. She just had to settle for sitting around drinking. He didn't dance. Karina would have done. Adele knew she would have had more fun with Karina. Old habits died hard in that respect. Karina could still entertain her, amuse her and piss her off, but she was in a class of her own. There wasn't anybody else like her, and particularly no man that could equal her in terms of being interesting, quick off the mark and a pain in the arse.

Bloody Karina. Adele wasn't holding her breath. She had a feeling that sooner or later Karina would take off again – no word of warning, no explanations. Just fuck off into the wild blue yonder without a damn thought for anyone else. Karina thought it gave her an air of mystique. It actually just annoyed and upset people, frustrating Adele further that one of her favourite people in the world had to be such a personality-disorganised fuckwit.

No, maybe something had changed. It wasn't like K to say sorry after all. Maybe at the grand old age of twenty-six, Karina had finally grown up. There was a thought. A version of K that was actually adult, instead of merely adult-rated. Adele got up off the seat. 'Another drink?' she yelled at Jude, holding up her empty glass.

He held up his pint, with a couple of inches left in it and nodded, mouthing thanks.

She made her way to the bar, glancing over at the dancefloor. A bunch of kids were pogoing and slam-dancing madly to a speed metal version of Michael Jackson's 'Smooth Criminal'. It made her feel even older when she remembered the original song, which she was sure had been released in the 80s. Most of the dancing crowd had probably been born then. Somehow it made a huge amount of difference between your date of birth being nineteen seventy something or nineteen eighty something, even if there were only a few years in it. The 70s' babies, the sprogs of prog and punk vintage years, were all turning thirty now and wittering their way beyond coolness by telling people ten years their junior that they remembered where they were when they'd heard that Kurt Cobain had blown his brains out.

The kids on the dancefloor got overexcited, and somehow their impromptu mosh pit collapsed in on itself into a heap of sprawling bodies. Adele laughed too loudly at the sight and realised she was probably more pissed than she'd thought, but the woman standing beside her at the bar laughed as well. She had a silver hoop through her nose and a bright green streak in her long blonde hair. She said something.

'Sorry?' Adele shouted over the music.

The woman leaned in closer and yelled in her ear. 'Said I reckon Michael Jackson moved a bit slicker than them lot!'

Adele laughed. 'Oh yeah,' she said, having to shout, and feeling only slightly self-conscious about screaming into a stranger's ear. 'I'm glad you said that. I was feeling old because I remembered the original.'

'About the only fucking thing people recycle, love,' said the woman. 'Crap music.' She had a hippiesh smell of patchouli and cannabis about her, and wore a black T-shirt and jeans with an unaffected air that didn't fit with the elaborately thought-out shock-tactic outfits of the usual Clarry crowd.

'You not from around here?' Adele asked.

The woman shook her head. 'Naa. Cornwall. Just passing through on the way up to Reading. It's Kate, by the way.' She held out her hand, dry and slightly rough skinned, fingers decked with cheesy-looking silver jewellery.

'Adele.'

'You from around here?'

'Yeah. Live just up the road.'

Cornwall Kate nodded appreciatively and glanced around, taking stock of her surroundings. 'Have to say, nightlife's kind of interesting. Not what I expected at all.'

Adele laughed, thinking of Karina. 'Is anything ever?'

'Sorry?' Kate cocked an ear over the music and frowned.

'I said "is anything ever quite what we expect?" '

'Amen to that,' Kate agreed, smiling. She had what looked like a small silver cap on one of her front teeth, and this gave her grin a rakish quality. Combined with the hoop in her nose and her tacky jewellery it gave her a pleasingly gypsyish, piratical look. It seemed just the job for a Cornish girl. Adele wanted to ask her if she was from Penzance.

One of Jude's friends had come in from the front bar to talk to him, and Adele wondered if this was her big chance to find something suitably big to lose him for.

'You asked me out, not your bloody mates.' She could imagine herself saying it; shrewish and irritating. It might be a valid complaint on some other woman's lips, but not her own. A valid kvetch for Jude, though. He could moan to his drinking buddies that she had expected too much of him and feel vindicated. If she said it, she'd be handing him the Get Out of Relationship Free card.

For all that it seemed silly, the dance of complaint and counter-complaint she had devised seemed funny and typical. Karina had reminded her that she could be a bitch if she wanted and it was liberating to shake off the burden of trying to be a good woman. It was no wonder that throughout history some women had lived their lives to the establishment's chagrin, living away from society and risking their lives by knowing the properties of herbs and delivering babies into the world with work-worn hands. Doing what they liked and saying what they liked, until instruments of torture were invented specifically for them – ducking stools and scold's bridles to clamp silent the nagging tongue of a woman who dared not to be contented with her meagre lot.

Cornwall Kate reinforced her present self-image; standing there at the bar with one foot on the rail with her pint at her elbow like a man, and her sea-witchy green streaked hair lit exotic colours by the dancefloor lights. Adele had liked Kate immediately. She seemed to give carte blanche to be wicked, cynical and outspoken.

Another of the men came in from the front and they appeared to be making themselves comfortable at the table. Adele paid for Jude's drink but let it stand on the bar. If he wanted it, he could come and get it. She wasn't going over there and bending over the table to put it down in front of him with that pair of leering wankers staring at her tits again.

'What's that? The chaser?' Kate asked, tapping Adele's rum and coke with the moonstone set in one of her numerous rings.

'Oh no. The pint's for him. He can get off his arse and fetch it if he wants it.'

Kate raised her eyebrows. 'Like that, is it?'

Adele screwed up her nose in thought and seesawed a hand in the air in a *comme ci, comme ca* gesture. 'It's like that. Just messing around really. Nothing serious. Even less serious would be cool, actually. I really don't know what I want from a man, but that isn't it.'

'Maybe you don't want it from a man at all,' Kate said, giving her a sly, naughty sidelong look.

'Maybe not,' Adele said, trying to coolly pretend she hadn't felt a gut-thumping thrill of shock and pleasure when she realised that Kate was flirting with her. It was like the raw feeling of terror and joy she used to feel in her late teens when she noticed a man's head turn in her direction and realised why he was staring at her. She hadn't felt it in years from a man because, when companionable banter turned to the inevitable pass, it just brought with it an amused, resigned feeling at how predictable men were. Being hit on by a woman was a surprise and, as such, a pleasing novelty. She wasn't sure that that was all it was because, while squeezing Karina's silicone, she had been kind of curious to see what her breasts looked like without the bra, and to pinch her nipples to see if they stiffened. Maybe it was just the natural curiosity that all women felt about boob jobs; even the ones, like herself, who swore they'd never do that to themselves were strangely, morbidly fascinated by what tits felt like and how they behaved when they'd been plumped up and artificially enhanced under the surgeon's knife.

She felt like she ought to say something. In a strange way, she supposed she had just been given a compliment. 'I never really thought about it,' Adele said vaguely. 'One of those things, I suppose.'

'One of those things?'

'One of those things you don't think about, you know?'

Kate nodded and looked her up and down. 'Yeah. You're straight.'

'I might not be,' Adele said. 'I don't know. I've never thought about it.'

'Then you're definitely not gay.' Kate gulped her pint.

'Because, if you're gay, you don't think about much else, especially when you're hitting puberty. Christ, honey, the fucking hormones. And the constant telling yourself you're going through a phase and you'll grow out of it.'

'I suppose.' Adele shrugged. 'But don't you think women are more open to trying new stuff than men?'

Kate grinned, flashing a sliver of silver. 'I think women are more open to following fashion.'

'Fashion?'

'It's the thing to do, innit? Dilettante dykes. Lipstick lesbians. Half of them are doing it to get more men, because men love that. Promise of a little girl-on-girl action in the bedroom and they'd run naked through a nettle patch to get some. Sad gits.'

'Yeah, but that's crap.' Adele leaned in close and yelled. 'That's not about women defining their own sexuality; that's women being exactly what men want them to be.'

'Amen, sister,' Kate said, holding up her glass. They clinked glasses.

The barmaid handed a couple of kids their drinks – two minuscule plastic pots the size of hospital sample vials. They were filled with clear liquid and covered with blue plastic lids. Adele wanted to ask what they were, but felt stupid asking sixteen-year-olds what they were drinking. She asked the barmaid instead.

'Schnapps,' the barmaid yelled, looking rushed and harassed.

'I'll take two, please ... no, four.'

The tiny drinks were placed on the bar. She paid and shifted two over to Kate.

'Now *that's* a chaser,' Kate said. 'Thanks. What's that in aid of?'

'In aid of getting drunker.' Adele took the lid off one of the drinks. It spilled on her fingers and she licked it up. It smelled like nail-polish remover and synthetic vanilla, and tasted like ice cream.

'Down in one?' Kate asked, drink poised.

'Down in one.'

They tossed them down. The stuff burned like tequila but tasted better. After the second, Adele felt like ordering more, but Kate insisted on buying the next ones. After downing four, the effect was powerful and seemed to make her thirstier. She started on Jude's pint, which had been sat sweating on the bar. He hadn't moved. He was talking to his friends, who were now glancing in her direction. Talking about her. Through a vanilla-alcohol haze, she watched him and his friends rise from the table and come to the bar.

'All right?' Jude said, laying a proprietal hand on her bottom. One of his mates said something to Kate.

'Forget it,' said Kate. 'I'm gay.'

Jude's friend backed up, holding his hands up as though he was about to be shot. 'Yeah, all right, love. Don't mean I can't buy you a drink, does it? I'm a lesbian too, actually.'

Adele laughed at Kate's raised eyebrows and wry expression. 'You were saying?' she said.

'Yep.' Kate sighed so hard she nearly blew the contents out of the ashtray.

'What's up?' Jude asked.

'I *was* having a good time,' said Adele, emboldened by the booze.

The arsehole friends cheered. 'Wahey! Hang on in there, Jules. Might get yourself some girlie action.'

Adele choked on her pint. '*Girlie action?*' she gasped, disgusted and amused by the phrase.

Kate laughed. 'Of course. Lesbians only exist to titillate men. I don't mean to be rude, but piss off.'

Jude looked outraged. Adele couldn't seem to stop laughing.

'What the fuck is going on, Adele?' he demanded, looking suddenly even younger; a petulant schoolboy.

She really couldn't stop laughing. It was ridiculous. 'Oh, God,' she said. 'Look, Jude, I'm sorry, but you know as well as I do that this isn't working –'

'Fine,' he snapped, cutting her off. He turned on his heel and walked out, the dogboy mates bringing up the rear.

'Whoops.' Kate pulled a face.

'S'all right. I've been meaning to do that for ages. Sick of the stubble rash on the inside of my thighs.'

Kate howled with laughter. 'OK, I take it back. You could be gayer than you thought.'

Sarah would just shit when he told her about this or, rather, when he didn't. Paul was smug in his knowledge of what was going on. Uncle Edward's second wife's transsexual boyfriend/girlfriend/whatever showing up here couldn't possibly be coincidence, not after Sarah had harped so long and loud on Paul's fantasies. The little bitch was setting Paul up for a tale of sexual exploits to make her mouth and her twat water. Paul had already made his mind up. Sarah was getting nothing, except a further demand for that long, outstanding divorce. He was sick of her machinations and he had pieced together what she was up to. She was screwing step-aunt Suki.

He doubted Suki was in the habit of having affairs with pre-op transsexuals and Karina was the 'she-male from Bangkok' in question. Typical of Sarah to generalise in order to make things sound more sensational. Karina was originally from Brighton. Paul listened to her futzing around in the hotel bathroom and idly wondered if she had taught herself to pee sitting down for appearance's sake.

Talk about hoisting Sarah with her own petard. It was clear to Paul that Sarah had steered Karina his way in order to make him cheat on Ieuan, and provide him with the kind of loveless sexual encounter that Paul would have no moral qualms about spinning into a tale for her entertainment.

That was what made the victory so much more satisfying. He hadn't cheated. In his own mind he knew it was unsalvageable and over with Ieuan; he knew whose photographs were in Karina's suitcase and he had the perfect ace up his sleeve to end the game with Sarah once and for all. And then there was Karina – his ultimate fantasy made flesh. She was simply devastating. He couldn't believe she had taken up his sleazy invitation to fuck in a hotel – an invitation largely born of practicality, since Karina was sleeping on Adele's tiny couch and Paul's own bed was a wrack and ruin of plaster, brick dust and ancient soot. Besides, it had been a complete joy driving out here. Karina had shown no contrition about what they had just done and bounced, smoked and flirted throughout the drive down the winding roads. It had been a beautiful evening, the sun dipping to a hazy, insect-buzzing golden glow that gilded hedgerows frilly with Queen Anne's Lace, and promised a sultry night to come; one of those summer nights where the prospect of excitement and transgressions hung in the air like a perfume. He was doing exactly what he shouldn't and it felt good.

The promise of further pleasure was there in Karina's sparkling black eyes, in the arch of her high, wide cheekbones, the tight tanned strip of flesh exposed at her waist. Paul was already fixated on the texture and taste of her fine, coppery skin, her pomegranate-round breasts and the ultimate surprise – the slender graceful cock that rose up at the juncture of her thighs. While caressing her he had wondered what she had been like as a man – a wispy-boned boy-man who would never look much older than late adolescence. He imagined her chest as it might have been before, flat, hairless, with delicate little nipples.

Her hands had strayed in the car, sneaking to his fly and attempting to gain entry. Paul had laughed it off and said no, that he couldn't drive and come at the same time, but secretly it was because he knew his sexual stamina was limited now. He wasn't twenty any more. Those five-times-a-night events were fifteen or more years behind him.

He didn't know how old she was. If she had reached her sexual peak at nineteen or twenty, then it didn't show. Her whole body was in defiance of nature's rules, and maybe even the set-in-stone rules of that loathsome old bastard Father Time himself. Paul couldn't place an age on her face or her body, any more than he could nail down her gender.

They had rushed up the stairs giggling like children and didn't pause to investigate the hotel room – too busy pulling each other's clothes off between kisses. Topless, she looked all woman, until he got down on his knees to pull down her trousers and tight panties. Then he was confronted by the male part of her. Dusty-soled little-boy feet made all the more piquant by sluttishly chipped blue toenail polish. Slender legs and barely-there hips. Then that beautiful, beautiful dick. It was the most perfect cock he had ever seen, slim and dusky rose-coloured, delectable as the raspberry shade of its rounded tip. He had feasted on it gluttonously, made greedier by the rich scent of her pubic hair and the velvet texture of the shaven balls that hung between her girlish thighs like a miracle. Hermaphroditus.

He had been on his back in seconds – too hungry to wait to do it with any degree of ceremony. The moment his bare arse had hit the sheets of that hired bed he had arched his back and flung his heels in the air like the slut he was, pleading with her to fuck him. He had always found hotels exciting anyway. It was somehow more erotic to fuck in a bed that wasn't your own, where the maid would inevitably know what had gone on the next morning when she changed the sheets. The hairs and stains would tell the full story – territory marked and leaving behind a weird animal tang of pleasure in knowing that a stranger knew you'd been there and fucked there.

He was nearly incoherent when he lay back and felt her delicate, lubed fingers probe his arse. When she had lined it up and pushed inside him, she had bit her lip, scrunched her eyes shut and let out a very boyish growl of 'oh, fuck, yeah' and Paul had been sure that in itself would send him over the edge. Instead he had angled his hips and invited her in deeper. She screwed as though it had been an age since she had done it last and, afterwards, when she lay blowing cigarette smoke across his nipples and dot-to-dotting the freckles on his body with her index finger, she admitted it could have been a matter of years since she had last had a man like that.

'The supposedly straight guys treat me like a pair of tits, a mouth and an arsehole; the gay ones say they're not into women, and the women insist they're not gay because I still have a dick. I can't fucking win.'

'You never can if you can't be pigeonholed and tidily labelled,' Paul said, sympathising.

'Nope. Can anyone? It's like Adele – we're neither of us quite right. I think she'd rather be a man: little Ms Macho. To be expected, I suppose. She *is* a fire dragon.'

'A what?' Paul asked, laughing.

Karina put out her cigarette and snuggled up, her body warm and smooth under the sheets. 'A fire dragon.

Chinese astrology. You have a zodiac animal and an element – earth, water, metal, fire or wood – determined by the year of your birth. She was born in the year of the dragon and that year's element was fire. I'm fire too, but I'm year of the snake.'

'What am I then?'

'When's your birthday?'

'December. Twenty-second. I'm on the cusp. Sagittarius and Capricorn.'

'Naa. That's western. Besides, Chinese New Year is in February. What year?'

'Year? Oh, sixty-six.'

Karina raised her eyebrows. 'You're a horse.'

'Thank you. I've had no complaints.'

She laughed. 'Yeah, yeah, yeah ... it has nothing to do with your wang. More to do with your yang.'

'Yang?'

'And yin. Fucking hell – sixty-six: that makes you a fire horse. Yow ... you're a handful.'

Paul peered under the sheets. 'Huh. One minute I'm a horse, the next I'm a handful. They must have a problem with the heating in here.'

She had rolled her eyes at the bad joke and gone down to demonstrate that he was more than a mouthful. Her mouth was silky and skilful, her fingers encircling the base of his cock and squeezing it to even greater hardness as her lips moved and her tongue lapped over him. He came slowly, the shocks muted by his previous explosive climax, and slid into a doze afterwards. When he woke up it was dark and she was gone, doing something in the bathroom.

She was lurking in the bathroom, and Paul realised that she was calling someone in there, speaking in hushed tones so as not to be heard. He could only make out fragments of the conversation, scattered words.

'Darling ... please ... must ... can't ... need ...'

She was speaking to her fucking lover. While he was in here waiting for her to come back to bed. Paul's satisfaction at being right again was tainted with the knowledge that he was being made a fool of. She was trouble. He'd had it nailed from the start. The problem with the kind of girl who had no problems about fucking you on the kitchen floor, sneaking off to hotels and being kind enough not to mention that you were supposed to be attached was that, if they'd do it all behind one person's back, they'd do it behind yours as well.

Exasperated, he lit a cigarette, contrary to hotel rules which banned smoking in bed. He felt stupid, quivering on the cusp of the inevitable mid-life crisis, if he hadn't already been there, done that, bought the T-shirt. Maybe he had fucked it up. He would miss Ieuan, who had at least had the virtue of loving him. Paul supposed that it was poetic justice that he should be here feeling tortured because he heard Karina calling some other lover. He deserved this. It didn't make it any better though, or wash the bad taste out of his mouth.

Karina turned off the bathroom light and looked as though she was trying to sneak into bed, hoping that he was asleep. In the orangey light from the floodlit garden without, Paul could make out her face, nose screwed up against the unexpected smell of smoke.

He switched on the bedside lamp. Karina darted under the covers beside him and looked covetously at his cigarette.

'You OK?' he asked, handing her a cigarette. She sat up and lit up, breasts bare and her hair swinging forwards over her cheek in a perfect black curtain, streaked with threads of scarlet. She looked exotic, duplicitous – utterly feminine.

'Yeah. Why wouldn't I be?' she said defensively. She

sounded as though she was making an effort to lighten her voice.

'Just asking.'

'I'm fine.'

Karina rolled over to lie on her stomach. She seemed tetchy, restless and guilty, as well she might be, but Paul wasn't going to mention it. Ultimately it was her business and, if he was just a one-night stand, then that made it even and less complicated. He had no intention of leaping headlong into another relationship. It had only been a matter of hours since the last one imploded. He was sure he was too old for break-ups, one-night stands, ex-wives and chasing sexual fantasies. The only thing most of his contemporaries chased were promotions and toddling children who were in the habit of tearing off on rubbery little legs. He thought it was bullshit that only women were supposed to hear the chimes of the biological clock. Paul was sure he could hear it bonging like Big Ben whenever he ran into an old schoolmate and they produced flourishes of baby pictures from their wallets, a deck of Happy Families. He could never decide if he was the lucky one or the male-menopausal wanker.

He glanced down at Karina, her shoulders cinnamon gold in the light from the bedside lamp. Given the choice between changing nappies or still exploring his sexuality with someone like Karina, he probably was the lucky one. He put out his cigarette and peeled the duvet away from her spine. Her arse was rounded, sweet and glossy. She sighed, perched her cigarette on the edge of the ashtray and swept her hair off the back of her neck. The nape of her neck was smooth, pretty, decorated with stray strands of straight black hair. Paul stroked it, leaned over and kissed it, his hand opening over the firm curve of her bottom.

'You know, I never got that until just now . . .'

'Got what?' Karina asked indifferently.

'The nape of the neck thing. In Japan. They have this fetish for the nape of a woman's neck. I didn't realise how sexy it was until now.'

She sniffed. 'I'm *Chinese* – if it makes any fucking difference whatsoever.'

'Sorry. Sorry.' He kissed, consoled. 'I'm an idiot.'

Karina sighed, hiding her face under her hair. 'No, you're not. I'm just sick of hearing it. The geisha thing. I've had it all my life. Other people's fantasies. Other cultures' traditions.'

'Yeah…' Paul wanted to pull away, but he was aware that would only show his guilt at committing the same crime she was accusing previous lovers of.

She pushed back her hair and retrieved her smoke. 'I used to bullshit people about Kyoto and Gion and cherry blossoms and blah blah blah. Lies, crap and bollocks. All of it. I figured if they were stupid enough not to know the difference between China and Japan they were fair game. I've never been to Kyoto. I've never been to fucking Beijing. The furthest east I've ever been is Bangkok, and even then I was too stoned to fucking remember half of it.'

She sounded depressed and resentful, and he kissed her between her shoulder blades, eager to offer some reassurance. She just blew out smoke and frowned.

'It was like too much trouble to explain. The truth, I mean,' she continued. 'So it was easier to let people believe I was what they wanted me to be. That seemed like the kindest thing to do.'

'Kind to them. Not to you.'

'No.' Karina sighed heavily. 'No. Because now I have absolutely no fucking idea who I am.'

13

'Maybe it's better if I get out here,' Karina said, peering up the street.

Paul chewed his lip and stared through the windscreen before giving an obviously considered reply. 'Only if you want to,' he said, meaning that he wanted her to.

'It's fine,' said Karina. 'I'm used to it.' Jesus, what a crappy thing to be used to – the sneaking around, avoiding jealous wives and husbands. She realised she'd been doing that all her life and it made her feel slightly grubby and depressed. Not any more, she told herself. Not when Suki arrived. Then it was going to be for real. Commitment. Children. And all at once. She excused herself over Paul; he was a final fling, like an alcoholic's last binge before booking into detox.

'Are you sure?' Paul asked.

'Yep. Sure.' She opened the car door and debated whether to kiss him or not. Fuck it, she thought. By the end of the day she hoped to be beyond reproach. She leaned over and kissed him good and hard and deep. Caught by surprise, he let out a startled little moan, an erotic reminder of the way he broke off from kisses to catch his breath while he was being fucked, but his tongue pushed eagerly into her mouth all the same. A few early morning tourists were already walking up and down the street and could clearly see them kissing, as blatant as he wanted to be secretive. Paul broke the kiss, frowning and licking his lips.

'Not here, for God's sake.'

She shrugged, pulled her suitcase from under her feet and put a foot on the pavement. 'Whatever. I'm used to that too. It's been a pleasure. Bye.'

She carried on up the street, holding her head up as he passed her in his car. OK, so maybe she was trading the old life in for something better, because this didn't help. Last night he'd had his tongue up her arse; this morning he wouldn't even stick it in her mouth because people were watching. 'Story of my fucking life,' Karina muttered, and punched up the hard-earned number on her phone.

It rang a few times, and then Suki's voice, sounding flustered and hurried. 'Oh, God, darling, can't talk for long. I'm driving – it's illegal, isn't it?'

'I'm not sure,' Karina said. 'Where are you?'

'I'm stuck at the damn Devil's Punchbowl. Be about an hour, hour and half ... wait.' Suki sighed and could be heard saying in her strained, harassed Mummy voice, 'No, darling, we're not nearly there yet.'

'I'll let you go then,' said Karina.

'Yes, yes,' Suki muttered abstractedly. 'Well, you should have had one before we left, shouldn't you? Darling, I have to go. Hannah needs a pee ... oh dammit ... not a pee? I'll call you as soon as we arrive, OK?'

'OK,' Karina said, and decided she should say something else. Try it on for size. 'I lo–'

She was cut off as Suki switched off her phone. And what the fuck was with the 'we'? The girls as well? 'Ease me into it slowly, why don't you?' Karina grumbled at the silent telephone, before putting it back into her pocket and trudging up the hill towards Shipworths.

The very worst thing was presenting herself at the front door and having to ask to be let in. Karina figured she may as well have tattooed GUILTY in block letters across her forehead for all the good any denials were going to do her.

When she knocked on the door of the flat, Adele opened it like a shotgun, glanced blearily at her with unfocused eyes for a second, and then bolted to the bathroom. Karina stood there, puzzled for a moment, until the sound of vomiting reached her ears. She knew Adele probably wasn't going to be delighted to see her, but that was kind of an extreme reaction.

Hoping to rack up some better karma after last night, Karina poured a glass of water and took it into the bathroom where Adele was hunched over the toilet, retching and spitting.

'You OK?'

Adele sniffed and held her hair back, gulping down another heave. 'Uh ... duh.'

'Yeah. Fair point. What's up? Oh God, you're not pregnant, are you?'

Adele peered up from the toilet and ripped off a stream of toilet paper. She blew her nose and pulled a face. 'Ugh. No. Chance would be a fine thing. Just drank too much. Way too much.'

'Oops.' Karina handed her the water.

'Thanks.' Adele flushed the toilet and leaned against the bathroom wall. She looked ashen, her skin stretched taut over the bones of her face and her eyes too large and shadowed from lack of sleep. Perversely, it gave her the fashionably wasted look of a catwalk model. She gulped the water too fast and Karina thought that she was probably still pissed.

'Where have you been?' Adele asked.

'Out,' Karina said, unconsciously regressing to a teenager. 'What the hell happened to you? You didn't drink yourself into a stupor over Jude, did you?'

Adele shook her head. 'Nope. I met this woman. Kate from Cornwall. Cornwall Kate. Got absolutely fucking plastered.' She grinned. Yep. Definitely still drunk. Her hair looked plastered too. Karina noticed dust in it from where Adele had obviously rolled, semi-conscious and oblivious, into her bed. The bed had been covered with a thin dusting of plaster that had back-drafted up out of the chimney when it had caved in. Adele hadn't mentioned that yet. Probably too drunk to notice. When Adele was really hammered she was completely and utterly single-minded about getting into her bed and sleeping it off.

'What about Jude?'

'Gone,' Adele said, hiccupping. 'Doesn't like lesbians who won't let him watch.' She stood up unsteadily and leaned on the sink, reaching for her toothbrush.

Karina rubbed her back and now wondered what the fuck she had wrought here. The old Adele was back, talking crap and raising hell, but Karina didn't especially want to have to be the sensible, grounded one. She'd spent the entire night misguidedly and stupidly fucking Paul in some strange Farewell to Dick ritual she had dreamed up before meeting up with Suki and hopefully embarking on a lifetime of blissful lesbianism. And now Adele was pissed as a fart and babbling about being gay, or something. The urge to take off was even stronger than before. Karina had come here looking for closure and stability – not even more confusion that she'd have to unravel in London, Bangkok, Glastonbury or wherever she happened to be at the time.

Maybe it was just her. Never mind Madam Butterfly. Madam Butterfly and Tornado. A walking, talking, breathing exposition of Chaos Theory.

'You're not a lesbian,' Karina said. 'I've never met anyone straighter.'

'Yeah, and I'd never met anyone *gayer* and look what

happened there,' Adele said, turning to look Karina up and down. 'You just never know, K. Nothing is ever what it seems.'

'Yeah, well. There is that,' Karina conceded.

'There you go then. I might be gay. Just don't know it – social conditioning.'

Karina sighed. 'Trust me. If you're gay, you know it.'

'How?'

'Well, it's not like "tonight, Matthew, I'm going to be a lesbian".'

Adele frowned and spat out toothpaste. 'Right. The same way you don't go "tonight, Matthew, I'm going to be a woman"?'

'That isn't fair,' said Karina. 'And no, you don't figure that kind of shit overnight.'

'Gathered that,' Adele said, walking out of the bathroom into her bedroom. Karina waited in the bathroom doorway for the shit to hit the fan.

'What the fuck?'

'It caved in,' Karina said unhelpfully. She peered in the bedroom door and saw Adele staring at the fireplace with her hands in her hair and a resigned, angry look on her face.

'Well, duh. I can see that. What the hell happened?'

'It's kind of my fault.'

'Now why doesn't that surprise me?'

'I just propped a suitcase in there!' Karina said, on the defensive. 'I didn't know it was that unstable.'

Adele peered down into the fireplace. 'You got that right. The whole bottom's dropped out. Fuck. It must have fallen down into Paul's.'

'Yeah. He returned the case.' Karina sounded more glib than she meant to, and prayed that she wouldn't be caught out. There wasn't a problem per se but, if Adele found out what Karina had done with Paul, she'd be disappointed, annoyed and, worse, vindicated in her belief that Karina couldn't and wouldn't change.

'Screw that,' Adele said. 'What about my fucking fireplace? I only moved in a week ago!' She groaned. 'Shit – I can't handle this now. I've got a lousy hangover, loads of work to do, crap in boxes and now this. What did Paul say?'

'About what?'

Adele stared at her. 'About selective foreign policy in sixteenth-century England. What do you think? About the fucking chimney.'

'Oh . . . he . . . um . . . well, he wasn't pleased.'

'You don't say?'

Karina sighed. 'You know what? You really shouldn't drink; I can't quite believe it, but you're actually more sarcastic with a hangover.'

'If you paid attention, you'd find the sarcasm is about the only way I can get a straight answer out of you.'

'Sarcasm isn't a good way to get a straight answer out of anyone, Adele. It only makes people angry and defensive.'

'Where the hell did you get that psychobabble from? Nothing makes people more defensive and pissed off as taking off without a word or disappearing for the entire night.'

'Oh fuck off! You didn't even know I was gone. You were so pissed you didn't even notice half the chimney in your bloody bedroom had fallen through the fucking floor!'

'Right – so I'm supposed to pay close and undivided attention to everything in order to spot the latest mess you've made? So what's new?'

'It was an accident!' Karina yelled.

'Everything is with you.' Adele shook her head and ran her finger through the dust clinging to the mantelpiece.

She sighed heavily enough to blow away the dust and raked back her hair. 'This is ridiculous,' she muttered.

'What is?' Karina asked, wrapping her arms around herself.

'This whole thing.'

'What do you mean?'

'It's nuts,' Adele said. 'I mean, what are you doing here?'

Karina shrugged, offended that that should even be a question. 'I came here to see you – and you weren't easy to find.'

'Why?'

'You'd moved and your old landlord wasn't very helpful.'

'No, I mean, why did you come to see me?'

'Because,' Karina said. 'I just ... I don't know. You deserved that much.'

Adele stared at the mantelpiece. 'Yeah. I did. But maybe we should realise it's never going to be the way it was.'

'No.' Karina had a sinking feeling in her gut, made worse by the impatient knowledge that she didn't have time for another psychodrama. She wished she had told Adele about Suki, but it had been too raw to tell, and now she didn't have time to spill it all out. She should have told Adele; to have that bulwark of support behind her now that Suki was responding to her telephone call and coming down to the coast.

'This is really difficult,' she said. 'But I have to be somewhere today.'

'Yeah, well so do I,' Adele said. 'Work. You know?'

'I get it.' Karina sniffed. 'Holding your proletarian conscience over me already?'

Adele shook her head. 'Christ, don't you start again.'

'You're the one making digs about work, which is rich considering you've barely handed in your own P45.'

'I'm sorry,' said Adele. 'I just don't feel too well. And I really didn't need a caved-in chimney on top of everything else. When are you going out?'

'About an hour or so. Waiting on a phone call.'

Adele nodded, still chilly. 'OK. I'll be here all day – either here or downstairs – if you need the key. I'm gonna go and get showered.'

'OK.'

She stood in the hallway, not knowing what to do with herself, and listened to the heaving, juddering noises of the plumbing as Adele turned on the shower. She knew she should have said something and come clean about the last year of her life. Maybe keeping secrets from your closest friends was a bad habit that took too much work to break, work that Karina had never had the stomach for.

She thought it was the plumbing at first. It knocked and rattled loud enough for someone to imagine that an earthquake was taking place. As the sound grew louder she realised that it was the front door. It was Paul, looking furtive and hunted.

'Hi,' he said breathlessly.

'What?'

'Hi. You know? Hello? Good morning?'

'Yes,' Karina said. 'What?'

He swallowed and licked his lips, still looking a little bedrumpled from the sex last night. 'Well . . . I just . . . I'm sorry. About before. Are you all right?'

'I'll live,' said Karina, not making any move to let him in. 'Like I said, used to it.'

'Yes, well.' He coughed and she realised that this was a shitty conversation to be having anywhere, but especially with Adele in the bathroom nearby. Mindful of previous mistakes for once, Karina took off her shoe and wedged it in the front door before stepping out onto the landing. It was echoey on the stairs and she was careful to whisper.

'It doesn't matter. It's fine.'

'It does matter. I needed to tell you: it's not you –'

'I know, I know,' she hissed impatiently. 'It's not you, it's me. Save it, sweetie. Do you think I haven't heard it a million times before?'

Paul shook his head, full lips thinning in frustration. 'Karina, please. It really is me. I just – I had absolutely no idea where I stood with Ieuan.'

'And you do now?' she asked archly, not caring.

'Yes. He's fucking left me.'

'My heart bleeds.'

'So does mine. The little shit's only gone and absconded with my David Gray CDs.'

Karina smothered a grin. 'That's ... not-very-gay of him.'

'I know. He doesn't even like bloody David Gray. To add insult to injury he left me with his fucking ABBA.'

'It doesn't change anything,' Karina said, determined not to be sidetracked. She didn't know how much of this she had time for.

'I know,' said Paul, nodding, a dark curl falling across his unshaven cheek. There were shadows under his eyes and his lips looked very smooth from a long night filled with kissing. It could have changed something, Karina thought, if she let it. She could call Suki and tell her to go home, that she wasn't ready, it wasn't appropriate in light of the court case. And all these fears would just go. Fears of fidelity, failure, kids. She could ditch everything and go back to the kind of comfortable, sometime-never, easy-going nothing she was good at.

'I know you have something lined up,' Paul continued. 'I overheard you talking to someone in the bathroom last night.'

'Oh,' Karina said dumbly, caught out in her duplicity. 'Um, yeah. Kind of.'

'Right. It's fine. Last night was fun.'

'Yeah. We're both adults, after all.' She met his eyes awkwardly. The skin of his heavy eyelids was only just beginning to crease slightly with age and the shade of his eyes was beautiful and surprising. In this light she could see gold flecks that she hadn't spotted last night, when his eyes had been so dark with dim light and lust that they appeared the colour of Chinese jade. His eyelashes were startlingly black and had brushed against her skin where he kissed – her cheek, shoulder, the base of her spine.

'Very much consenting too,' he said, with a wry, slight lift of one eyebrow and a knowing twist curling the corners of his impossibly pretty mouth. She listened to the plumbing creak and the distant spatter of Adele's shower and felt the surge of excitement rise in her gut like the sensation of a slowly ascending roller coaster. Yeah, she had a problem, hence the detox, but wasn't the first step of recovery admitting that you had a problem?

'Uh huh.' She nodded and stared into his eyes. That curl of hair was bothering her. She wanted to push it away, along with his clothes. Have him stark naked on the stairs where they could have been caught *in flagrante delicto*, humping and grinding like animals. His gaze was a little vacant and greedy, the lines of his mouth softening to kiss so that his already sensual lips looked as irresistible as plump, ripe berries – something red and shiny that woke the childish desire to want to put it in your mouth. She reached out and brushed back his hair.

His head tilted and their lips bumped. She knew she

shouldn't be doing this, but she also knew how his lips burst open in heartfelt gasps against her skin. She had felt his tongue lap the sweat from between her breasts as she straddled him; felt it trace the tendons on the sole of her foot and fill the hollow behind the bone in her ankle. It had been so good to have a lover so unashamedly dirty and still be able to surprise him. He moaned as she opened her mouth and she pushed her tongue eagerly into the kiss. Such a good kisser – soft, rain-wet and succulent. His hands slid around her waist and his arse hit the wall as he stumbled backwards. She listened out for the sound of the shower, thinking that this was the descent, the freefall of the roller coaster. Paul shivered, stiff against her, squeezing her arse with both hands. Had to stop – had to. With a fierce effort of will, she pulled away, prised his hands off.

'Sorry,' she said, looking at the floor.

'No, my fault. Sorry.'

'No. It's mine. I shouldn't –'

Paul sighed. 'Look, can I give you my number?' He responded immediately to the shake of her head and jumped in. 'You don't have to call. I'd just like you to have it. If you . . . need anything.'

She programmed in the number he gave her to keep him happy, meaning to erase it from her phone later. It was too much like temptation.

'Whatever you're doing, good luck,' Paul said uncomfortably. He sounded very young, a schoolboy despite his years. 'But, if things don't go to plan, I hope you'd give me a call.'

'Yeah.' Karina nodded, staring down at the phone in her hand. 'Thanks.'

'I'd better go.'

'Yep.'

She watched over the edge of the banister as he went downstairs. He didn't look up. Self-control sucked.

Karina stared down the length of the crowded beach, packed with the candy stripes of deckchairs, shrill with the seagull screams of children and smelling of hot sand and hot sun lotion cooking on nearly naked bodies. How she was supposed to find one woman and two children in this mass of women and kids she didn't know, and was annoyed with Suki for not wanting to meet at the seaside hotel she had booked into an hour ago. The beach had probably been the girls' idea and Suki had caved in to their pressure.

She took off her shoes and stepped carefully across the sand, ducking dive-bombing kids and tiptoeing between girls who lay as if dead on beach towels, their eyes covered with dark glasses, their faces impassive and their pale English tits turning perceptibly pink despite the sunscreen. Karina winced in sympathy, wondering why they did it when sunburned nipples were so painful. Too many damn people. Where the fuck was Suki?

'Darling!'

She followed the yell to the waving figure and picked her way between bodies to the blanket where Suki was standing. Suki had had all her hair cut off. It was snipped into a pixyish crop that Karina hated on sight, thinking it made her face look hard with her enormous eyes masked with Chanel sunglasses. She wore a blue bikini top and Gucci jeans and looked older for it – skinny and underdressed in an unfetching, footballer's wife kind of way.

'Darling, it's so wonderful to see you!' Suki crooned and (Karina could scarcely believe it) airkissed.

'Are you all right?' Karina asked, holding onto Suki's

upper arms. They felt too soft and thin, and Karina worried that Suki had been using booze as a substitute for food again. It made her heart skip a beat to think of Suki behind the wheel of a car with her daughters in the back.

'I'm fine, darling. Never better. Well, except for Edward. The bastard is going to take me for every penny, you know – but I shall be fine. It's this nostalgia thing: I had a word with my old record company and some girlie from a soap – not *EastEnders*, one of the ones on Channel 4 – well, she wants to do a cover version of my song and that means royalties for me. Awful thing though, you should see her. All bleached blonde hair and so much fake tan she's practically orange, but the earnings will be enough to keep me afloat, I think. Hate to think of it, of course – money is so boring. Lucky for me I've still got pots in my own account – old royalties, you know – amazing to think it mounts up like that, and Sarah's been absolutely super about deferring my legal expenses –'

'Yeah, I'm fine. Thanks for asking,' Karina interrupted sarcastically, setting down her suitcases.

Suki pouted, somehow managing to be charming even in the depths of self-absorption. Her lips were covered in a frosted pale-pink gloss the colour of a Barbie ballgown. It looked like it should taste of marshmallow. 'Oh, don't be like that. I've come all this way to see you,' she said. 'The girls have been absolute bears as well – foul moods.'

'Where are they?' asked Karina, sitting down and glancing into the supermarket carrier bag that contained sugary treats and crisps designed to placate the girls. An orange plastic spade and blue sandcastle mould shaped like a tortoise were discarded at the edge of the beach-mat, maybe dumped there in petulance at being a lousy substitute for a real tortoise and pet ponies, a swimming pool and all the other luxuries they were accustomed to.

'Over there.' Suki pointed to where Hannah, in a red bathing suit, was being instructed to dig in the sand by her elder sister, who stood brandishing a spade in an unpleasant echo of her father with his shooting stick. Elisa looked almost unrecognisable, appearing to have shot up in the past couple of weeks, and the small bumps that might have been the beginnings of breasts under her pink bikini looked disconcerting and incongruous on her gangly, little body. Surely she was only nine, nearly ten? Karina felt old just looking at her.

'I'm glad you came,' Karina said sincerely, wanting to ask what was going to happen now. 'And I'm glad you decided to get rid of *him*.'

'Yes.' Suki peered out to sea. 'So am I. It's wonderfully exciting, actually. This could be my big chance to make a comeback. Show the world I'm not just another blonde *avec* tits and arse.'

Karina grinned. 'Su, that's fantastic! I *told* you. Didn't I tell you that you had a beautiful voice?'

Suki squeezed her wrist and smiled. 'Yes, darling. You did. Bless you for that. This has all completely opened my eyes. I've been speaking to the guys at the record company and it's all changed – like a revolution. About seventy per cent of their best-selling artists are female singer-songwriters and the PR people are raving. They think this entire unholy mess can be turned to my advantage – women don't feel so threatened by women who have a broken marriage behind them and children, and apparently there are simply tons of lesbian artists selling nowadays. It's not a big deal any more.'

Karina struggled to keep pace. 'What . . . I don't . . . you mean you're *out*?'

Suki bit her lip and looked evasive. 'Well, not yet. It's all a matter of judging the right time. I'm trying not to let it come out in the court case.'

'I'm co-respondent in the court case,' Karina said. 'And it might have escaped your attention, but having me as a co-respondent makes you look ... kinda gay.'

'Yes, but darling –' Suki sighed. 'You have a *penis*.'

Karina tried and failed to close her mouth.

'Well, you do, don't you?' Suki prompted. 'Unless you've done something drastic in the past fortnight?'

'No, I bloody well haven't!' Karina shrieked, more offended than she had ever been in years of offensive remarks. 'I'm a fucking woman!'

'But you're –'

'Hung?' Karina pouted. 'Thank you for noticing, baby. I've lived with this gender for seven fucking years. I think that makes me qualified.'

'Genetically,' Suki said.

'Genetically I'm male and in the wrong frigging body.'

'Yes, but with you I'm not really a lesbian, am I?' Suki explained, with playground patience that made Karina fume. 'Not while you're still ... you know.'

'You didn't know when you met me!'

'No. I thought you were a girl.'

'*Yes*,' Karina snapped, patronising right back. 'So doesn't that make you a teensy bit *gay*?'

'Not technically.'

'You weren't attracted to me as a *man*, were you?' Karina said. 'If I'd walked into your house in a suit and tie and you'd jumped on me, then, yeah, I'd say that was pretty heterosexual.'

'Yes but –'

'I was wearing a fucking evening gown and to all effects and purposes, and for all you knew, I was a woman.'

'Yes, I know that.' Suki sighed. 'I do know that. That's why I realised I liked girls too. Because of you. But it's not really gay, is it, because you're not ... well ... it's not really lesbian.'

'So how can you be a lesbian if I'm not the real deal?' Karina demanded. 'You can't just slap a label on yourself because the PR people think you'd make a cool gay single-parent icon. Not if it's not *true*.'

'Well, it is true,' Suki said petulantly.

Karina snorted. 'Yeah right. Eaten any good pussy recently, k.d. lang?'

Suki hid behind her sunglasses and licked her upper lip. She squirmed and Karina noticed the symptoms of betrayal. She didn't know why she hadn't seen it before. Suki had been sleeping with someone else. A woman. A woman with a cunt.

'You fucking cow,' Karina said slowly.

'I didn't do it intentionally. You know how things just happen.'

'Yeah,' said Karina, wondering if now was a good time to mention that she had spent the previous night shagging a beautiful man up the arse. She decided not to. She preferred Suki's guilt untainted with any sense of vindication. Suki didn't deserve to be handed an advantage on a platter. 'Shit happens. And you want me to stand up in a Court of Law and help you out with your divorce?'

'Nothing's going on. It was just the once, I swear. We were in her office.'

Karina gawped. 'Oh, this just gets better.'

'Well, how was I supposed to know if I was *really* a lesbian?' Suki wailed. 'I'm so confused.'

'Join the club, darling,' Karina spat. 'So what? You're going to find yourself some cute little gay girl to bolster your new earth-mother image? Because I don't fit into this picture of yourself, do I?'

'I –'

'"What shall I wear today? The Gucci or the girl-friend?" Jesus, I can't believe you.'

'If you *were* a girl, I swear –'

'What? That it would all be different?'

'Well, yes,' Suki said lamely. 'It would. But you're not, and there's no changing that.'

Karina blinked, wondering why she hadn't seen this before. Love was certainly blind if it failed to let you see that your beloved obviously had the intellect of a disadvantaged donkey and the depth of a child's paddling pool. 'No. It *can* be changed,' Karina said, explaining as if to a five-year-old. 'The clever doctors at the hospital are like the Blue Fairy in *Pinocchio*, you see – they can make me be a real girl.'

'There's no need to be sarcastic,' said Suki. 'I do know what happens.'

'It doesn't matter anyway.' Karina stared at her suitcases and wondered what the hell happened now. She felt as though she were permanently in between one state and another – neither male nor female, gay, straight or bi, struggling to realise that it couldn't be the same with Adele again, preparing herself for the biggest commitment of her life, and now finding that she wasn't really wanted.

'It does matter. If it's what you want.'

'I don't know what I want,' Karina said sullenly, digging her toes into the sand. 'Knowing what I want would involve some kind of understanding of the concept of *I*, and I have no fucking idea who or what I am any more.' She sighed and pushed her hair out of her face, struggling with the pain as she speculated whom Suki had been having sex with in 'her office'.

'Who is this fucking woman you're seeing anyway?' she asked. 'Your lawyer, I suppose?'

Suki flushed. 'Darling, I . . .'

Karina rounded on her. 'Don't fucking *darling* me. That's how long it took, was it? Just over a fortnight to get over me?' Her own guilt suddenly needled her, and she forced herself to ask the unbearable, unaskable question. 'Do you love her?'

Suki hesitated. That was all the answer Karina needed. She was sure she felt something break irreparably inside of her, her own karmic curse caught up with her at last. She swallowed back the tears and stared out to sea, determined that Suki should not see her cry. Time to get moving again, Miss May.

'I'm sorry.'

'Fuck off. Your fucking *lawyer*? Isn't that illegal?'

Suki gulped. 'You wouldn't say anything, would you?' she asked pathetically.

'Noooo,' Karina spat, sarcastically. 'I'll just take it like a good little transsexual and stand up in court and back up all your claims of unreasonable behaviour against your husband, so you can get your divorce and cop off with your bitch barrister.'

'All right –' Suki's lips pinched together in an ugly line that Karina had never seen before. She dug in her Prada handbag. 'I have children, you know.'

'Don't plead them as an excuse for your shitty behaviour.'

'I'm not,' Suki whined. 'It would just be easier for them if this was done as smoothly as possible.'

To Karina's disgust and horror, Suki produced a chequebook from her handbag. Karina saw her in a whole new light – the kind of woman for whom everything came at a price, and Karina was no exception. A soppy little posh Gucci-clad madam who only had to bat her lashes and wiggle her tits to have the world at her

French-manicured feet. Well, fuck *her*. Nobody was playing Karina May for a fool. Not when the last laugh rightfully belonged to her.

'How much?' Suki said tersely.

Karina gulped down her own disgust and gave her a sickly, sneering smile. 'Let's say ten grand should cover it. Make the cheque out to Kim Qing. Q-I-N-G.'

14

Whatever Karina was up to now, Adele didn't want to know. Karina didn't know anyone in this town, or so Adele had thought. She kicked herself for thinking Karina had come here for her. 'Probably doing a fucking drugs run,' Adele muttered, swallowing down an acidic burp and staring into the fridge, wondering if she could face food. There was nothing but cream cheese, a carton of milk and a bag of lychees. Typical chef's fridge, she thought, closing the door. People assumed that, if you cooked for a living, you cooked at home. Usually you came home unable to look food in the face and having to summon up a huge effort of will just to shovel a bag of tortilla chips down your throat to still the rumblings in your stomach. If she ate anything she'd only throw it up again. The vanilla schnapps stuff seemed to encase her in a cloud that smelled of ice-cream and nail-polish, and it hadn't tasted at all pleasant on the way back up. She had a million and one things to do, drawing up menu plans and running them past Paul so that she could get on with the vital business of stocking the kitchen. What she'd been thinking the night before, she didn't know. It was never going to be a day she could handle with a raging hangover.

She rinsed off the worst of the greasy, sicky hangover feeling under a cool shower, frustrated by the crappy water pressure on the top floor. It was a sullen little trickle of water when she needed cold hard needles to slam into her scalp and skin and clear away the hot, gassy feeling that went with too much booze. The weather was already warming up too, and she realised that this top-floor cubbyhole of a flat could get fiendishly hot with the sun on the flat roof all day. She would have to buy an electric fan and damn the expense of running it.

As she dressed, she kept her back to the fireplace, refusing to deal with it or even think about it. Another hassle she didn't need. Typical of K to find the thing that could be most easily broken and home in on it like a destruction-seeking missile.

She put on a light shirt and three-quarter-length jeans, tied up her hair under a red paisley scarf and went downstairs, hoping Jude wouldn't be there. He wasn't. Most of the woodwork was finished now and she surveyed the sanded, varnished surfaces with a sense of satisfied closure. She picked up pen and paper from Paul's office and scooped a bucket of ice chips from the machine to take the bad taste out of her mouth and let the cold, glassy fragments dull the edge of her nausea.

Adele sat down in the kitchen to work, picking at ice chips and scribbling on the page as she figured out the important question of what people would like to eat. The time passed fairly rapidly once she got into her stride and she was reminded that she loved this – considering vegetarian dishes, the matter of which fish was fashionable, whether warm salads were now passé and if the trend for reinventing British 'classics' as actual, edible food was still going strong. Cooking was fifty per cent instinct, thirty per cent common sense and twenty per cent innovation. Innovators made their names famous, but innovation was just sticking foods and techniques together and seeing if they worked. Bugger fashion, she thought, striking monkfish off the page. The poor things were probably nearing extinction after being scoffed by the whole of Islington and the Home Counties. Give people a new flavour. They would never know they liked it until they tried it.

'Are you busy?' Paul interrupted, poking his head around the door, hand on the lintel. He had a cigarette between his knuckles.

'Yes, but I can take a break. And you can't smoke in here any more.'

He ducked into his office and put his cigarette out, then came back. He looked tired and blinky eyed behind his glasses, but he still looked good. Secret crush material.

'Glad to see you're a stickler for discipline anyway,' he said, perching on a kitchen stool. 'How's it going?'

She tapped the pen against her lips, craving a cigarette now that she'd smelled his and the tobacco scent clinging to him. 'Pretty good, I think. Wrangling with fish.'

He raised his eyebrows. 'Fish wrangling? Do tell.'

'Depends if you want to pay through the nose for monkfish. I was just thinking it's about time mackerel made a comeback.'

'OK . . . was it ever *the* thing?' Paul wrinkled his nose.

'It is if you cook it right. Stuffed mackerel with orange. And I do a mean smoked mackerel kedgeree.'

'Kedgeree? Seriously? I didn't know anybody ate that any more.'

'They don't, which is silly,' Adele said. 'It's Anglo-Indian, multicultural – fusion food before the term was even invented. And it tastes gorgeous. Dash of lime pickle with the lime juice, toss paneer in with the butter and cream and add a little palok sag for that extra touch of India.'

He licked his bottom lip. 'You temptress. My mouth's watering now.'

She laughed, flirting. 'You'll love it.'

'I'm sure I will.'

'The idea is to draw up these dishes, make a few and see what you think.'

'You can definitely do me that kedgeree,' said Paul. 'It sounds fabulous.'

'It is.' She peered into the melted ice bucket and decided it was time for a cigarette break. 'I must have a fag. You coming?'

'Hmm. Yeah. I keep smoking too much lately,' Paul said, following her lead outside. 'Ieuan's pernicious influence. Little shit.'

Adele picked a roll-up out of her tin and lit it. 'What's up?'

'I think he's left me,' Paul admitted, with a rueful scrunch of his nose.

'Oh, God, I'm so sorry,' Adele said, touching him on the arm. His skin was even smoother than it looked.

'I'm not.' Paul lit a cigarette and shrugged. 'He was insanely jealous and completely possessive. If you can't trust someone, then what's the point?'

'If you can't talk to someone,' Adele said, thinking of Jude.

'Exactly.' Paul sighed. 'How's that going, by the way?'

'It's not. I committed the cardinal sin of embarrassing him in front of his friends.'

'From what I've seen of his friends that's something of a pot and kettle situation, but do go on.'

'Nothing to tell, really.' Adele shrugged. 'I was getting seriously pissed with a Cornish lesbian, and we were on an "all men are wankers" roll, and then, when Jude and his friends came over and started talking about girl-on-girl action, I literally couldn't stop laughing when this girl Kate attacked them.'

'Attacked?' Paul laughed. 'She attacked them? Who is this woman? She sounds a scream.'

'She is. Gone though. Reading Festival.'

'Shame.' Paul sighed, then said suddenly, 'Oh my God . . . do you know what this means?'

'What?'

'We're both single,' he said, waggling an eyebrow suggestively and grinning through cigarette smoke. 'What on earth will happen?'

'Nothing, probably.' Adele laughed. 'I'm not the kind of woman who causes mothers to lock up their sons.'

'Oh bullshit! You had Jude in minutes. Right here. I know you did.'

She flushed furiously and covered her embarrassment with a laugh. 'And you still hired me?'

'I'd have been stupid not to. I read your CV, remember?'

Adele tossed him a sidelong look. Yeah, right. She'd walked in here trussed up like a chicken in lacy drawers and pin-thin high heels and he'd been hiring her for her credentials? 'If you weren't gay my bullshit radar would be bleeping CRITICAL right now.'

'Oh,' Paul said. 'Well, that's got me kind of worried for your bullshit radar.'

'Why?'

'I'm not gay.'

She snorted. '"Lady Marmalade"?'

'I like that song. A lot of people do.'

'OK, backtrack – forget "Lady Marmalade". What about the man you were having sex with?' She wanted to get him back for mentioning Jude and, wickedly, added, 'Extremely noisy sex, at that.'

Bingo. He blushed. 'It's only polite. Motivational.'

'Motivated me,' she said, the words popping out of her mouth before her brain engaged to stop them. Shit.

Paul yelled with triumph and bounced up and down on his toes. 'Ha! I *love* you! You *always* manage to dig yourself deeper in the shit. I love it – too funny!'

'Fuck off,' she said, laughing. 'I didn't say that.'

'I think you'll find you did.'

'I didn't.'

'Did.'

'Look, it's very hard not to get ... motivated when you've got "do me baby" moans echoing up the chimney. And that's something else I've been meaning to speak to you about, actually.'

'Actually –' Paul held up a hand '– "do me baby"? I have never. I'm being misquoted here. I have never said "do me baby" during sex. Ever.'

'Well, it could have been "fuck me", but there were definitely a few babies in there somewhere.'

'Medically I think that's impossible, isn't it?' Paul wrinkled his nose. 'Ugh. Better be. If that little bastard hits me with a paternity suit in nine months' time –'

'Damn you. Stop making me laugh. Seriously – the chimney. What are you going to do about it?'

'It will be fixed,' Paul said, hand on his heart. 'I promise. I'll make the necessary calls today.'

'Good.'

'I don't think you need worry. I think it's structurally sound, otherwise it would have caved in by now. That or that fucking surveyor lied his arse off and the whole place is about to go down like a house of cards.'

Adele stared up at the building. 'Thank you for those words of reassurance and comfort, Paul.'

'Yes. Sorry. I'm just looking at a worst-case scenario here.' He looked up too. 'Not a very pleasant thought, is it?'

She blew smoke up into the boughs of the wisteria. 'Nope.'

'I'd best call someone about that, hadn't I?'

'Yep.'

'OK.' He nodded. 'I'll go and do that.'

'You do that.'

'I shall. And book that restaurant.'

She tilted her head back to normal and frowned. 'Restaurant?'

'I thought we could have dinner tonight. Where would you recommend?'

'Oh,' she said, thrown another curveball. Keeping pace with Paul's conversation felt like being on a helter-skelter. 'Well . . . Amadeo's, I suppose.'

'Excellent. Get your gladrags on.'

'Wait a minute!' she said. 'I didn't say yes!'

He pouted. 'You didn't say no.'

'I think it's very rude of you, actually,' she said. 'How do you know I don't already have vastly more important plans?'

'I don't. I'm just taking a shot in the dark. Are you busy?'

'Well . . . no.'

'OK. Say about eight?'

'OK.'

There was a note stuck to the front door. It simply said SORRY. WILL CALL YOU. Adele only just resisted the child-ish desire to shred it into tiny pieces and flush the scraps down the toilet. She couldn't believe she had been so stupid as to imagine K had changed or grown up in any way, shape or form. Still taking the piss. Still ripping out hearts and stomping on them. She was probably wanted by the police or a drug cartel: nothing could surprise Adele any more where K was concerned, and she was determined that she would no longer care. The old clichés about leopards and spots, once bitten, twice shy, rattled through her brain. That was the fucking end of the matter. She had done bereft where-did-I-go-wrong weeping eight years ago, and she wasn't going there again. It wasn't her problem.

She thought about cancelling dinner, but that made anger surge up again like acid reflux. Why should she not enjoy herself? Why should she mope at home getting pissed and furious to old Nirvana CDs? For the first time in months she wanted a joint – a little something to take the edge off and put things back into perspective, but she had ditched that set of acquaintances too messily to call on any of them. Besides, she had no desire to sit around on a hash-burn-pocked armchair and listen to 'In A Gadda Da Fucking Vida' fourteen times in a row because some ancient wreck of a hippy was determined that she should 'y'know . . . really, like . . . feel it'.

On with the show, she told herself. On with the gladrags and on with the warpaint.

She remembered painting her lips scarlet and striding into school sporting a brilliant poppy pout when she was just seventeen. That had shut them up for at least the length of a morning, which, while it wasn't much, had felt like a blessed respite. The bitches simply hadn't known what to say, momentarily stunned silent by Adele's defiance of realpolitik. The hush had been so wonderful that Adele kept inventing new things to cause it – heavy metal tour T-shirts, homemade batik hats, studded wristbands and grungy plaid shirts. She had probably looked extraordinary, but she hadn't cared. So long as it kept them on their toes thinking up the next taunt to throw at her.

She knew what to wear. She was glad she had found time to put her clothes away, otherwise she would have gone out smelling of brick dust and soot. The whole room smelled like a chimney sweep. The dress was a little musty from long storage, but it would air out quickly enough. Every woman, she reflected, had a 'That Dress'. The showstopping number that was their personal version of Marilyn's white crepe Travilla or Liz Hurley's safety-pinned Versace. The dress that turned you instantly into the big-mouthed, big screen goddess of the movie of your own life. Hers was one of a kind, a muted green-blue silk that she had created with dyes and hot wax in her first year of art college. A fashion student friend had sewn it into a simple sheath dress for her. Every part of the fabric was unique. She had spread out the huge sheet of silk on the floor, spattered it haphazardly with hot wax, dip dyed and dried it, hurled more wax, dribbles of dyes – turquoise, peacock and green. She had chucked all her anger at the silk until she was staring at a sheet smothered in it, violence described in traditionally calming colours. It had made her uncomfortable enough to boil the fabric back to something she could feasibly work from scratch on, but the result was unexpectedly beautiful once the colours were muted.

She went downstairs feeling not only better but pretty damn good. Paul gawped when he opened the door.

'Oh my God –'

Adele gave him a twirl, feeling coquettish and delighted with his reaction. 'How do I look?'

'Amazing. Like a million dollars. And I am so underdressed. I had no idea Amadeo's was dressy.'

She looked at him, dressed in pale chinos and a maroon shirt, and stupidly realised the opposite was true. 'No,' she said, feeling deflated. 'It's not really. I'm overdressed. I should change.'

'Don't you dare,' Paul said, unbuttoning his shirt. 'I'll change. We'll both do dressy. I never liked having dinner casual anyway. Give me a moment, and help yourself to a drink. There's some wine in the fridge.'

'OK, thanks,' she said, cheering up again. Her moods seemed all over the place, and for a moment she had thought she was going to cry at something so stupid as wearing the wrong dress, until she had remembered that she was wearing mascara and thought better of it. Sometimes it felt as though mascara had been invented expressly to remind women that they mustn't cry. She peeked in the fridge and found the open bottle of Semillon inside the door, but she couldn't find a glass and didn't want to swig it from the bottle and leave her lipstick there. God knows, Paul was probably in enough trouble with Ieuan as it was for taking her out like this, and she didn't want to be part of their next row if and when Ieuan came to pick up his stuff.

'Paul?'

'Yeah?'

'I can't seem to find a glass.'

He walked into the kitchen, shirtless. Strictly speaking, she knew she wasn't supposed to stare, but Paul was so often flashing scraps of his skin that to see him walk in topless felt like a shock. If he'd peeled off his shirt in front of her it would have seemed like a natural conclusion to the extreme slow-motion striptease he always seemed to be absent-mindedly performing. She felt a little bit cheated at not having seen him take it off. He looked harder than Jude, his darker skin lacking that pale redhead transparency that Jude's had. He looked opaque, solid, full grown – no wispy boy-man you could cuddle and cosset and belittle in bed. He didn't have as much wiry muscle as Jude, but paradoxically it made him look more masculine. The sloppy, don't-give-a-fuck softness around his waist was male, negligent, lazy, and spoke of someone comfortable in his own skin.

He was comfortable – comfortable enough with himself to take men into his bed as well as women. Nothing, no amount of fleeting youthful prettiness, no washboard bellies and buffed-up biceps could turn her on like a light the way it did when she witnessed someone who radiated that cool, inner knowledge that they were beautiful.

'Let me...' he said, taking the bottle from her and opening a cupboard above the sink. His back was turned, a smooth, pleasing curve disappearing into the waistband of the black trousers he had changed into, his arse wrapped like a gift in the cloth. There were scratch marks on the back of his shoulder, not deep, but distinct enough to be noticed. The first time she had seen him he had been sporting a love bite on the small of his back, carrying the marks of sex on his body like an Indian aristocrat who had read his *Kama Sutra* well enough to remember that such markings demonstrated that you were desired and reminded people that they might feel the same.

The marks had clearly been made by human fingers – a series of four pinkish parallel lines etched into the back of his shoulder blade. The skin of his back was otherwise smooth and dusty pale-tan in colour, handsome and glossy in texture. The look of it drew her hand the way the fur of a cat might and before she could reign back the impulse, her fingers were touching the marks of fingernails, matching the tips to the top of the lines. Paul didn't jump or stiffen, but he turned his head slightly and gave her a quizzical, frowning smile.

'What have you done there?' she asked, frozen and unable to pull away for fear of looking even weirder.

'Hmm. What's that?'

'You've got scratches on your back. What have you been up to?'

'Scratching myself?' he suggested.

She looked down at his hands, nails bitten down to nothing. 'Must have been one hell of an itch then.'

'Something bit me, I think.' He turned around and handed her the wine.

'That was lower down,' she said, mouth once again engaging before brain. Dammit.

'Lower down?' He laughed.

'Um, yeah. First time I met you you had this huge lovebite kind of low down on your back.'

Paul leaned back against the kitchen surface, the posture pushing his belly and crotch forwards. 'That was probably Ieuan. Had a habit of sucking on parts of my body.'

'I gathered that.'

'You don't miss much, do you?'

'Always did have a good eye for detail,' she said, backing up and sipping her wine. 'Got me so far through art school before I realised my hands wouldn't follow through with what my eyes wanted.'

He raised his eyebrows and stood up straight. 'Oh, I don't know. I'd say you were following through.' He gave her a sly, dirty, flirty smile. 'Nothing wrong with your hands at all.'

15

She stumbled on the stairs. They seemed to lurch like a scene from *Titanic* and she reached down to try and take her shoes off, get some of that balance back. 'Fucking, stupid, shoes.' The straps didn't seem to want to let go of her ankles and she yanked them fiercely, not caring if they broke. She wanted them off her feet.

'Let me help,' Paul said, kneeling at her feet. His tie was askew and he had faint wine stains at the corners of his mouth.

Adele tugged at the strap, swatting away his drunk, clumsy fingers. 'I got it ... it's emancipation, y'know ... fuck this *Sex and the City* shit. Bullshit Manolo Blahniks ... Blah blah blahniks. Crap. Crap to the power of crap squared.' She pulled off the shoes, furious with the way they'd chafed her ankles. 'Fucking women chaining themselves to railings and what the fuck do we get? Stupid pointy shoes that hurt my fucking feet!'

She spinbowled them down the stairs, over Paul's head. He was laughing so hard that he was almost sliding off the stair where he was sitting, threatening to slip down them like a human slinky.

'It's not funny,' she said, laughing because he was laughing. 'Stupid pointy shoes on stupid pointy women who are all like "money, marriage, money, shoes, sex" and eating *nothing* and thinking they're so radical because they're saying somehow it's fun to be a woman. It fucking well isn't. I hate it.'

'You don't,' Paul said patronisingly, scrambling up off the stairs.

'Yes I do. I hate period pains and smear tests and men having conversations with my breasts and men who think they're sooooo shit hot and liberated because they eat pussy. I mean, do you know how boring that gets? For hours? Slurping away and chafing your inner thighs with a fucking big stiffy between their legs because they think they're *such* a sexual god because *whoa* ... they actually *care* that they're getting a woman off?'

'Your lot started it, madam,' Paul remonstrated. 'You and *Cosmopolitan* – demanding orgasms all over the place.'

'I had nothing to do with that,' Adele snorted. 'Those women make me puke. How to get thin so you'll get fucked. How to be independent to please your man. How to get married. How to have a lovely home. God, I need a drink.'

'Yep.' He swayed towards his front door and unlocked it. They both almost fell through it, wobbling through into the living room. She flopped down gracelessly on the couch and fumed.

'Scotch?' Paul asked, holding up a bottle.

'I get aggressive when I drink Scotch,' she said, shaking her head. 'Fuck it. Make it a double.'

'You'll turn into fucking Boudicca,' he said.

'And why not? Big whirling scythes – that's what a woman needs. Bollocks to babies and couches and stupid pointy shoes. I don't want any of that shit.'

'So what do you want?'

'I don't know,' she said, taking a glass of Scotch and searching for her cigarettes. 'I just want to be me. Is that really too much to ask?'

'What if –' Paul said, tumbling down onto the couch

beside her. 'What if the person you really are really likes pointy shoes?'

'Then I'd have to consider killing myself before my feet did,' she said, lighting up. 'Oh, Christ – I'm drunk. And making a bloody fool of myself.'

'Don't worry about it. I won't remember in the morning anyway, I am so drunk.'

'This is the second night on the trot.'

'I'll bear that in mind when I book us into the Betty Ford clinic,' Paul said, hiccupping. 'I think you're a very bad influence.'

'I think you were the one pouring the Chianti, mate,' said Adele. She swallowed down her Scotch and stared at Paul's arse, which was making a noise. 'Did you know your bum was bleeping, by the way?'

'Ah. I thought I was sitting on something.' He sat up and fished in his back pocket, producing his phone. 'Hello?' he said, still giggling, and rolled off the sofa, laughing hysterically. 'It's for you,' he said, holding out the phone.

'It's your phone –' Adele said, taking it from him. He seemed to find that hilarious.

'Hello?' she said, holding the absurdly tiny phone to her ear.

'Hey, babycakes.' Karina's voice sounded surprisingly clear to come from a phone the size of a Tic Tac box, and sounded off centre, drunk or something. 'Said I'd call you, didn't I?'

'This isn't my phone.'

'I know. You haven't got one.'

'Yes, I know I haven't. This isn't my phone.'

Paul appeared to be having difficulty breathing.

'What's so funny?' asked Karina.

'Nothing. He's just drunk. So am I, I think. Where the hell are you?'

'It doesn't matter,' said Karina. She sounded tired and depressed. 'I'm off anyway.'

'Off where?' Adele asked, poking Paul with her foot. He rolled onto his back and grabbed hold of her skirt. She pulled back, laughing, trying to stop his playful attempts to peer under it. 'Ow ... Paul, get off ...'

'How the fuck should I know?' Karina said. 'Fucking Casablanca or whatever. Sorry to disturb you.' Her voice cracked but Adele chose to ignore it. She was too drunk to deal with one of K's passive aggressive turns.

'No problem. We'll always have Paris.'

Paul had wrapped his arms around her knees like a supplicant and was moaning drunkenly into her lap. She patted his head. Good boy. Pissed as a fart.

'Yeah. Whatever.' Karina sighed. 'It's better this way. I'll know who I am.'

'Oh God. You're not going to go off and find yourself again?'

'Yep. I think I'm in Casablanca, somewhere. So here's lookin' at you, kid.'

Adele sighed. If she wasn't mistaken, Paul's lips were doing something to her left thigh. What was it with her and gay men? 'Look – you can't just fucking call me when I'm drunk and start babbling about Casablanca and shit, you know. You show up out of the blue after eight fucking years and you're pissing off again without giving me a single straight answer about what you've been doing? For God's sake, when are you –?'

The line went dead. 'Fuck you too,' Adele said, to the phone. 'Dozy cunt. She always fucking does this.'

'Whassat?' Paul muttered, peering up from where he was resting his chin on her knees.

'Goes off to find herself,' Adele said. 'Did that. Fucked off to Thailand, found herself OK ... swapped addresses but lost touch.'

'That's a shame. Not even the odd Christmas card?'

'Apparently not. What are you doing down there?'

'I prefer my centre of gravity closer to the floor,' Paul announced, sprawling out on his back on the rug. He was flushed, booze stained and his dark curls had defied the gel he had smeared on them and stuck out in mad configurations. He looked pretty good, she thought. Monochrome brought out the green in his eyes and the olive tints of his skin – better than that lime green shirt he was so attached to. She could second guess what he'd been up to while tugging playfully on her skirt and burying his head in her lap, and she decided to provoke him. She put her bare foot on his chest and wiggled her toes.

'What are you up to?' she asked.

'I don't know. I'm up for anything after this amount of booze.'

'You're gay.'

'No I'm not. I told you I'm not. I was married. To a woman.'

'Yeah, well.' She scrunched her toes into his shirt front. His flesh felt solid beneath it and she couldn't deny that she was hungry for the touch of another warm human body. 'I tend not to trust gay men who tell me they want to be with women. The last one wanted to *be* a woman, never mind with one.'

'No danger of that with me,' Paul said. 'I've got legs like a rugby player. I'd look shocking in fishnets.'

'Being married doesn't prove a damn thing anyway,' she said, thinking better of it and trying to move her foot. Paul held her around the ankle and grinned, teasing. His thumb stroked the hollowed out spot on her ankle, just in front of the Achilles tendon.

'It proves a lot,' said Paul, rolling onto his side so that he was staring directly up her leg. 'It was my wife's idea that I start fucking men anyway. She liked to watch.'

'No way!'

'Uh huh. Come on.' He dipped his head as if he was about to kiss her foot, but teasingly just let his breath drift and tickle over her instep. He peeked up from under dark eyelashes and smiled. 'Admit it – it cuts both ways, doesn't it? Men fantasise about two women; women must fantasise about two men?'

'Occasionally,' she said, sounding prim, determined not to let on that her knees were turning to liquid and that she was already aching for his dick. That was all she'd wanted from Jude – damn him and his stupid condom phobia and his pride at being some kind of *soi-disant* muff-munching aficionado.

'You listened, didn't you?' Paul asked matter of factly.

'It was hard not to,' she admitted. 'You know that already.'

'I don't know the details.' His tongue slithered over her instep and she groaned, the tension palpable in the air by now. 'Did it get you all wet?'

'What do you think?'

'Don't be coy. I'll tell you anything if you want me to. I'm very good at telling dirty stories, actually. It was my ex-wife's little kink – still is. She got pissed off with me for refusing to give her all the filthy details about Ieuan.'

'Why didn't you?'

'I was in love with him. And it was none of her business any more. She'd refuse me because I wouldn't tell her.'

Adele frowned. 'OK – that sounds . . . twisted.'

'It was. From the start. Before I married her, Sarah was my step-sister.'

She laughed incredulously. 'You're joking.'

'Nope. She had this completely warped incest kink. I was eighteen and perfect to carry it through – I was her brother, but not a blood relative. Fresh out of school as well. She'd just finished at Cheltenham. Head girl, model pupil, blonde hair, blue eyes. English rose by all appearances, but she just hid the nasty streak well.'

'Tell me,' Adele said, leaning back further on the couch. She wanted to throw down the gauntlet and see if he'd follow through and reveal all. Her internal muscles twitched impatiently at the mental image of a shy, beautiful, eighteen-year-old Paul gasping with shock and pleasure as he penetrated his smug, blonde step-sister.

'I thought she was foul at first; horrible. A really stuck-up little bitch. But the day my mother married her father I caught her shagging some guy in the laundry room. She didn't see me; there was a sort of slatted door, but I saw her. She was sitting on top of the tumble dryer with her skirt up and her legs wide open, and I could literally see this cock going up inside her as he pulled back to shove it in her again.'

Adele shuddered, caught off guard. She hadn't expected anything quite so explicit. She glanced furtively down at his fly, but the lighting and the drape of the dark fabric didn't allow her to gauge if he was aroused too. She wanted him to take his cock out and touch himself, if only to give her permission to do the same. 'What did you do?' she asked, her voice sounding hollow and analytical to her own ears.

'Crept out of there with my heart in my mouth. She would have gone mad if she'd spotted me. I sneaked through the kitchen, sure I was going to come in my pants there and then, made it to the downstairs bathroom and came so hard I think I saw stars. Looking back, I think she knew damn well I was there, because the next day, when our respective parents had gone off on their honeymoon, she came down to breakfast wearing this tiny baby-doll nightie and matching knickers – hideous shocking pink, but it was the 1980s, so that wasn't really her fault. She sat down on the kitchen table, being deliberately confrontational – totally aggressive about her sexuality. She was bitching the air blue about how she hated this house, she hated her father, she couldn't wait for university to start so she could meet some real men, and all the while she had her legs wide open, and this nightie covered *nothing*. I could see hair at the edges of her knickers and she knew I was staring because she was getting off on it. They were satiny fabric and showed this wet stain growing on her crotch. I thought I was going mad, that I'd do something terrible, like rape her or something. I was a virgin. I had no idea how to control myself.'

'What did you do?' she asked breathlessly. She was sliding deeper down the sofa cushions and her long silk skirt was riding up over her knees and thighs. She didn't care. The sooner he recognised her need the better, however much she was enjoying this slow build up. The slower, the more measured it was, the bigger the explosion when they did fall on each other. She thought hungrily of demented, ravenous, furniture-trashing sex – fucking madly against walls, over chairs, sweeping objects off the table in order to throw each other down on it.

She knew for sure he wasn't lying about not being entirely gay, whatever her doubts beforehand. He was playing expertly with kinks she didn't even know she had had until he tongued her ankle and started talking dirty.

'What do you think?'

'I don't know. Tell me.'

'Wanked off in the bathroom again. She was so sick, and I was loving it. She teased constantly, saying it would be wrong because we were brother and sister by marriage, but she was always careful to add that I'd like that, wouldn't I? I'd like it if we really were brother and sister because it would be even more wrong to fuck your own sister. She was good, incredibly good, at the off-the-cuff headfuck. I was an only child, and she played on my natural protective instincts. I suddenly had a sister and, no matter who she was, I'd want to protect her from other men. She came downstairs to go to the pub one day wearing this dress which looked totally demure at first glance, a little print shirtwaist thing, but then the light caught her from behind as she was coming downstairs and I could see she was naked underneath it. I could see the lips of her cunt quite clearly defined in the light.'

'Christ,' Adele muttered. Her skirt had ridden up and the small, silly thong, which was all she could wear under the dress, felt damp between her legs; a twist of fabric that chafed teasingly against her sex and yet didn't manage to touch her clit. She realised her knees had been slipping apart, trying to angle the cloth to nudge against her clit and maybe give her a chance in hell of getting off.

Paul's hand slid up the back of her knee, his brilliant, intense eyes fixed on her face, his lips a little parted, sensual and suppliant as he knelt at her feet. She looked at him from under her lashes, and moaned when he pushed her skirt higher. 'You want these off?' he asked, his thumb tracing the edge of the fabric, tantalisingly close to where she wanted his hand to be squeezing, cupping and pushing inside.

She nodded, her tongue sticky with booze and heavy breathing inside her mouth.

'Take them off then,' he said.

She arched her back and took them off, then decided to shock him, if such a thing were possible. She stood up unsteadily, worried for a moment she might plunge headlong into the coffee table, and pushed the straps off her shoulders. The dress slid down and off and landed in a perfect Hollywood-sex-scene puddle at her feet. He lifted his eyebrows, appraising her tits, her thighs and her bush, but he didn't make any move. She sat back down and spread her legs, her clit pulsing in tandem with the beat of her heart.

'You're naked,' he said, smiling.

'That's what I love about you. You're quick on the uptake.'

To her intense frustration, Paul leaned back, picked up his Scotch from the coffee table and lit up a cigarette, staring right up between her legs with a cool interest, which was a thousand times more erotic than the number of times Jude had crammed his tongue up her snatch. 'Do you want to hear about how I fucked my step-sister?' Paul asked. 'Or maybe you should have a turn. I want to know what you got up to the day I first met you. Will you tell me?'

'I want to hear about your sister,' said Adele.

'Not just now,' he teased. 'Let's save some for later, shall we? I *know* you were up to something with Jude in the back yard that day. I could smell it on you . . .'

She arched her back impatiently, the movement spreading her thighs wider. He lifted an eyebrow and grinned, but carried on smoking his cigarette.

'You started this,' she said, beginning to feel slightly irritated.

'So I did.' Paul nodded and put down his drink. He ran his thumb behind the back of her knee, startling her with how sensitive the skin was.

'I don't kiss and tell,' she said, turning her failure to articulate the filthy words into something secretively feminine and, hopefully, seductive.

'Good for you,' he said, and kissed the inside of her

thigh, high up enough to make her muscles contract involuntarily with anticipation. She gasped and he left his cigarette abandoned on the side of the ashtray as he leaned closer and pressed his mouth to her hip, teasingly avoiding her aching, soaking crotch. He stopped talking, at last. She could feel his breath coming faster against her skin as he kissed each hip, her belly, the dip of her navel. She pushed her fingers into his dark curling hair and his hands came up to grip her arse, stroke her thighs, a gluttonous touch that was so fucking *welcome* after all that deprivation and teasing. She thrust her hips eagerly, moaning as her cunt pressed against his shirtfront, the friction delicious but still unsatisfying.

She wanted his mouth. For all this fooling around, she hadn't even kissed him yet. He was working his way up to her tits, his hands moving under her breasts to cup them, squeeze them and press them together. She wanted his clothes off, and scrabbled for his shirt buttons because she could feel the heat of his flesh under the cotton and craved skin under her hands. Paul rushed ahead of her, scrambling over her to kiss her on the mouth at last. His kiss was fucking beautiful, tremulous with panting breaths, greedy, sloppy, messy and delectable. She moaned around his tongue, shuddering fiercely with lust. She could smell herself on his shirt and the garment was riding up under her fingers, baring his spine to her hands. His skin was warm, smooth and wonderful to touch after all the glimpses he'd proffered in the past few weeks. He was hard in his trousers, the firm bulge of his dick pressing between her wide-open legs and smearing her juices all over the fly of his trousers, branding him with her scent. She wanted him naked, tugging frantically at fastenings, buttons, cloth. His shirt was off, his tan nipples and the smooth expanse of her chest so tempting that she had to kiss, suckle and bite, licking skin, endless skin, under her lips and tongue as she moaned incoherent broken endearments against his shaking, half-naked body. You're beautiful, gorgeous, incredible, want you, want you so fucking much . . .

He cried out as she pinched and bit his nipples, and then she howled in reply as he finally thrust his fingers inside her. No preamble, no more teasing, just a good, strong fingerfucking, almost exactly what her body had been screaming for. When his thumb rubbed her clit she reacted like she'd received an electric shock it was so sensitised and swollen. She kissed his mouth again, stuck on the sexy, breathless way he kissed, rocking her hips into his touch. He was moaning filth between kisses, whispering that she was so good, so tight, how much he loved her hot, wet cunt.

'Fuck me,' she moaned, reaching for his cock. She'd take her time to get to know it better later, when she'd come.

'Wait, wait . . . one second . . .' he panted, and broke off for a moment to retrieve his wallet from the table. His trousers were round his knees and he took the opportunity to strip fully while he carefully rolled on a condom. His arse was hairless, firm and perfect. He leaned over her again for more kisses, warming up the mood again after the inevitable but necessary break in the action. There were no more obstacles, no more reasons not to and she ground her hips against him, thrilled when she felt his dick pressed against the lips of her sex, desperate to feel it inside her. He pushed it in and she moaned gratefully – it felt like forever since she'd had a good, hard, eager prick inside of her.

As he pushed, he cried out too, his eyes scrunched shut and his teeth digging into his wet lower lip, gritting out a soft, choked 'oh fuck' at the sensation. She prayed he wasn't going to come too fast because she was so turned on that this had the makings of a perfect fuck. When he began to thrust into her, his pubic bone was at just the right angle to put pressure on her clit, his dick darting and gliding back and forth inside her. His face was flushed, his shoulders beautiful as they supported the weight of his body above her. He was panting, his lips red and full and eyes almost black. He ploughed forwards and kissed her again, heightening the pleasure to fever pitch. She was so wet that his cock moved silkily, pounding away as it sought and sometimes found the right spots where the friction was so slick and sweet she had to shudder and groan. He gasped in her ear, panting out his appreciation in a series of cracked obscenities that made her head spin.

Her body was no longer under her own control, bouncing enthusiastically along with his and straining further towards climax every time his cock thrust forwards and his hips hammered between her legs, jarring nerve endings. 'Oh fuck...' she whispered, astonished at how horny her own voice sounded. 'Oh my God ... oh yeah ... oh yes ... I'm gonna come...'

Paul leaned back, his eyes intent on her face, licking dry lips and thrusting harder and faster. A drop of sweat ran down his temple, his breathing as hoarse as her own. 'Come on, come for me...' he urged excitedly. 'Want to watch you come...'

She bucked madly at the sound of his voice – so sexy and nasty it turned up the heat to the point of no-return – and she felt her climax burst behind her clit, radiating waves, ripples, convulsions of pure sensation. Her throat was caught and refused to let the sound out as she rode the orgasm out, shuddering as Paul fucked her with sharp, terse jabs of his hips. When she relaxed her throat enough to scream, he was coming, his mouth open, head thrown back. He made a choked, whimpering sound and flopped forwards, his body solid and sweaty, the weight of him deepening her satisfaction as her still-twitching muscles tenderly hugged his spent dick.

They had somehow humped themselves halfway over the back of the couch, and her head and shoulders were almost hanging off the sofa. She stared up at the ceiling, tingling from lips to toes, drenched with pleasure. Paul moaned softly and ran his tongue up her outstretched neck to her lips. His mouth was as dry from panting as her own, but it became a nice, slow, sated kiss when their mouths became wet again. She clenched her muscles around him, laughing at the way he flared his nostrils and winced at the touch. He rocked slowly once or twice into her, with deep, contented noises, before slipping out.

'Whoa,' he whispered.

'Mmm-hmm.' Definitely *whoa*. Oh yeah.

'That was . . .'

'Yep,' Adele sighed. 'Sex. If I remember correctly . . .'

16

Paul opened his eyes and immediately thought better of it. His stomach lurched and his head throbbed. He had no idea when he had last drank so much and there and then made the traditional morning-after vow of 'Never Again'. Adele rolled over and groaned next to him, her dark curls spread in a debauched-looking tangle on the pillow. She pushed her hair back from her face, still fast asleep. Her eyes were shadowed from last night's make-up and her lips stained their customary pink. Paul smiled to himself as she snuggled up and pushed a thigh between his under the covers. He hoped she wouldn't regret this – at least not the sex side of it. He regretted the booze already and knew she probably would too when she woke fully. It was high time he realised he was far too old to chuck it back like that, although moderation smelled distastefully of old age.

He yawned and cuddled down under the duvet. Adele was warm and silky smooth, as substantial to hold as she looked; big round breasts that dropped like pale pink-tipped fruit when she bent over, and a rounded pink and white arse, although he had never asked if it was still as virginal as it looked. She had been more interested in being fucked the conventional way, obviously bored rigid by Jude's inexpert vanilla attempts to prove what an unselfish and wonderful lover he was. Poor woman; after all the fumbling and bedroom tricks of boys who occasionally peeked at women's magazines in the doctor's waiting room, it was no wonder all she wanted was a man who would fuck her like he really meant it.

She had been completely into it from the start, turning so soft and sweet in his arms that he wondered how much of the angry smart-arse Adele was a defence mechanism. She could be diffident in bed, sucking her lower lip into her mouth in a slight frown that resembled concentration as she handled his dick. Then she had *asked* if she might go down on him.

'Oh my God – you don't need *permission!*' Paul had laughed incredulously. 'I am a man, you know.'

'Ah. I wondered what this was.'

She was a tease, getting her own back on him. She tickled his balls and his dick with her fingertips, with light feathery touches, with her breath and little flickers of her tongue until he begged, pushed a pillow under his arse and gently, with hints and hands, directed her fingertips to his arsehole. She stroked it thoughtfully as if contemplating a puzzle, her cheek resting against his hip, her lips lightly touching the shaft of his cock. When he was left with no alternative but to hand her the lube and spell it out for her that way, she pushed a finger inside his body with a cool curiosity that made him shiver. She felt her way analytically, finding the spots that made him arch and moan until she had him wide open – three slender fingers crammed up his arse and slowly fucking him from the inside. He didn't know if she knew what she was doing, but it must have been obvious to her what she was doing to him; he had been drenched with sweat from head to toe, thighs in the air and muscles quivering from the effort of being brought time and time again to the brink of climax but unable to get enough stimulation to take him over the edge.

The moment she put a little extra pressure on his prostate, he exploded – his balls tensing and the pressure forcing hot thick spurts of come out of his untouched, aching cock. She watched him moan, grip the sheets and scream, and looked surprised and pleased by the way his muscles spasmed around her fingers; but it wasn't until he was determined to return the favour that he realised how aroused she really was. She was soaked and swollen when he pushed his tongue between her legs, his head still reeling and his breath still coming in ragged gasps from his violent climax. She moaned when he suckled on her clit, her hips bucking and shaking with the need to come. She was seashell smooth inside and beautifully hot and wet, her muscles twitching eagerly as he pushed inside with his fingers. He pressed a finger against her arsehole and she was so wet that the tip of his finger popped effortlessly inside. She cried out and came almost immediately, her muscles contracting in deep, slow waves, her clit pulsing under his tongue. Fucking gorgeous.

Adele stretched and opened her eyes, giving him a shy, morning-after smile.

'Hello.'

'Hey,' she said, and grinned a little awkwardly.

'How are you feeling?'

'Um . . . pretty crap, now that I think about it.'

'Me too. How much did we drink?'

'Too much.'

'Whoops.'

'Yeah,' she said, and he was unsure she meant the booze or him was the whoops involved. He gave her a light, dry kiss on the mouth, hampered by morning breath from being any more demonstrative than that.

'Coffee?'

'Coffee sounds good.'

'I'll go put some on. Don't go anywhere.'

'Wasn't planning to,' she said, to his relief, making herself comfortable.

He got up a little unsteadily and felt sick, counting on

the recuperative powers of an intense caffeine fix to carry him through the hangover. He drank several glasses of water and wanted to curl up on the kitchen floor as a rush of nausea hit him. The second time in two days he had been naked on the kitchen floor. Oh God – that was something Adele probably wouldn't take well: that he had slept with Karina. He didn't know why he thought she'd flip; it was just a sense that she would. Now was probably not the best time to tell her. He didn't know what the deal was with the two of them. Neither woman had let on about how they felt about each other or how long they had known one another, although Paul guessed that it had been a long time.

The phone rang; he hurried into the lounge to answer it, more to shut it up rather than out of any desire to discover who it was on the other end. As it was, he wished he had just unplugged it altogether.

'What the fuck's going on?'

'Good morning, Sarah. How are you?'

'Paul, what the hell are you fucking playing at?'

'I might ask you the same question,' he said, deeply confused. He sat down and tried not to puke.

'Where is she ... he ... it ... whatever?' Sarah demanded, fuming down the phone line.

Paul would have usually bitchily envisioned her kicking some puppies or taking the flying monkeys out of their cage, but her last statement put paid to all flippancy. 'Who?'

'Kim Qing. Alias Karina Fucking May. I know she's down there in that armpit of the South Coast you decided to inexplicably relocate yourself to.'

'Whu?' Paul rummaged in the debris of the coffee table for something that resembled a smokeable cigarette. There was only Adele's battered tobacco tin and Rizlas and he rolled one inexpertly, holding the phone in the crook of his shoulder. 'Sarah, I really don't know what you're talking about.'

'Yes you do. Suki has told me she's staying at Shipworths. I don't know what poison you've been pouring into that tranny's ear but ten grand, Paul – that's how much worse off my client is this morning. It's blackmail, plain and simple, and I know damn well you'd do this just to make life difficult for me.'

'Whoa ... wait. Slow down.' Paul lit his cigarette, a pathetically constructed thing that was eighty per cent Rizla and bore no resemblance whatsoever to one of Adele's perfectly rolled smokes. A scrap of burning paper fluttered loose and almost set his pubic hair alight. He swore and swatted it off onto the floor. 'Ten grand, a transsexual and Uncle Edward's soon-to-be-ex and now apparently lesbian trophy wife? I'm making some kind of mental notes of the key points here, Sarah, but it *is* eight o'clock on a Sunday morning and I do have a fucking stinking hangover.'

'You have always had it in for Suki. You and your fucking mother!' Sarah raged.

'I have not! In my opinion, getting dumped for a bimbo was the best thing that ever happened to Aunt Virginia.'

'Suki is not a bimbo!'

'Whoops, pardon me,' Paul said smugly. 'Forgot I shouldn't diss your client –'

'*Diss*? You're from Hertfordshire, you twat. There is nothing more unattractive –'

'– who you happen to be fucking –' Paul yelled over her.

'– than a middle-aged man talking like bloody Ali G.'

'– against all legal codes of practice, Ms Professional, and if you'd like me to keep my mouth shut about that then I would like those fucking divorce papers in the post first thing tomorrow morning, if you can take some time out from your busy schedule of leading me around by the dick and waxing yours and Suki's Hers and Hers matching Brazilians.'

Adele appeared in the doorway, trailing a bed sheet like a shroud and frowning. On the other end of the line, Paul could hear Sarah hissing and spitting like a pissed-off teakettle.

'Done,' she said furiously.

Paul inhaled triumphantly on his crappy home-made fag and punched the air exultantly. 'Yes!'

Adele's frown deepened. 'All right?' she mouthed.

'I'm a free man!' Paul yelled.

'Yeah –' Adele chewed on her lower lip. 'That's nice. But I think your sofa might be on fire or something.'

'Shit!'

The corner of the rug was smouldering. Adele dropped down stark naked at his feet and smothered it with the sheet. Sarah was still screaming down the phone.

'Is there someone there with you? That fucking boyfriend?'

'That fucking boyfriend has left me,' Paul announced. 'Which fits precisely with the plans I am now making to get myself a life.'

Adele glanced up from the floor where she was choking out the last traces of smoke. He had never had cause to contemplate it before, but there was something very sexy about a beautiful naked woman who had just stopped your house from burning down around your ears. He smiled. She smiled back, making his toes curl.

'Need I remind you that blackmail is a crime?' Sarah demanded, in her haughtiest bar voice.

'Who's blackmailing?'

'Kim Qing, you fucking idiot. Suki handed over a cheque for eight grand and two grand in travellers' cheques to him yesterday. Ironically, for the same titbit of information you're holding over me now...' She trailed off into an angry and frustrated sigh.

'Well, there you have it. I did always tell you it wasn't nice to brag about your sexual conquests.'

'You sanctimonious little cunt!'

'Sarah, if you have a problem with blackmail, I suggest you call the police. As for Kim, I haven't seen him since yesterday.'

Adele jumped, whacked her head on the coffee table and stared at him.

'Sarah, I have to go.'

'I know you're behind this, you bastard.'

Paul unplugged the phone and switched off his mobile the second it started ringing. Adele was curled up on the carpet, knees drawn up over her tits, looking worried and wary.

'Kim?' she said faintly.

'Karina.'

'OK –' Adele nodded, exhaled. 'I think you need to tell me what the hell she's done now? Blackmail?'

'That was Sarah.'

'I got that.'

'Sarah can't stand either her own family or mine. She loves causing trouble. My aunt – Mummy's sister – was divorced by her husband about ten years ago, when Uncle Edward traded her in for a younger model – you know that pop singer, Suki?'

'One Hit Wonder Barbie? Yeah. I know. What the hell does this have to do with Karina?'

'Well, Suki's been having an affair with her.'

Adele blinked. 'With K? A woman?'

'Yes. But now it seems it's all turned ugly after Karina found out Suki's been sleeping with Sarah, which is off limits as Sarah is Suki's lawyer.'

Adele shook her head. 'You do know your family are severely and intensely fucked up, don't you?'

'Yes. I had an inkling.' Paul sighed. 'But apparently Karina is being accused of making off with ten grand. You don't happen to know where the hell she's got to, do you?'

Adele's eyes widened. She grabbed her dress from the back of a chair and pulled it on. 'Oh fuck,' she said, struggling with the sheath of fabric and searching for her knickers. 'Fuck, fuck, fuck.'

'What?' Paul asked, puzzled as to the reason behind this sudden panic.

'She said Casablanca,' Adele said, breathless and ashen. 'Last night. Didn't she?'

'Yes. I believe so.'

Adele groaned. 'Shit. She wouldn't. She always threatened to go and have the job done on the cheap in Casablanca ... she wouldn't. I mean, she's had the operation already.'

Paul's stomach lurched. Time to give away the truth or let Karina risk cheap sex-change surgery in Morocco. There wasn't really a choice. 'No. She hasn't.'

'How do you know?' Adele asked, rounding on him fiercely, then shook her head again. 'No. Forget it. It doesn't matter now. I don't care how you know. I just need to know – does she still have a dick?'

Paul nodded, amazed how he could turn a good thing into a catastrophe so damned fast.

'She couldn't –' Adele said, pacing and thinking aloud. 'She doesn't have the money –' She spun on her heel and turned to look at Paul.

'She has the money,' they said together.

Adele went so pale even the colour drained from her lips. 'Oh shit.'

'Wait. I have her number!' Paul switched his phone

back on and punched up Karina's number. It rang while Adele stared maniacally, and rang. And rang. Then the plummy recorded voice of the network answering-machine woman. He listened for the beep and knew he was clutching at straws, but he had to say something.

'Karina . . . it's Paul. I'm with Adele.'

Karina picked up. 'That didn't take you long,' she said, sounding vague and drugged.

'Karina!'

Adele snatched the phone. Paul caught only Adele's end of the conversation. 'Don't you dare tell me it's a crappy signal, K . . . you swore you'd never do this to yourself – for fuck's sake, you stupid bitch. Don't do it! . . . What the –'

She dropped the phone and let out a small scream. 'Cut off. Shit shit shit.' She sat down heavily on the couch. 'Oh God. She means it. She's in fucking Casablanca. What the hell am I going to do?'

'Pack a bag?' Paul suggested. 'Come on. I've always wanted to go to Casablanca anyway.'

'I don't care,' Adele said, for something like the fourth time in ten minutes. She sat awkwardly in the window seat of the plane, still wearing the same dress as the night before and feeling like she'd walked onto the set of come bizarre movie. 'Will you stop apologising? Because I don't care. It doesn't matter to me.'

'It must matter,' Paul pleaded. 'To some extent –'

'It doesn't fucking matter. Really. We're all adults; we're all single. Shit happens.'

'So last night?'

'Was very nice, yes.' She sighed impatiently and craved a cigarette. 'We'll work out whatever needs working out in a slightly less weird situation, OK? Right now I have other things besides who you sleep with on my mind.'

'Yes, of course. I'm sorry.'

'Paul!'

'Sorry.'

She rolled her eyes. 'Just shut up, OK?'

'OK.'

She put on the headphones and tuned the in-flight radio to a classical station. Bach was playing, *Air on a G-String*. Smooth, soothing and absolutely nothing like her present mood. She stared out over the banks of cloud, listened to the silky strings and wondered why the fuck it was that, for every something that went right in life, there were about a million things that went heinously wrong to follow it.

This was all Kim's fault. This was the reason she had spent so many years smoking herself stupid and drifting along in a state of hemp-addled boredom – because boredom was the opposite of the endless state of chaos that seemed to follow K around and trail in her wake. Adele had resigned herself to letting go again when K had taken off once more, and now she knew she was really and truly screwed. She did still care. She couldn't shut off her feelings any more than she could become a lesbian to give free reign to them with Karina. But that too, like so many other things with K, turned out to be a crock of shit. K wasn't all woman after all, and Adele hated to think what she might be if they didn't catch up with her in time.

Paul only added further confusion and a heady dose of lust. She couldn't believe he had let her do that – push her fingers inside him like that. He had felt so soft in there – smooth and hot. And the way he came was just ... wow. She was sure she had never seen a man moan like that before, head thrown back, mouth open, forehead creased in a tight little 'fuck me' frown. There wasn't a hint of aggression in it, just total surrender. The sounds that had erupted out of his open mouth were as masculine as any she had ever heard, but so drenched with lust that they almost sounded like sex itself, transcending gender.

She sighed, stared at a break in the clouds and took off the headphones. She hadn't had enough sleep. What sleep she had managed to snatch had been a series of small, sullen catnaps grabbed between moments when her body hadn't wanted Paul's. In the dead of night, sated and sleepy, they'd done it a third time; a plain old-fashioned fuck that made her think that the missionary position was a classic for a reason.

She dozed with her head uncomfortably pillowed against the fuselage, craving a soft pillow and a warm bed so desperately that the sense memory drowned out the music, the hum of the plane's engine and almost crowded out her fears about Karina. Almost. It was as though she could feel her troubles lurking down there in some deep level of her mind, but they were cushioned by the dreams that lay just under the surface of sleep. When she breathed she felt aware of every long slow breath – her own and Paul's, his chest rising and falling in sync with her own, his cheek brushing her shoulder and his breath touching her throat, warm between her breasts as he sighed.

They had to get to Casablanca, but it didn't matter. She was dreaming, but that didn't matter either. His hands moved light as water, like something unlearned and instinctive, fingertips drifting airily over skin. Dreaming was good – no obstacles, no anguish, no worry – somewhere she could enjoy his body without fretting that this was yet another complication she didn't need. She could smell his hair, black threaded with a few strands of silver, smelling of smoke and sweat, curling sweetly against the background of his tan neck, framing the dip at the base of his throat. The fringe of his eyelashes, sooty dark under closed lids only slightly crumpled with years and laughter, the slope of his nose, the gentle pout of his lips and the rough scratch of his stubbled jaw. Just lips and lashes and day-old beard, breathing close against her face, beautiful and vulnerable as men could be in sleep.

The plane jarred, stirring her into striplighted, foul-tasting reality. She licked her lips, the inside of her mouth so dry from the pressurised cabin that she was aware of the feeling of every tooth in her head as she moved her tongue around to moisten her mouth. She instantly felt grubby, ugly, angry and desperately tired at being jerked roughly out of sleep.

Paul was sat beside her, listening to the voice informing them they'd soon be landing in Casablanca. He looked so intent she imagined him squatting on his haunches with an ear cocked, like the HMV dog. He fastened his seatbelt and glanced at her. 'Oh. You're awake,' he said.

'Just,' she grumbled, raking her hand through her hair. It felt thick and dirty and she wished she had a hair band handy to tie it off the back of her neck, but she felt too tired to root through the sluttish fudge of hairpins, old notepaper and crumbling cracked powder compacts in the bottom of her bag. Just leaning forwards to fetch it from under the seat felt like an effort.

'Thought I was going to have to wake you. Buckle up. We're landing.'

Paul hadn't been idle. He'd been compiling a list of all the main hospitals and clinics in the city.

'Aren't you a godsend?' she murmured, closing her eyes at the sickening bump as wheel touched tarmac. 'Don't suppose you speak Arabic as well?'

'Sorry, no,' Paul said. 'But I suspect we can get by in French.'

'You obviously haven't heard me speak French,' Adele said.

The heat was unbelievable when she stepped off the air-conditioned plane, a remorseless dry heat that immediately parched her throat further still, and made her head throb with dehydration aggravated by the tail end of a monster hangover. The delay at customs was even more baffling. Surely people smuggled drugs out of Morocco and not vice versa? She made up her mind to kill Karina when she laid hands on her, for dragging her to North fucking Africa in the middle of August – a place where no sane person would usually travel. Paul was clearly not sane, judging by the mad-dog fervour with which he dashed about the airport launching himself at customs officials, check-in clerks, telephone booths and tourist information, demanding pointers in French that he dismissed as 'schoolboy', but which sounded much more fluent than her own.

It was going to be like finding a needle in a haystack – a teeming haystack full of goats, trucks, snake-charmers, beggars, hustlers, taxi-drivers and tourists. She was scared the way she hadn't been scared since she was a child losing her mother in a crowd. She still dreamed about it now, about calling shrill-voiced through a crowd towards the figure of her mother as she remembered her in her earliest memories – straight backed with a big mop of black curls, before the disease had robbed her of her hair, her straight shoulders and round breasts, turning her into a gaunt creature so frightening to a six-year-old that Adele had sometimes shrunk back in terror. She feared hospitals for the same reason and felt as though she was in a nightmare where nobody understood what she was saying. Crowds swarmed oblivious around her and, no matter how loud she screamed for her, Karina would not come. She was terrified of the feeling of impotence, of being unable to do a thing to help.

'I've got it,' Paul said, taking hold of her arm.

She started and blinked. 'Got what?'

'Where she's staying. She's just across town. We'll get a cab.'

'Oh God.' Adele's heart seemed to speed unbearably in the stifling heat. 'How come? I mean, what happened?'

'I don't know. All I know is that she's left her phone as insurance with the desk clerk at this hotel and he said she's staying there. *Une petite femme Chinoise*, he said, which sounds like Karina.'

'Did he say she'd been at the hospital?' Adele asked, following him through the crowds and glancing around the massed ranks of battered cars. 'Oh fuck it ... what's the French for taxi?'

'Er ... I think it's taxi, actually.'

The taxi driver was named Yusuf and talked about his children in a combination of French and English ('*Trois garçons et deux filles*, all *beau* – Allah be praised') on the way to the hotel. Paul nodded and followed the conversation in pidgin French. Adele felt stodgy, provincial and stupid. She knew Karina would fit right into a melting pot like Casablanca, with her sharp, highly tuned ear for music and languages. She wondered what on earth an exotic, exciting creature like K had ever seen in her – a lumpy, fleshy-lipped girl from nowhere.

The hotel had a faded glory about it. Moorish arches tiled in cracked blues and greens, a tired neglected version of the Alhambra. The desk clerk to whom Paul had spoken was a heavy-set man with eyebrows that met in the middle, and carried on a conversation with Paul in French that she only picked out various words from. Her heart nearly stopped stock still when the clerk picked up a tiny pink mobile phone that she recognised as Karina's.

'Oh shit, that's –'

Paul shushed her briskly and nodded, picking up his conversation. If his French was indeed 'schoolboy', he had clearly paid more attention in class than she ever had, driven to muck about at the back with Kim who had used to say that being bilingual was worthless and could tell you that in two languages.

'*Merci. Vous etes tres gentil.*' Paul nodded to the clerk and turned back to Adele. 'OK, I got it. Come on.'

He headed back out of the hotel to where they had asked Yusuf to wait. 'The clerk thinks it's this clinic about twenty minutes away,' Paul said, as they got back into the taxi. He showed scribbled notes to Yusuf, who nodded and started the car. Adele was so hot, tired, scared and hungover that she couldn't think straight any more or even try to understand what was being said. She was angry at herself for letting Paul take charge, for being useless, but her body was at the stage where it was close to quitting. Two drunken nights on the trot without adequate sleep; food grabbed on the fly; a flight to North Africa; and now the devastating heat of this dusty, foreign place. She felt like she would have sold her soul for a cool shower, a set of clean clothes and a square meal.

They arrived at the clinic, which was battered with balding paintwork that didn't inspire confidence. More babbled conversations, more confusion, Paul dragging her down a hall.

'What's going on?' she asked.

'*Elle est ici* ... I mean, she's here ...' he said breathlessly. 'Come on!'

She ran down the hall, doubtless an unlikely-looking heroine in trainers and homemade evening dress. They rushed into a room, where two doctors were bent over a figure lying on a bed. Karina.

Adele screamed at them, struggling to find her long-forgotten French to yell, *ne touche pas, ne touche pas*. Get the fuck away from her. Don't touch her. The two doctors looked at her in puzzlement, Paul attempting to mediate. Karina must have been unconscious, or worse, because she didn't wake at the commotion in her room, her face boyish and young without make-up. She looked absurdly tiny under the sheet where she lay perfectly still. Shocked and exhausted, Adele began to sob, her knees giving underneath her. Paul ushered her to a plastic chair and sat her down. She knew she was wailing like a mad-woman, but she couldn't stop and it surged even stronger when she gripped Karina's limp hand and received no answering squeeze. The doctors were beating a baffled exit and Paul rubbed her shoulder reassuringly.

'It's OK, it's OK. We're in time . . . it's all right.'

'In time?' Adele sputtered, accepting a proffered paper tissue.

'They were just putting her under when we arrived. She's just anaesthetised.'

'Huh?'

'Nobody's operated on her. She's just under anaes-thetic. I think I've explained the situation adequately to the surgeons. If not . . . well, we'll just have to take her out of here ourselves, but I think it would be better if we can stay here so they can monitor her until she comes round.'

'I'll wait,' Adele said, not relinquishing her grip on Karina's hand. 'Are you sure she's all right?'

'I think so,' said Paul. 'Talk about timing, huh?'

'You said it.'

He sighed and pushed her hair away from the nape of her neck so tenderly that she wanted to be able to do the right thing, the storybook thing, and accept him as her knight in shining armour, the love of her life. She wished she could do that for all the lust she had for him, for all he made her laugh, but she couldn't foist that foolish hearts and flowers crap on him now she'd come to care for him. The love of her life was unconscious and had B-cup tits and a dick, and she didn't care one way or the other.

'Do you want me to go?' Paul asked quietly.

'No,' she said, although she did, because he made her even more confused. 'It's OK.' She blew her nose, cleared her throat and thought for a moment about what she needed to say. 'You've been great ... I don't know how to thank you for everything you've done.'

He shook his head. 'It's fine. Gay man does his bit for penis protection ... or something. Oh God, I'm sorry. That's a terrible thing to say.'

'You're gay again?'

'I don't know. If you feed me after midnight I might turn straight again.'

'Paul –' She shot him a reproachful look over her shoulder.

'Sorry,' he said, raking a hand through his hair. 'Just trying to inject a little humour into ... well ... what's been a hell of a day, really.'

'Yeah.' She sighed. 'Could have been worse.' She looked down at Karina, obliviously dozing off the drugs, and decided she was going to either kiss her or strangle her when she came round. Wasn't sure which.

'It could, but it wasn't.'

'Yeah. Thanks for that.'

'Well ... you know ... good chefs are an absolute bitch to find.'

She smiled this time, partly in disbelief that he could keep laughing. He rubbed her shoulder gently.

'You two,' he said seriously. 'I mean – this goes way back, doesn't it? Between you?'

Adele nodded, sure she was going to cry again. 'Oh God, yes. Fucking years. If I told you what you'd walked into you'd never believe me.'

'You're talking to a man who spent the last two years trying to divorce his step-sister. It terms of general fuck-uppage, it takes a lot to surprise me.'

'Oh, I could a tale unfold –' Adele sighed, and sat up straight when she saw Karina stir in the bed. She squeezed her small hand tighter, tiredness evaporating in her eagerness to speak to her again, to worry about her again.

Karina opened her eyes and blinked groggily. '– The fuck –?' she groaned, her voice so cracked it was almost nonexistent.

Adele's eyes filled again, snorts and sniffles erupting from her nose.

'Is it over?' Karina moaned, ever the drama queen.

'It never started,' Paul said.

'Del, what are you doing here?' Karina said, looking blurred, confused; a drugged stranger.

Adele tried to speak, so overcome with relief and exhaustion that all she could do was cry. 'I love you,' she blurted, barely able to see for crying. She thought maybe she was laughing too – mad or hysterical; in need of the smelling salts or a slap.

'Congratulations, Miss May,' Karina said, imitating a midwife. 'It's a lesbian.'

Adele choked. 'Stop making me laugh, you bitch.'

Karina searched for water. Paul handed her a plastic cup with a straw and she sipped gratefully. 'Babycakes.' Karina sighed, her voice smoothed with water and her hand tight in Adele's. 'Why on earth would I want to do that?'

17

Paul knew what was in the letter before he even opened it. He had already decided to savour the moment and realised he had a whole bar at his disposal to help along his enjoyment. The sign on the door said CLOSED FOR REFURBISHMENT – GRAND REOPENING 1ST MAY, but he had the keys in his pocket and unlocked the big glass-fronted doors to Shipworths and entered the empty bar. The work was going on upstairs where his old flat was being converted into extra restaurant space. At first it had seemed insane to do it after such a short space of time, but he stuck his neck out on the extra investment and the prospect of no longer having to pay maintenance. Even at the arse end of last summer the business had been phenomenal, largely due to the women.

He opened one of the fridges and popped the cork on a bottle of Taittinger, swilling it from the bottle. It was icy, fizzy and ludicrously expensive but, today, it didn't matter. He slurped his champagne and opened his letter, smiling with satisfaction when it confirmed that he was finally divorced. He tried to remain on good terms with Sarah but she accused him of gloating, which he did, frequently. When he met up with her she had changed beyond recognition – her long fair hair scraped back into an Eva Peron knot at her nape – and during their conversation she talked about 'the girls' and swore even more than usual. She had even cracked a fingernail and tore off the irritating segment of nail with her teeth and spat it across the room into the dustbin, something the old

Sarah would have rather died than done. The everyday encumbrances of a relationship and children had turned Sarah into an ordinary person, with eyebags and chipped nail polish. Adele had gone down like a ton of shit with Sarah when Paul had taken her to London to meet up. Sarah had immediately pronounced Adele a 'fat moustachioed cow'.

'Ain't sisterhood grand?' Adele had said, with a big shit-eating grin that Paul suspected was borrowed from Karina. Then she had blinked quite ingenuously and twisted the knife, telling Sarah with patronising sympathy that it was so hard for a woman to hold down a family and career, and that she was sure one side-effect of feminism had been for women to be stuck with all the fucking work. So sad.

Paul had taken her back to the hotel under the impression that all women were somehow fundamentally evil, but he wasn't going to argue, because his buxom brunette Adele was celebrating putting one over on a skinny career blonde in the best way she knew how – bouncing cheerfully up and down on Paul's dick until he was hanging on to sanity by his fingernails and pleading with her to come so that he could at least be a gentleman about coming second.

'Patronising bastard,' she panted, grinding away on top of him.

'Ladies first. I insist,' Paul gasped through clenched teeth, then she closed her eyes and bit her lips while he felt her muscles clench and ripple around him in a quiet climax that belied all her previous energetic and noisy bump and grinding.

He thought it was probably serious between them, and he thought she felt the same way, although he knew she wasn't given to emotional outpourings that weren't to do with anger or irritation. He would have liked to flatter her and charm her, but she hated flattery, saying it was insincere.

Paul took his champagne out into the garden, which could now safely be called a garden-in-waiting, he supposed, rather than a junkyard. The wisteria had been pruned back and the heaped earth shovelled and power-hosed off the flagstones. Beds were taking shape, to be lovingly edged in white pebbles and planted out with night-scented stock.

Karina was out there struggling with a dead forsythia, a boot holding the root steady while she sweated and whacked it with the cutting edge of the spade. The spring was shaping up to be warm already and she wore jeans and a sweatshirt, black hair tied in two schoolgirl braids. Her hair had grown, long enough to cover her nipples like a thick, bang-cut curtain when she sat up straight in bed to roll a joint or light a cigarette. She complained she looked like Yoko Ono but didn't know what else to do with it, and couldn't be bothered when she had the garden to deal with. She'd become surprisingly devoted to it and, even more surprisingly, good at it.

'You never told me she was keen on gardening,' Paul had said to Adele when Karina once again picked up her shovel and gloves and strutted out into the mud.

'I didn't know,' Adele said. 'Probably even she didn't know either. Of course, she has to be fucking good at it – you'll find that with K. She's one of those annoying people who's good at everything they try.'

Karina had got quieter and more reflective since returning from Casablanca, carving herself an irreplaceable niche around Shipworths, doing the garden, washing the pots and providing the entertainment. Paul thought maybe she had mellowed because her act gave her an excuse to vent her twisted, fucked-up side with a vengeance and gave it an outlet. When she was doing her routine she was monstrous, vicious, deliberately disgusting and rib-achingly hilarious. Already Paul was worried that someone might hear of her through the London grapevine and she would be seduced away from him by promises of becoming the next Eddie Izzard. It had come naturally to her when she was heckled at karaoke and some missing link had yelled out that he hadn't realised it was a drag night.

Karina had come back at him with aplomb. 'Of course you didn't, darling. If you had this place would have been fucking empty – *you* in taffeta and sequins? Ugh. On behalf of all visual thinkers in this place, I would like to apologise for giving form to that image.'

And that was that. The audience had convulsed and Karina got into her stride, improvising, bullshitting, bitching, being herself. 'My mother was like "Oh Kim, why you no marry some nice Chinese girl?" and I was like "Oh fuck … uh, Mum … I want to *be* a nice Chinese girl." Only, I mean, for fuck's sake. Did she not see it coming? Even my name is gay. Kim Qing. I was signing documents K. Qing. K'Ching? Christ – bad enough being *transsexual*, never mind having a name that sounded like I was *born* to be a drag queen.'

Paul watched her attack the roots of the dead shrub and coughed to get her attention. Karina turned around, wiping her face with the back of her arm and raising her eyebrows at the bottle in his hand. 'Are we celebrating something?' she asked.

'Most definitely.'

She liked doing the garden. It gave her time to think, while mindlessly whacking weeds and tearing up old flagstones. She came up with some of her best-received material while she was on her knees. Don't we all, dearie?

said a voice in the back of her head – the camped-up, fucked-up version of herself she paraded to make people laugh until they hurt. It came easily to her, having had what could best be described as an interesting life. You simply tilted your head and looked back on your life askew, and it looked funny from that angle.

Karina mentally rehearsed as she slammed the spade into the roots, determined that one way or another she'd have the last laugh on Mother Nature. She seemed to be rehearsing all the time now that she had a chance to perform, and it dimmed a lot of the frustration that had dogged her in the past. Paul interrupted her when he came out into the garden carrying a bottle of champagne and wearing a smug-as-hell grin.

'Are we celebrating something?' she asked.

'Most definitely.' Paul held up the bottle. 'You thirsty?'

'Oh God, yeah,' Karina said enthusiastically. She shoved the spade into the dirt and took the bottle, gulping the cold, fizzy liquid as if it were Diet Coke. It tasted sour when she craved something sweeter, but it was cold and wet and that was good enough.

'So what's up?' she asked, handing back the bottle.

Paul took a breath and beamed. 'I got my divorce.'

'Fabulous!' Karina hugged him ecstatically, knowing how much he had been looking forward to it. 'Does this mean you're free?'

He smiled, his hand planted firmly on her arse. 'For the time being. Are you busy?'

'I'm tired, I'm sweaty and I stink.'

He leaned in and sniffed the side of her neck, lightly brushing his lips against her ear. She could feel his hips sway closer and bump gently against her. 'You smell fine to me,' Paul whispered in her ear. 'A little musky, but nothing I couldn't stand.'

'You wait until I get these clothes off,' she warned.

'I wasn't planning to, actually. Patience isn't one of my virtues.'

He slid a hand up her sweatshirt and under her T-shirt. Karina winced at his touch, his hand icy from the champagne bottle, but when his fingers reached her nipple and pinched, the chill made her shiver deliciously and her nipples stiffen and chafe against the inside of her shirt. The cold was a pleasing contrast to the heat of his mouth and his tongue, which carried the taste of celebration.

'Where's Adele?' she asked, pulling away and heading towards the door. Paul followed and managed to squash her between himself and the door frame, hard, horny and obviously feeling the effects of the champagne already.

'Meeting with a supplier,' Paul said, pushing up Karina's shirt and teasing her by touching the side of the cold, wet bottle to her skin.

'Ow, fuck off!' Karina wriggled free and darted up the back stairs to the first floor, where the builders had been transforming Paul's old flat. She stood and stared for a moment, having not been up here for a while, indifferent to the sound of Paul's footsteps on the stairs behind her. She was fascinated by the way the space had changed. Walls had been knocked through, the old chimney bricked up and shored up, floorboards laid. Unrecognisable as the place it had been before.

Paul came up behind her and wrapped his arms around her waist, planting a kiss on the nape of her neck.

'They've been busy up here.'

'Yep. Looks a bit different, doesn't it?'

'Does it ever,' Karina said. 'Looks like ... well ... like a restaurant. Sort of.'

'That's a relief. That's what I wanted it to look like.'

'It's quite weird. To think it all used to be different,'

she said, turning around to take a better look. 'To think that people are going to be eating their lunches right where we had sex.'

Paul laughed. 'I never thought of it like that before.' He leaned back against the waiter's station. 'Don't think I'll ever think of it in the same way again now.' He grinned. 'Maybe we should do it again.'

'And get splinters up my arse? Piss off.'

He pushed his bottom lip out in a little-boy sulky look that she would have been inclined to slap off the face of a man less downright pretty. 'Adele won't be back for a while –' he wheedled.

'She might be back early,' Karina said.

'Well, if she does come back early, I'm sure you'll find a way to win her round,' Paul said, taking her hand. 'I'm told you can be quite charming when you put your mind to it.'

'You're *told*? You know it – cheeky fucker.'

Adele wound down the windows and turned up the radio as she steered Paul's car through the spring bright countryside. R.E.M. were jangling happily through 'Pretty Persuasion' on the radio; the weather was just that kind of muted tryout of full summer to be perfect, and all was right with the world. She had a couple of punnets of forced early strawberries on the passenger seat of the car and carefully steadied them as she turned a corner. She would have brought Paul along to hold the punnets if she'd known the nursery was giving out samples. She popped one into her mouth, delighted with the flavour of the fruit. If these were forced then the strawberries would be magnificent in season, and the supply deal she had cut with the nursery would turn out to be lucrative.

Strawberry tarts, fresh strawberry ice cream, strawberry cream teas – everyone's favourite summer dessert.

Her mouth watered when she thought of strawberries and cream – red berries sitting on top of heaps of white like the nipple of a breast. Bright red fruits; the auspicious colour, the lucky colour, streaked with dribbles of cream, staining the cream pink with their sweet juice.

The radio changed its tune, the idiot DJ babbling about a comeback single from Suzanne Hausmann – formerly known as Suki. Adele resisted the urge to turn it off out of a trainwreck fascination to see how bad Karina's ex would fare. It was a cover, like so many songs, a piano-accompanied reworking of the old Smokey Robinson hit 'Tracks of My Tears'. Adele was forced to admit that the bloody woman could sing, and was actually delivering the song convincingly, but she had to grin at the lyrics – the ones about being seen out with another girl who doesn't measure up to the original.

'It's your own fucking fault, you silly cow,' Adele told the radio. 'She's mine. You blew it. Deal.'

But she sang along anyway as she drove back into town. She was unable to park outside Shipworths and had to put the car round the back and walk round the block. Karina would probably be digging her garden and Paul would be poring over his accounts, grabbing some peace and quiet before the builders returned tomorrow and started hammering and crashing all over the place. Adele was thankful that Paul had been sensitive enough not to rehire Jude as a carpenter, but the two Daves were back working for them, since they were used to Karina and didn't wind up getting the rough side of her tongue when they ogled her.

'I'm taken and I have a penis. Now fuck off.'

There had been no more talk of surgery since Casablanca. Karina had admitted that she had done it because she was upset, because she wanted to get at Suki, not through any genuine desire to be a woman. Adele had warned Karina that right now, where her head was at, no respectable surgeon would carry out gender reassignment until she was psychologically adjusted. Repelled by the thought of psychiatry, Karina carried on the way she was and seemed contented enough, but Adele kept her nerves braced for the day Karina might decide to go all the way. Her only regret was that Karina hadn't given her the chance to be supportive years ago.

She entered through the side door and went up the stairs, the old door to Paul's flat bricked over but not yet plastered. She'd had to move out for a while, and had spent several uncomfortable nights in hotels worrying about her home while the builders carried out the biggest structural alterations downstairs. Fortunately nothing else had caved in after the now infamous chimney incident.

As she approached the door she heard voices inside the flat, even more distinctly when she opened the door. The sounds were coming from the bedroom and she set her face in an acceptably pissed-off expression as she walked into the room. Karina was peering owlishly over the edge of the duvet, shoulders bare and the covers tangled up between Paul's legs. Paul's arse was hanging out of the covers and he looked unrepentant, and even a little optimistic.

'What do you think you're doing?' Adele asked, putting down the strawberry punnets on top of the chest of drawers.

'I plead the Fifth Amendment,' Karina said.

'In *Britain*?' Paul queried. 'Adele, I can explain –'

'Really?' She peeled off her T-shirt. 'All I can say is you two better have a damn good reason for starting without me. Move up.'

Visit the Black Lace website at
www.blacklace-books.co.uk

**FIND OUT THE LATEST INFORMATION AND TAKE
ADVANTAGE OF OUR FANTASTIC FREE BOOK OFFER!
ALSO VISIT THE SITE FOR . . .**

- All Black Lace titles currently available
  and how to order online
- Great new offers
- Writers' guidelines
- Author interviews
- An erotica newsletter
- Features
- Cool links

**BLACK LACE — THE LEADING IMPRINT
OF WOMEN'S SEXY FICTION**

**TAKING YOUR EROTIC READING
PLEASURE TO NEW HORIZONS**

LOOK OUT FOR THE ALL-NEW BLACK LACE BOOKS – AVAILABLE NOW!

All books priced £6.99 in the UK. Please note publication dates apply to the UK only. For other territories, please contact your retailer.

THE BLACK LACE SEXY QUIZ BOOK
Maddie Saxon
ISBN 0 352 33884 9
£6.99

- What sexual personality type are you?
- Have you ever faked it because that was easier than explaining what you wanted?
- What kind of fantasy figures turn you on – and does your partner know?
- What sexual signals are you giving out right now?

Today's image-conscious dating scene is a tough call. Our sexual expectations are cranked up to the max, and the sexes seem to have become highly critical of each other in terms of appearance and performance in the bedroom. But even though guys have ditched their nasty Y-fronts and girls are more babe-licious than ever, a huge number of us are still being let down sexually. Sex therapist Maddie Saxon thinks this is because we are finding it harder to relax and let our true sexual selves shine through.

The Black Lace Sexy Quiz Book will help you negotiate the minefield of modern relationships. Through a series of fun, revealing quizzes, you will be able to rate your sexual needs honestly and get what you really want from your partner. The quizzes will get you thinking about and discussing your desires in ways you haven't previously considered. Unlock the mysteries of your sexual psyche in this fun, revealing quiz book designed with today's sex-savvy girl in mind.

Coming in July

WICKED WORDS 10 – THE BEST OF WICKED WORDS
Various
ISBN 0 352 33893 8

Wicked Words collections are the hottest anthologies of women's erotic writing to be found anywhere in the world. This is an editor's choice of the best stories from the first five years of this immensely popular series. With settings and scenarios to suit all tastes, this is fun erotica at the cutting edge from the UK and USA. Combining humour, warmth and attitude with imaginative writing, these stories sizzle with horny action. **A scorching collection of wild fantasies.**

THE SENSES BEJEWELLED
Cleo Cordell
ISBN 0 352 32904 1

Eighteenth-century Algeria provides a backdrop of opulence tainted with danger in this story of extreme erotic indulgence. Ex-convent girl Marietta has settled into a life of privileged captivity, as the favoured concubine in the harem of Kasim. But when she is kidnapped by Kasim's sworn enemy, Hamed, her new-found way of life is thrown into chaos. **This is the sequel to the hugely popular Black Lace title, *The Captive Flesh*.**

Coming in August

SWITCHING HANDS
Alaine Hood
ISBN 0 352 33896 2

When Melanie Paxton takes over as manager of a vintage clothing shop, she makes the bold decision to add a selection of sex toys and fetish merchandise to her inventory. Sales skyrocket, and so does Mel's popularity, as she teases sexy secrets out of the town's residents. It seems she can do no wrong, until the gossip starts – about her wild past and her experimental sexuality. However, she finds an unlikely – and very hunky – ally called Nathan who works in the history museum next door. **This characterful story about a sassy sexpert and an antiquities scholar is bound to get pulses racing!**

PACKING HEAT
Karina Moore
ISBN 0 352 33356 1

When spoilt and pretty Californian Nadine has her allowance stopped by her rich Uncle Willem, she becomes desperate to maintain her expensive lifestyle. She joins forces with her lover, Mark, and together they conspire to steal a vast sum of cash from a flashy businessman and pin the blame on their target's girlfriend. The deed done, the sexual stakes rise as they make their escape. Naturally, their getaway doesn't go entirely to plan, and they are pursued across the desert and into the casinos of Las Vegas, where a showdown is inevitable. The clock is ticking for Nadine, Mark and the guys who are chasing them – but a Ferrari-driving blonde temptress is about to play them all for suckers. **Fast cars and even faster women in this modern pulp fiction classic.**

Black Lace Booklist

Information is correct at time of printing. To avoid disappointment check availability before ordering. Go to www.blacklace-books.co.uk. All books are priced £6.99 unless another price is given.

BLACK LACE BOOKS WITH A CONTEMPORARY SETTING

☐ SHAMELESS Stella Black	ISBN 0 352 33485 1	£5.99
☐ INTENSE BLUE Lyn Wood	ISBN 0 352 33496 7	£5.99
☐ A SPORTING CHANCE Susie Raymond	ISBN 0 352 33501 7	£5.99
☐ TAKING LIBERTIES Susie Raymond	ISBN 0 352 33357 X	£5.99
☐ A SCANDALOUS AFFAIR Holly Graham	ISBN 0 352 33523 8	£5.99
☐ THE NAKED FLAME Crystalle Valentino	ISBN 0 352 33528 9	£5.99
☐ ON THE EDGE Laura Hamilton	ISBN 0 352 33534 3	£5.99
☐ LURED BY LUST Tania Picarda	ISBN 0 352 33533 5	£5.99
☐ THE HOTTEST PLACE Tabitha Flyte	ISBN 0 352 33536 X	£5.99
☐ THE NINETY DAYS OF GENEVIEVE Lucinda Carrington	ISBN 0 352 33070 8	£5.99
☐ DREAMING SPIRES Juliet Hastings	ISBN 0 352 33584 X	
☐ THE TRANSFORMATION Natasha Rostova	ISBN 0 352 33311 1	
☐ SIN.NET Helena Ravenscroft	ISBN 0 352 33598 X	
☐ TWO WEEKS IN TANGIER Annabel Lee	ISBN 0 352 33599 8	
☐ HIGHLAND FLING Jane Justine	ISBN 0 352 33616 1	
☐ PLAYING HARD Tina Troy	ISBN 0 352 33617 X	
☐ SYMPHONY X Jasmine Stone	ISBN 0 352 33629 3	
☐ SUMMER FEVER Anna Ricci	ISBN 0 352 33625 0	
☐ CONTINUUM Portia Da Costa	ISBN 0 352 33120 8	
☐ OPENING ACTS Suki Cunningham	ISBN 0 352 33630 7	
☐ FULL STEAM AHEAD Tabitha Flyte	ISBN 0 352 33637 4	
☐ A SECRET PLACE Ella Broussard	ISBN 0 352 33307 3	
☐ GAME FOR ANYTHING Lyn Wood	ISBN 0 352 33639 0	
☐ CHEAP TRICK Astrid Fox	ISBN 0 352 33640 4	
☐ THE GIFT OF SHAME Sara Hope-Walker	ISBN 0 352 32935 1	
☐ COMING UP ROSES Crystalle Valentino	ISBN 0 352 33658 7	
☐ GOING TOO FAR Laura Hamilton	ISBN 0 352 33657 9	

BLACK LACE BOOKS WITH AN HISTORICAL SETTING

BLACK LACE ANTHOLOGIES

BLACK LACE NON-FICTION

To find out the latest information about Black Lace titles, check out the website: www.blacklace-books.co.uk or send for a booklist with complete synopses by writing to:

Black Lace Booklist, Virgin Books Ltd
Thames Wharf Studios
Rainville Road
London W6 9HA

Please include an SAE of decent size. Please note only British stamps are valid.

Our privacy policy
We will not disclose information you supply us to any other parties. We will not disclose any information which identifies you personally to any person without your express consent.

From time to time we may send out information about Black Lace books and special offers. Please tick here if you do <u>not</u> wish to receive Black Lace information. ❏

Please send me the books I have ticked above.

Name ....

Address ....

....

....

....

Post Code ....

Send to: Virgin Books Cash Sales, Thames Wharf Studios,
Rainville Road, London W6 9HA.

US customers: for prices and details of how to order
books for delivery by mail, call 1-800-343-4499.

Please enclose a cheque or postal order, made payable
to Virgin Books Ltd, to the value of the books you have
ordered plus postage and packing costs as follows:

UK and BFPO – £1.00 for the first book, 50p for each
subsequent book.

Overseas (including Republic of Ireland) – £2.00 for
the first book, £1.00 for each subsequent book.

If you would prefer to pay by VISA, ACCESS/MASTERCARD,
DINERS CLUB, AMEX or SWITCH, please write your card
number and expiry date here:

....

Signature ....

Please allow up to 28 days for delivery.